THE TERRITORY

THE TERRITORY

TRICIA FIELDS

MINOTAUR BOOKS

A Thomas Dunne Book
New York

A THOMAS DUNNE BOOK FOR MINOTAUR BOOKS.
An imprint of St. Martin's Publishing Group.

THE TERRITORY. Copyright © 2011 by Tricia Fields.
All rights reserved. Printed in the United States of America.
For information, address St. Martin's Press, 175 Fifth Avenue,
New York, N.Y. 10010.

www.thomasdunnebooks.com
www.minotaurbooks.com

Library of Congress Cataloging-in-Publication Data

Fields, Tricia.
    The territory / Tricia Fields. — 1st ed.
       p. cm.
    "A Thomas Dunne book."
    ISBN 978-0-312-61378-5
    1. Lower Rio Grande Valley (Tex.)—Fiction.   2. Mexican-
American Border Region—Fiction.   I. Title.
    PS3606.I366T47 2011
    813'.6—dc23

                                                    2011026224

First Edition: November 2011

10 9 8 7 6 5 4 3 2 1

Dedicated to Todd with love

ACKNOWLEDGMENTS

Special thanks to my GD3 writing pals: Linnet, Mella, and Merry. Your collective guidance and friendship were more appreciated than you will ever know. And thank you to my mentor and friend, Sandra Scofield, for helping me to slow down until I finally got it right. And finally, to Peter Joseph, for your infinite patience, kindness, and editing expertise. Thank you all for helping bring this book to life.

THE TERRITORY

ONE

Chief Josie Gray sighted down the rifle scope at two black sedans prowling the empty streets of Piedra Labrada. She was posted atop a fifty-foot-high watchtower, looking across the Rio Grande into a two-block area of squalid bars. For forty-five minutes, Josie had listened to gunfire coming from inside the Garra del Tigre, one of the five bars on the strip, but there had been no movement until the sedans came into view. The watchtower, used jointly by Border Patrol and local police, stood on the U.S. side of the river, just a quarter mile from downtown Piedra. From her vantage point, Josie could see an access road that followed the Rio, then a half dozen blocks of factories fanning out from the collection of bars situated directly south of the tower. She lowered her rifle, slowly scanning the area for a reaction to the cars. Something was about to open up.

The sedans rolled to a stop in the middle of the empty street in front of the Tigre. Although the occupants' identities were concealed behind black tinted windows, Josie was certain the cars belonged to either Medrano or La Bestia. The Medrano cartel was a family-run drug operation that had terrorized northern Mexico into submission. La Bestia was a newly formed cartel with enough money and firepower to pose a threat to Medrano: a death sentence for anyone caught in between.

Garra del Tigre's front door hung from its hinges, the wood splintered with bullets. The inside of the club appeared dark and still, but she knew the gunmen maneuvered at night with the ease of cockroaches.

Josie rubbed her neck and rolled her shoulders, trying to ease some of the tension from them. She could feel blood humming through her veins, the tingling of nerve endings on her scalp: Her body was on alert. She was thin, with arm muscles strong enough to surprise a full-grown man if the occasion called for it, and was above average height for a woman. At thirty-three years old, she knew she was attractive, but lately she felt that side of her served little purpose.

Heat lightning snaked across the night sky, and she caught a glimpse of the blue and white jeep patrolling River Road below her with its headlights off. She pulled her cell phone out of her uniform shirt pocket and called the driver, fellow officer Otto Podowski. She disliked leaving him on the ground with no backup, but they were the only officers on duty that night.

Otto answered on the first ring. "Anything?"

"Two sedans just pulled up in front of the Tigre. They're watching. This has to be a battle between the cartels. Any movement on our side?"

"Not a soul in sight."

"You see cars pushing across the river? Don't be a hero. Get out of their way."

"Backup on the way yet?"

"Are you kidding?" She and Otto made up two-thirds of the Artemis Police Department. The three-person police force should have been enough for a border town with a population of 2,500. But given the current violence across the border, she needed at least triple that number of officers. Without constant vigilance by police agencies, the violence would spread like wildfire through the Southwest.

One block south of the nightclubs, Josie watched two uniformed Piedra police officers approach the east side of the strip, on foot with guns drawn.

"Jesus, there's two cops ready to run right into the middle of it. They're walking up the side street. They can't see the cars yet."

Josie hung up on Otto and tried the Piedra Labrada police dispatch but received the same busy signal she'd heard for the past two hours. She called her local dispatcher, Lou Hagerty. Lou was a fifty-year-old chain-smoker with a voice like gravel, but no one handled stress better than she did.

"I can't get through to dispatch in Piedra," Josie said. She could feel the panic in her throat as she watched the officers approach the corner of the building. Then the panic turned to dread. She grabbed her binoculars off the deck railing and focused them with one hand.

"Every phone line in Mexico must have been slashed. I can't even get through to the gas station," Lou said.

Josie focused on the officer who stood almost a foot taller than the other man, and recognized Lorenzo Marín. She had worked with him frequently on cross-border issues. He was a good-natured officer, with a million stories to tell and a loud, high-pitched laugh that could get even the most cynical cop to smile. He had a wife and twin boys at home. It was all she could do to keep from screaming his name, but her voice would never carry.

Josie quickly summed up the gunfire and officer location. "You find a way to get through to someone. Let them know Marín's walking into an ambush."

She hung up and found Marín in her cell phone contacts. She had to warn him. The sedans were almost certainly carrying gunmen, cartel members who would not hesitate to shoot a police officer.

Marín didn't answer, his phone probably silenced. At the corner of the bar, he and the shorter officer stopped and leaned their backs against the side of the building. She could barely see their outline in the shadows. Her stomach clenched as she watched the passenger-side doors of both sedans open and four men exit, each holding automatic weapons. They hunkered low behind the cover of the cars and faced the Tigre.

Josie watched Marín walk cautiously around the front of the building, now in full view of the gunmen crouching behind the sedans. The gunman closest to Marín slowly raised his head above the rear of the sedan and brought his gun up, aiming toward the cop, who was now pressed against the front of the nightclub, his gaze on the front door. Josie heard the shots first, then watched as Marín's body jerked, hit the wall of the nightclub, and slid down the cement wall, where bullets continued to riddle his body. She screamed and grabbed the deck railing to keep from falling to her knees. The second officer remained around the corner of the building, edging around to open fire on the sedan. The four gunmen disappeared into the cars within seconds, and the sedans rolled off, heading away from the Rio into a darkened residential neighborhood, where Josie lost sight of them. She watched the other officer crouch over Marín, who now slumped against the building, his legs splayed out on the sidewalk.

Her ears buzzed in the sudden silence. Stunned, she watched the other officer lean his head down to Marín's chest and check his neck for a pulse. Three cars exited the alley behind the nightclub, making their escape before reinforcements could ever arrive.

Josie repeatedly dialed the Piedra Police Department until finally reaching a dispatcher through sheer luck. She reported an officer down, and within minutes the ambulance arrived. Josie watched as Marín's lifeless body was loaded into the ambulance. They were treating him like he had a chance, but she had little hope.

She leaned her rifle against the deck railing and forced her breathing to return to normal. She rubbed at the knots in her neck and felt the tension pulling the muscles in her back and shoulders. Thirty-three years old, and she wondered if the dark circles under her eyes would ever fade.

She unbuttoned her uniform shirt and lifted the bulletproof vest and her T-shirt away from her chest, sighing in relief as the air touched her skin. She unclipped her shoulder-length brown hair and finger-combed it back into place. It was four o'clock in the morning. Her body felt numb; her thoughts flatlined.

Josie pushed open the rickety wooden door into the boxy room at the center of the watchtower's platform and found the water bottle in her backpack. She drained the contents and searched her cell phone for Sergio Pando's phone number. A single father who obsessed over his teenage daughter's safety, he was her closest contact on the Mexican police force. His wife had been killed, a bystander to a car bomb explosion when Benita was just a baby. It had nearly destroyed him.

Josie finally made contact with him. "What's happening over there?"

"Josie, it is insanity. We've lost all control. Benita? She's in the cellar, scared out of her mind." Sergio's English was excellent, but his accent was thick, slowing his speech.

"Is she home by herself?" Josie asked.

He sighed heavily and took a moment to respond. "You know where I am? Posted on the International Bridge. As if anyone in their right mind would want into this city right now."

"The gunfire has let up." Josie realized how inadequate it sounded. How do you talk to a man whose city is dying?

"For how long?" Sergio's voice was bitter and tired. "All those government soldiers going to save the villages? Where are they? The Federales are so outmanned, we can't keep up. It's a joke."

"I requested Border Patrol and DPS all night. It's no good. Dispatch has been nonstop."

Sergio made a dismissive sound. "The landlines are down, probably destroyed like the rest of the city."

"Border Patrol is monitoring scanner traffic. They set up defensive positions at the main points. They're preparing for a mass crossing."

"They aren't stupid. The cartels won't cross tonight." Sergio's voice caught. "Thirteen people murdered. One police officer in critical condition. It's territory and drug routes. Always what it comes to."

Josie listened in silence as Sergio went on, listing one horrible act after another. She stared down at the river and wondered how long before the chaos spilled over the banks and into the U.S.

After Sergio calmed somewhat, Josie called Otto, dialing his cell phone to keep the radio frequency clear. "Where are you?" she asked.

"Intersection of River Road and Scratchgravel."

"Any noise?"

"Nothing. It's too quiet now."

"Everything's shut down," she said. She raised her binoculars again and scanned the city, almost deserted at an hour when third-shift and first-shift workers should have been passing in the streets. An underground system of communication, neighbor to neighbor, spread information throughout the city when trouble started. Lights went out; windows and doors shut. Piedra Labrada went into lockdown.

The radio on Josie's belt hissed. Lou Hagerty said, "Forty-two twenty-two, location check."

"Rio watchtower," Josie replied.

"Mayor Moss requests all units to the Trauma Center, stat."

Josie hooked her backpack over her arms and took the wooden stairs that zigzagged down the fifty-foot descent as quickly as she could.

Lou had not been provided any details, and Josie dreaded to find out what lay ahead. She shoved her department-issued jeep into four-wheel drive and sped toward the center of town via a dried-up arroyo that also served as a county road. The smell of baked earth and desert scrub blew in through her open window.

The radio forecaster said the overcast sky held no hope for rain and little chance of lowering the record-breaking temperatures. Looking in her rearview mirror Josie noticed the wall of dust she stirred up, and ran her tongue across her lips, tasting the layer of fine sand that coated her skin. The heat had the locals wishing for the monsoon season, but it would be dangerous when it hit. The ground was so hard and dry, the water would wash down arroyos like this one to the Rio, flooding everything in its path.

The Artemis Trauma Center was located south of the center of town, near a neighborhood of small cinder block homes. As she pulled up, Josie saw the mayor's white pickup truck enter the empty lot, dingy under the charcoal-colored sky. He parked in front of the center's entryway, climbed out of the truck, and approached Josie like a drill sergeant. He was a short stocky man with an underbite like a bull-dog's.

"An ER surgeon from El Paso is on his way. He was already on call in Marfa, so he should be here within a half hour. Two scrub nurses should be here any minute. They'll start setting up for surgery." Moss's voice was clipped and too loud for the silent parking lot.

"What's going on?" Josie felt her face flush in irritation.

He pointed toward the door. "Let's get inside. We shouldn't be out here."

Josie grabbed his shoulder as he turned from her. "Has someone been shot?"

He glared at her and turned back toward the building, forcing Josie to follow behind him.

The Trauma Center was a one-story brick rectangle with a glass front door and green awning above it. The building housed the town's Health Department and a one-room surgical unit that had been paid for with a Homeland Security grant the previous year. Artemis supported one family doctor and now a trauma unit, thanks to the drug cartels pushing north.

Using a key from a silver ring with at least a hundred other labeled keys, Moss unlocked the door and pushed it open, flipping on the entry lights to the left of the door, obviously familiar with the building. For the past ten years, he had micromanaged every agency in town, down to the bid orders for paper towels and toilet paper. He ran Artemis like a city manager, at times using authority he did not officially have. Moss and the city council appointed the chief of police, and he had the authority to fire Josie: a fact Moss was not above reminding her. Running unopposed gave him the type of unchallenged power that Josie worried was not in the best interest of the city.

Moss turned on a second set of lights, and fluorescent bulbs lit up the white waiting room, revealing two rows of blue plastic chairs linked together by a metal rail. Low coffee tables on either side of the chairs were littered with various tattered magazines. The room smelled of bleach and Pine-Sol.

Josie pointed ahead to a dimly lit hallway where they could talk in a more protected space, away from the glass entryway and two windows in the waiting room.

Moss leaned against the wall in the hallway and rubbed the stubble on his face. Usually impeccably dressed, he wore a wrinkled shirt that looked as if he had picked it off the floor on the way out of his house.

"I got a call from the Federales. The Medrano ranch is under attack. Five to eight gunmen from La Bestia went there after the gunfight in Piedra. They shot three front men for Medrano, as well as the old man himself. He's in critical condition." He paused, looked away from her. "The ambulance is headed our way."

Josie leaned her head against the wall. She had been warned it would happen eventually. "Wasn't he shot in Piedra Labrada?" she asked.

Moss nodded. "I had no choice. He's got dual citizenship. The Federales said La Bestia already has men surrounding the hospital in Ojinaga. There's not a hospital in Mexico safe enough to take him. The Federales are certain La Bestia's set to finish the job."

"So we let them finish the job here? Let our doctors and nurses be killed?" She stopped and forced herself to slow down, lower her voice. "Do you have any idea how many innocent people that man has killed in Mexico?"

Moss took a step forward and pointed a finger toward her chest. "He owns a cattle ranch in West Texas the size of our town! Until our suspicions are confirmed, we treat this man like the U.S. citizen he is. We offer him protection and medical care like we do any other citizen."

Josie laughed in disbelief. "I can't cross the border to help a fellow law officer, but we allow criminals to cross the border for medical care? How screwed up is that?"

"You don't like the rules? Write your congressman."

Josie bit back a sarcastic barb. "I've called Border Patrol and Department of Public Safety for assistance countless times tonight. They're swamped. We'll get no help here. Have you called the sheriff yet for backup?"

"I got the call from Mexico and called dispatch. I called our Trauma Center team leader to round up the ER staff and drove here," Moss said.

"Call the sheriff. Tell him we need every man he can find to surround this building." Josie paused and listened as she heard an ambulance siren approaching the center's side entrance. "Otto's en route.

I'll have him start setting up the perimeter for backup. I'll work with the surgical team. You have any contacts you can tap for extra help?"

The mayor flipped open his cell phone to begin making calls while Josie met the ambulance.

The two attendants opened the back door of the ambulance and unloaded Hector Medrano, founder of the Medrano cartel. His chest and abdomen were shredded, and blood leaked through the bandages. His large square face was also bloodied and smeared with black dirt. He was as large in life as he appeared in the frequent newspaper and Internet articles that featured his crime sprees. Josie noticed the two Mexican attendants keeping a wary eye on the unconscious patient, stepping back from the gurney as soon as it was rolled into the operating room. Even with his approaching death, Josie could feel the evil that surrounded the man.

Within minutes, the two ER nurses had arrived. Vie Blessings parked and got out of her car, talking on a cell phone, already dressed in blue scrubs. She was a busty forty-year-old woman with spiked hair and vibrant makeup and jewelry. She commanded attention and got it. A younger nurse whom Josie didn't recognize got out of the passenger seat of the car; she looked pale and terrified and stayed behind Vie's back.

As soon as the nurses walked into the operating room, the ambulance attendants turned and left without a word.

"How bad is this?" Vie asked.

"I'll get your team locked in as soon as the surgeon gets here," Josie said. "How long?"

Vie looked at her watch. "Ten minutes at the most."

"I'll be in the room with you. Otto will be in the lobby near the front entrance. We're waiting on backup to surround the building."

Vie called over her shoulder to the younger nurse. She was a small-framed girl with slumped shoulders and round glasses.

"Carrie, this is Josie. She's the officer that will be in the room with us throughout surgery."

Josie shook the girl's clammy hand. "Good to meet you, Carrie. Don't sweat this. We're going to be okay."

Carrie offered a weak smile, and Vie told her to get the surgical table set.

After the girl left, Vie planted her hands on her hips and narrowed her eyes at Josie. "You never answered my question. Must mean it's pretty bad." Without waiting for a response, Vie turned back to the surgery room, already shouting orders.

When the surgeon arrived, Josie followed him into the prep area, where he scrubbed for surgery and dressed in sterile gear. He was tall, early thirties, and rail thin with a calm demeanor that impressed Josie immediately. She gave him a quick summary of the situation.

Before they walked out of the prep area, Josie stopped him at the door. "My first priority is the medical staff. You have control over the surgery. I have control over your safety. If I give you and the nurses an order, I need you to follow it. No questions asked. These people are murderers. I want to keep you safe."

He paused, considering his words, and then reached into the breast pocket on his scrub top. He handed Josie a picture of a baby.

"She's three months old," he said, his voice strained.

The baby's hand was wrapped tightly around her father's little finger, her lips forming an *O*, as if the camera had caught her by surprise.

"Keep us safe," he said. He squeezed Josie's shoulder and pushed open the door into the surgery room.

Within fifteen minutes, Hector Medrano was prepped, and Josie and Otto had done what they could to secure the building. She had sent the mayor back to his office to reduce his risk and keep him out of the way. Otto was positioned at the front door, crouched behind the receptionist's desk, while Josie stayed in the operating room.

Her biggest fear was the unmanned door at the back of the clinic. It was locked, but they were wide open for attack. There were so few police officers in the region that backup was unlikely. Artemis was surrounded by towns with populations under eight thousand. Odessa was the nearest large town, at ninety thousand people, but it was 240 miles away. She had requested Border Patrol and DPS backup, but time was not on her side.

As surgery began, Josie listened for voices or activity outside the operating room. She stood behind the surgical table to keep a clear view of the door, and attempted to avert her gaze from the bloody mess in front of her. Hearing the suction of body fluids made her realize she had not eaten since a half can of fruit cocktail for supper. She glanced down and watched the gloved hand of the surgeon, slick with blood, exit the man's chest cavity. Her peripheral vision turned black, and she pressed her hands flat on the cool concrete wall behind her, bent her knees, and breathed in the pungent mix of antiseptic and blood. She forced herself to take slow, deep breaths.

Vie, standing opposite the surgeon, called Josie's name. "You're looking a little peaked. You're not going to drop on us, are you?" Vie asked.

Josie shook her head, hoping Vie would leave her be.

Focusing on the door, Josie listened to the surgeon's steady voice and the measured blips and whisking of machines as her nausea subsided.

The surgeon walked Carrie through the process of inserting a chest tube to stabilize the patient's breathing, and Josie wondered at his bravery. He was one of twelve surgeons from El Paso and Odessa who served the trauma needs of several West Texas border towns on a rotating basis. With so few resources, the surgeons were required to take a course in triage. During emergencies, they were taught to determine which patients would live and which would die, regardless of treatment, so they could focus on the patients who would most benefit from immediate care. Josie feared the knowledge might be put to use that day.

Each person on the surgical team understood the danger they were in; operating on one of Mexico's drug cartel elite after a failed assassination attempt—one that would most certainly be completed in the future—seemed suicidal. And at what cost? Three decent human beings in exchange for a man suspected by authorities to have plotted the deaths of more than twenty rival gang members in the past year. For the assassins, an order to kill was an order, not a suggestion. The international border was no obstacle. La Bestia ran an organization as structured as, and certainly more ruthless than, any government military.

"The bullet struck bone. The fragments have to be removed. This will take longer than I'd hoped." The surgeon lifted his head and looked to the ceiling, either to stretch or offer a prayer. He took a steel instrument from Vie as the other nurse rattled off numbers that meant nothing to Josie.

Carrie checked the monitors. She pulled her scrubs away from her chest and twitched as if her clothes irritated her skin. Behind the blue mask, Josie saw the fear in her eyes.

"Pressure's dropping," the girl said. "There's blood in the breathing tube."

Josie heard muffled voices outside the building, and Vie lifted her head, her expression wary.

With her back braced against the wall, her muscles taut and focused, Josie strained to decipher the noises from outside the unit. She reached Otto on his cell phone, not wanting the conversation on the public frequency.

"I hear voices outside the building. DPS arrived?"

"The front parking lot is empty. I just checked with Lou. DPS has two officers on their way, but they're still thirty minutes out. The voices are coming from the east side of the building. They're moving toward the back door." Otto hesitated. "It's about to get ugly."

Josie knew Medrano would not have made it through surgery in Juárez. Retaliation in trauma units was common there. It was ranked the deadliest city in the world. Just a month ago, Mexican authorities charged two members of La Bestia for the murder of a high-ranking police commander in Juárez who refused to pay the demanded protection. He took a bullet through his chest as he entered the grocery with his wife. When the bullet failed to kill him, the assassins followed the ambulance to the hospital and killed the officer, the ambulance driver, and three bystanders.

Josie heard a car in the rear of the building, shut her cell phone, and slipped it in her shirt pocket. Within seconds, bullets pelted the back of the building, and glass shattered. The sound echoed down the hallway and filled the operating room. They had shot the back doors open. Voices were shouting, obviously inside the building now, speaking rapid-fire Spanish. Josie's chest tightened under her vest, and she gritted her teeth, every thought focused on her actions.

"Flat on your stomachs!" she said, waving to the floor.

The surgeon looked wide-eyed at the man on the gurney. "I can't leave him. He'll die!"

Josie pointed toward the corner of the room with her gun. "Now! They'll spray this whole room with bullets if they can't get in."

Gunshots echoed down the hall, just outside the trauma room, and Carrie screamed and dropped to her knees. Vie and the surgeon both looked to Josie for an answer. She motioned for them to cover their heads and lie on the floor in the corner.

More shouts from the hallway, then two additional gunshots, single caliber, that sounded like police rounds coming from the front of the building, where Otto was stationed. The three medical personnel lay flat on their stomachs. Josie heard the young nurse crying and Vie praying aloud. The doctor was between both nurses, his hands held protectively over their heads.

Josie crouched in the opposite corner. She had two guns, one on her thigh, cocked and ready for backup, the other trained on the door, both with a bullet in the chamber and a full magazine. The police-issued sidearms were little consolation in combat with automatic weapons that could sweep a room in a matter of seconds.

The trauma room echoed with the pounding of fists on the door and shouts in Spanish, but Josie couldn't shoot without knowing who stood beyond the wall. With her gun trained on the door, she thought of Otto in the front of the building and hoped he hadn't been hit. She shoved the image from her mind, forcing herself to keep focus.

The cries of the young nurse on the floor turned to sobs.

Bullets hit the door, ringed the handle, and the door flew open with a kick. Three gunmen screamed as they opened fire on the man lying on the table. Josie fired her pistol, hit one man in the chest, then a second in his upper arm. The first man stumbled backwards into the hallway; the second man fell back against the wall as the third man turned and fled, still yelling as he ran down the hall, spraying the walls with bullets.

She heard the clinic's back door slam and tires blow gravel through the parking lot. Josie leaped from her crouched position on the floor, yelling at the injured man to drop his weapon. He leaned against the wall, holding the other hand over the bleeding wound, the automatic rifle at his feet.

Josie pushed him to the floor, kneeled on his back. He cried out in pain as she pulled his arms back and snapped handcuffs on him. Stepping into the hallway, she pushed at the gunman lying on his back on the floor. From the chest wound, she was certain he was dead. She put her backup weapon inside the concealed holster under her shirt and carried his AK-47 with her. Otto ran down the hallway to the back entrance as Josie stood, leaving the wounded man moaning on the floor. The two nurses and doctor stared up at her from the floor.

"Anyone hit?" she asked them.

They began to pull themselves up into sitting positions, still too shocked to know if they were hurt. They all appeared fine to her, and she told them to stay down. She glanced at Medrano on the operating table. He was no longer recognizable.

With her back pressed against the wall in the hallway, she moved quickly toward the rear entrance. Otto rushed back inside, sweat dripping down his face, his coloring so red, she worried he might be having a heart attack.

"It's clear. No one back there, no cars or people in the parking lot or in the yards across the street."

"You okay?" Josie asked. Her voice echoed in her head as if in a box, and the smell of gunpowder burnt her nose.

Otto wiped the sweat off his forehead with his shirt sleeve. "Jesus, I thought you were all dead. The staff okay?"

"They got the patient. That's it."

The two stood in the silence of the hallway, ears still ringing in pain from the gunfire.

Eight hours later, Josie sat in the mayor's office, along with Moss and Sheriff Roy Martínez. Moss had requested a debriefing to discuss the shooting. His office was located in the Artemis City Building, which was connected to the left side of the police department in downtown Artemis. The mayor's office was located in the back of the long, narrow building, and was walled in brown 1970s-style wood paneling and beige shag carpeting. The conference table, large enough for eight people to sit around, dominated the office. A mahogany desk the size of a twin bed took up the space in the back. Josie could smell the cigar smoke on Moss's clothing from across the table as he plugged a laptop cord into a wall socket.

Built like a linebacker, with wide shoulders and a squat stance, the mayor held himself in great esteem and was not shy about sharing that opinion with anyone who would listen. Three years ago, when Josie applied for the position of chief of police, she had the support of the city council, the other officers in the department, and Sheriff Martínez. Moss was the hold-up. He had told her to take her name out of the running, that she did not belong, that she was not strong enough mentally or physically for the rigors of the job. It wasn't personal, he said, but women were not "built" for police work. She had ignored his demand and was appointed shortly thereafter. Josie had never learned who put the political pressure on Moss to hire her, but she knew he resented her presence and would relish her dismissal.

Josie connected her digital camera to the mayor's laptop, downloaded the images, and clicked through the set as she provided a description of the pictures she had taken, inside and out at the Trauma Center, as the Artemis PD and Texas Department of Public Safety officers processed the crime scene. She explained that she had hit one of the gunmen in the chest and he had died at the scene.

Moss interrupted her. "That is not good. Not good at all." His eyebrows furrowed, and he stared hard at Josie.

She ignored the comment and pointed to a picture of the gunman she had shot in the arm being loaded into an ambulance. "The Arroyo County Sheriff's Department took this man, the second gunman, into custody and transported him to the Arroyo County Hospital. The bullet was removed and the wound dressed. He was transported to the jail about an hour ago." She made eye contact with the mayor. "Our jail. The surgeon said the man needed to remain in the hospital overnight." She gestured to the sheriff sitting across the table from her. "Martínez fought and won."

Roy Martínez said, "After the hit on the Trauma Center, I won't risk another unsecured situation." Martínez shifted in his chair. A burly former marine, he was a large, muscular man who barely fit between the arms of the wooden captain's chair. He often looked uncomfortable in his uniform, as if he needed more space to breathe. He cleared his throat and said, "There's a nurse outside his cell to keep track of his medical needs. He's a Mexican citizen, so we'll have to figure out who's going to pay for this mess."

"We can't afford the phone bill, let alone the medical bills for a fugitive," the mayor said.

Josie pressed the space bar on the laptop and showed the last picture, a wide-angle shot of the operating room. The gurney and body had been removed, but blood splatter remained on the walls and floor. Yellow stickers, numbered one through fifty-eight, were scattered about the room near pockmarks and holes in the white cinder block.

"Fifty-eight bullets used to kill a man who was already half-dead," Josie said. "It's a miracle we didn't lose the entire medical staff."

Moss stood and walked to the window, then turned to face them. "This has to stop. I will not allow my town to be overrun by terrorists."

Sheriff Martínez cleared his throat and pushed a finger in between his neck and his brown uniform collar and tugged. He leaned forward in his chair toward the mayor. "Allow? You think the law officials in this town are allowing these people to shoot up the town?"

Moss stared back at Martínez and didn't speak. His expression changed, as if he were recalculating his next move.

"The city police department has three officers, including myself. The sheriff's department has four, and they have to run the jail," Josie said. "You have drug cartels across the border with million-dollar arsenals. You patch one hole in the border, and they just blow through another. They dig under the fence, they go over it in biplanes, they scramble the radar. We're in their line of traffic right now. And we don't have a tenth of the officers we need to fight back."

"Then patch the crack. Blow their asses down the border. I don't really give a damn, but I don't want them here," Moss said.

"Then don't allow medical transports across the border!" Josie said.

"Do you understand what kind of political hell we'd get if he died because we wouldn't allow him access to a surgeon?" Moss asked. "A U.S. citizen? The media would eat me alive!"

"We have two thousand miles of border with Mexico, and only a third of it is controlled. I just read a briefing last week from Homeland Security stating that West Texas was put on the national watchlist for high-intensity drug trafficking. We're a designated port for weapons transportation and terrorist entry." She let her words sink in. "We need more officers."

"Whose paycheck do you plan on squeezing? Yours?" He pointed directly at Josie. "I'm telling you, either get a grip on this situation, or I will find someone else who can."

Martínez interrupted. "I don't like your threat or your tone of voice. You don't have the power to replace me or her, so knock off the meaningless bully tactics."

Moss's eyes bulged in anger. He looked at Martínez. "That's fine! Let the voters deal with you. But the commissioners and I can and will run her out of town if she isn't doing her job."

"You need to be reminded of your place." Martínez leaned forward in his chair toward Moss. "You're a figurehead who can be voted out. You have absolutely no support to remove Chief Gray. And if you try, I'll personally run a campaign against you like this town has never seen."

After thirty minutes of talk that left everyone angrier, the mayor dismissed both officers with a wave of his hand and a vague order to catch the sons of bitches. Josie and Martínez exited his office and walked across the street to his car, which was parked in front of the courthouse. It was six o'clock, and the smoldering July sun intensified the misery. The grass around the courthouse lawn had been brown for a month, and even the massive oak trees that ringed the courthouse looked faded to Josie.

Martínez leaned against the hood of his sheriff's car and stroked his mustache. "You still shook up over the shooting?" he asked.

Josie stared at the pavement and considered the question. She respected and liked Martínez as a person. She was a foot shorter, but he never tried to overpower her with his physical presence, a tactic he used often—and effectively—with others. Josie stood at a thin five feet seven and carried herself with assurance. Most people had no doubt when looking at Chief Gray that she was capable and in charge, but that afternoon, she had begun to worry for the first time in her career that the criminals were getting the upper hand.

She pointed in the direction of the clinic, just a block away from the courthouse and police department, and stared at the yellow police tape that surrounded the building. "I kneeled on that floor, waiting for a hundred bullets to spray across the room. I'm thinking, these three people are lying there and looking to me for answers. For safety. But I felt like a caged animal locked in that room. I basically waited for us to die. What do you do when you have no options left?"

"You got them on the floor and offered protection. Wasn't much else you could do," Martínez said.

"I keep hearing Vie praying in my head. I swear I could hear her voice above the bullets." Josie paused for a minute and finally nodded toward the courthouse. "I can't take another meeting with that guy."

"He's an idiot. Don't sweat the idiots."

"The idiot makes statements in the newspaper about the lack of law enforcement in his great town. I look at the guy, and I want to throw a punch. He doesn't even need to speak, and I want to snap his arrogant—"

Martínez slapped Josie on the back and opened his car door. "He's scared to death and has no idea how to solve the problem. He sees his reelection floating down the Rio. And when you don't have solutions, all you have left is blame."

TWO

The Artemis Police Department faced the courthouse square from across the street, couched between the City Office and the Gun Club. The brick buildings surrounding the square were a mixture of one- and two-story flat-roofed structures, most with plate glass windows on either side of a glass entrance door. Several buildings sat empty while others were in need of a fresh coat of paint or a good scrub. Josie had noticed that downtown had begun to suffer over the past few years. The economy was tough, jobs were scarce, and people had bigger issues to deal with than keeping up appearances.

Josie walked into the PD and felt the welcome blast of stale cold air.

Dispatcher Lou Hagerty sat behind the dispatcher's desk and slammed her phone down. She scooted her rolling chair back to get Josie's full attention. "You'd think the gates of hell just opened into Artemis. The phone's ringing off the hook!" After forty years of Marlboro Lights, Lou's strained voice came out in a raspy whisper, but her irritation carried with no effort. "I've had half of Artemis on the phone today. Old Man Collier called and said Armageddon was on us. I believed him for a while there." She handed Josie a stack of pink papers with phone messages written in Lou's scrawling hand. "Jim Hankins, over at *Big Bend Sentinel*, wants a phone call ASAP. He's got the paper going to print, and he wants an update."

Josie stood at the front counter and sorted through her messages, asking Lou to clarify some of her notes. She passed several slips back to Lou and asked her to make follow-up phone calls, and then she called Jim. The *Sentinel* newspaper was located in Marfa, but it supplied news for several border towns, including Artemis. Jim provided a good pulse on local border issues, and his reporting was fair and accurate. He was a slight man with a ponytail and a limp earned during the Vietnam War. She gave him a brief explanation of what she knew as fact: Hector Medrano, the leader of the Medrano cartel, had been shot by a member of the La Bestia drug cartel during surgery in the Artemis Trauma Center. Gunfights took place in Piedra Labrada throughout the night, and thirteen people were confirmed dead. Jim thanked her and promised to keep her informed if he heard any local scuttlebutt on the cartels.

Josie hung up with Jim and grabbed a stack of file folders from Lou and walked toward the back of the office. The dispatcher and intake computer were located downstairs behind the front lobby area. The officers' desks were upstairs in a large shared space with a long oak conference table used for interviews. Beyond the table were three metal desks used by Josie, Otto, and Marta Cruz. Marta was the third-shift officer for the city police department and had been out of town during the shooting at the Trauma Center.

Before Josie could reach the stairs, the bell on the front door rang and she turned back to see a tall woman who looked to be in her early thirties. She wore a spaghetti strap tank top, cut-off jean shorts that revealed long tanned legs, and flip-flops. Long brown hair hung in tangles around her shoulders as if she had just been riding a motorcycle with no helmet.

"Can I help you?" Josie asked.

"There's a dead man on my couch."

Josie stifled a sigh. "Any special reason he's dead on *your* couch as opposed to someone else's?"

"Is that cop humor?"

"No. I'd like an answer."

"None to give. All I know is he's left a hell of a stain on the couch. Isn't even mine."

"The couch?"

"Not the couch or the trailer."

"Why didn't you call 911?" Josie asked.

The woman glanced at her watch. "I got ten minutes before I'm late to work. Six to midnight. If I called from the trailer, you guys would have kept me there for hours. I need my paycheck." She held up a set of house keys. "Make yourself at home."

Josie ignored the keys. "Do you know the dead man?"

"Red Goff."

Josie shook her head in shock. The woman smirked.

"How did he die?" Josie asked.

"Gunshot. In the forehead."

Josie couldn't believe what she was hearing. "You're telling me Red Goff was shot in the head inside your trailer?"

"That's exactly what I'm telling you."

"Do you know who shot him?" Josie asked.

"I have no idea." She held her keys up again. "I have to get to work. Can I pick my keys up here when I get off?"

"You have a dead man on your couch, and you can't tell me why?" Josie let the question hang for a beat, but the woman didn't respond. "Where do you work?"

"Value Gas."

"Call your boss. Tell her you won't be in tonight."

"You guarantee I won't get fired after I miss work?"

Josie felt a tension headache starting at the base of her skull. "Is Leona still a manager?" she asked.

The woman nodded.

"I'll call Leona. She owes me one."

She sighed loudly and slipped her keys into her shorts pocket.

"I'll have to take your statement." Josie gestured for the woman to enter through the swinging half door that led behind the front counter. The counter extended across the front of the office and separated the lobby from the booking and intake area.

Josie turned to face Lou. "Get an ambulance out there and call Otto. Tell him we've got a probable homicide and we need him there now. Ask him to secure the scene and call the coroner. Tell him I'll be there within the hour."

"It doesn't take a degree to figure out dead. He ain't coming back."

Josie turned to the woman. "Just a precaution. Have to do things by the book."

"Whatever suits you," she said.

Josie walked past Lou and led the woman to a desk with a computer that the officers shared for intakes and statements. She pointed to a chair across from the desk and pulled up the form on the computer. "Name?"

"Pegasus Winning."

Josie glanced up and saw the woman was serious. "Address?"

"I don't have an address."

"The address for the trailer," Josie said.

"There isn't one. My brother said he never had an address for it."

"Does your brother have a P.O. box?"

She shook her head. "Nope. He didn't want mail."

Josie looked up from her computer. "Work with me here, okay? I need to get out to your place, and you need to get to work."

"It's off Farm Road 170, just in front of Red's place. Use his address. He's dead, anyway."

"What's your relationship with Red?" Josie asked.

"Limited." She grimaced. "He'd wander down to my place to tell me the world was coming to an end. How I needed guns and dead bolts. Like anyone in their right mind would want what's inside my trailer. He'd rant about the government and the police state. Then he'd try to get me to go to his place to look at his guns. Show and tell. He was a leech."

"You're living in your brother's trailer?" Josie asked.

"I moved here about three months ago to live with him, but he was gone. He left me a note and said he had to cool off. Couldn't take the Texas heat anymore. He left me an address to mail the trailer payment each month. That was about it."

"Think he was in trouble when he left?"

"He's never been out of trouble."

Because the murder was committed outside the city limits, Josie had called the sheriff's department to pass the case off. Technically, it was their jurisdiction, but dispatch had said all their officers were tied up. Josie agreed to take the case. With a budget so tight it barely covered salaries, the two departments often operated out of jurisdiction in order to cover calls. Considering the territorial drama among agencies in some small towns, she took pride in the relationship the city police and sheriff's department shared in Artemis. She also worked well with most of the Border Patrol agents, and with the occasional Department of Public Safety officer, though DPS rarely showed up so far out of the city.

Josie followed Winning's 1980s Cadillac Eldorado to her trailer. The car was the size of a boat with a mottled black and gray paint job. Josie thought it was one of the ugliest cars she had ever seen. She followed Winning down Farm Road 170 west toward Candelaria, a ghost town and dead end for the 170. After the Mexican Revolution ended, the cavalry pulled out and the city had faded.

Josie had once talked with an old rancher who raised his family in Candelaria back in the seventies. He said there were no border issues back then. People crossed the river at will and traded basic goods among the small towns. Families were buried on both sides of the river. Josie gazed out across the Chihuahuan Desert and tried to imagine the freedom and lack of fear that families like that once felt.

Winning was living alone in one of the most remote places in the United States, down the lane from Red Goff, a man rumored to have an arsenal of several hundred guns, including high-powered rifles and automatic weapons. Josie had no doubt that Winning knew more than she was telling, but Josie needed to deal with the dead body before the heat destroyed it. Just as important, Goff's house had to be inventoried and locked before the vultures ransacked it for the rumored arsenal.

As the leader of the Gunners, a right-wing group of Second Amendment nuts who thought guns would solve the world's ills, Red was known throughout West Texas. He was an arrogant hothead. Before he turned into a hermit, Josie would occasionally roust him from various Democratic rallies for shouting obscenities and causing a public disturbance. Josie had gathered intelligence on Red's organization, the Gunners, for years. They had too much firepower to let it get into the wrong hands.

Ten minutes outside Artemis, Josie followed Winning down Davis Pass, a gravel road prone to washouts. The drive stirred up a thick layer of white desert dirt that recoated the ocotillo and prickly pear cactus that dotted the roadside. Large boulders, gray green agave, juniper, and Spanish daggers marked the white, sandy foothills for miles. The Chinati Peak could be seen in the distance, a grand backdrop to the ramshackle trailer propped up on two dozen cinder blocks in the rocky dirt. Josie wondered what kept the trailer from washing away in a heavy downpour.

Otto's Artemis PD jeep was parked out front, the navy blue

paint barely visible under the nearly permanent layer of dust. The jeeps were a perk of the job: four-wheel drive, no-frills, stripped-down retired army models capable of driving anywhere, on road or off. Otto stepped out of the trailer as Pegasus parked her Eldorado beside the jeep and got out of her car looking angry and hot. Her car windows were down, and Josie figured she had no air-conditioning.

"It's Red Goff in there, sure enough," Otto said with a frown as Josie stood and slammed her door shut.

He smoothed down the flyaway gray hair on top of his head. Otto weighed forty pounds over the department limit for patrol work, but it had never been an issue. He had served as chief of police for twelve years before giving it up for a slower pace. He was still an excellent officer, slow and methodical.

"Murder or suicide?" Josie asked.

"There's a nice piece of irony," Otto said. "Gunshot through the head. Unless he's been moved, angle's wrong for suicide. Five hundred guns in his closet to save him from the government, and what do you want to bet one of the other gun crazies shot him?"

Josie introduced Otto to Winning, who still looked hot and annoyed.

"Let's go over this again. What time did you get off work?" Josie asked her.

Winning rolled her eyes. "My shift ended at seven o'clock this morning. I got home at seven fifteen. I took a shower and went to bed."

"You slept here all day long?" Josie asked.

"Yep."

"A guy gets shot on your couch and you don't hear it?" Josie asked.

"Nope."

"You might want to lose the attitude. You're a suspect for murder on a pretty short list."

Winning laughed. "A short list? The guy's threatened to kill half of Texas, you included. You got more suspects than you can count."

"Difference is, he's lying on your couch," Josie said. "Now, tell me how it is a man gets shot in your trailer and you don't hear it."

She scowled and crossed her arms over her chest. "If I knew, I'd tell you. Maybe someone shot him with a silencer. Maybe they shot him while I was in the shower with the music up."

"You have a stereo in the bathroom?" Josie asked.

Winning walked to the trailer and stepped inside her front door. Josie followed her up the stack of cinder blocks that made for a front stoop and entered the trailer. Otto had propped the door open, but the heat was stifling.

The corpse was lying on the couch with a hole in the center of his forehead and three dried blood rivulets that ran down the side of his nose and right cheek. His face was covered in stubble that matched the gray of the military haircut on his head. Red's eyes were open and vacant, the old arrogance extinguished.

Red Goff had been a thin man, standing about five feet five inches, but in the heat of the trailer, his face and arms were already beginning to bloat. It gave him a distended look, as if he were reflected in a fun house mirror. He wore black polyester dress pants and a white button-down shirt that was pulled up on one side, exposing a pale, hairy stomach that somehow looked more obscene than the bullet hole through his head.

The couch was up against a wall in the living room, the only room to the left of the front door. To the right was a small dining room and kitchen.

Pegasus pointed down a short hallway through the kitchen. "Bathroom and bedroom are down there."

Josie entered the bathroom and saw a duffel bag–sized stereo perched on a wooden shelf on the wall facing the shower. She pushed the power button, and the Kinks blasted out from the speakers. She turned it off. She stepped back out into the hallway and saw that Red's body couldn't be seen from the hallway area in the back of the trailer. The couch sat behind a four-foot-by-four-foot half wall that separated the front door entryway from the living room.

"Satisfied?" Winning asked.

"Otto?" Josie called. "Give me twenty seconds, then shoot off one round."

Josie ignored Pegasus standing in the hallway and shut the bathroom door. She turned the shower on and pressed the power button on the stereo to hear a head-splitting *La-la-la-la Lola*. Ten seconds later she heard a dim pop, but if Winning had been singing with the music, she could have missed the sound. Her bedroom was to the right of the bathroom, so she could have taken her shower and gone to bed without seeing the body.

Josie opened the door.

Winning cocked her head but said nothing.

"It's pretty flimsy. What time did you take your shower?" Josie asked.

"Seven thirty."

"Exactly?"

"I get off work at seven. I come straight home. Drink two or three shots of tequila. Depends on how bad the shift was. I take a shower, brush my teeth, and go to bed."

"You lock your door when you're home?"

Winning pulled a rubber band off her wrist and ran her fingers through her sweaty, tangled hair to pull it into a loose ponytail behind her head. "Can I at least turn the air-conditioning on? I turn it off when I leave for work. I can't even breathe in here."

Josie nodded toward the living room and watched Winning walk by the body on her couch, grimace down at it, then turn the wall unit at the end of the room on high.

Otto had come back into the trailer and was on one knee by the couch, getting a carpet sample. He cursed as sweat dripped from the end of his nose and onto the plastic evidence bag in his hand.

"It already smells in here. Can't you get him out?" Winning asked, her nose wrinkled in disgust.

"The coroner should be here soon. We'll get him out as soon as we can. Let's step outside," Josie said.

Outside, Pegasus led Josie to a small picnic table under a clump of gnarled cedar trees that offered a surprising amount of shade from the setting sun. "I can give you a glass of well water that tastes like nails, or you can have a beer," Winning said.

She crossed her forearms in front of her and leaned on the picnic table. Josie noted the sprinkling of freckles across her nose and high, pronounced cheekbones. She was prettier than she let on.

"Nothing, thanks," Josie said. She pulled out her steno pad and opened it. "Do you lock your doors when you come home, Ms. Winning?"

She smirked. "One swift kick's all you need. Red claimed Kenny used to padlock the door. I can't see why."

Josie studied her for a moment. "Back at the office, why did you need to give me the keys to your trailer if it wasn't locked?"

Winning tilted her head and paused long enough to consider the question, or her answer. Josie couldn't tell.

"Don't you think it was wise to lock the dead man inside until the police could get here? You wouldn't want the body tampered with, would you?"

Josie gestured toward the trailer. "How did Officer Podowski get inside?"

"Beats me. Have to ask him. Probably the extra key under the mat."

"You ought to consider being more careful with who has access to your trailer."

Winning shrugged.

"Can you think of anyone who would want to break in?" Josie asked.

"Nope."

"Have you made any enemies since you moved here?"

"Only enemy I have is back in New Orleans."

"Who's that?" Josie asked.

"My ex."

"Any chance he could have paid you a visit? Found Red up the road and got jealous?" Josie asked.

"No way. He was strictly knives. They're clean and easy. No jacking around with bullets. His words, not mine."

Winning stood and stepped back from the picnic table. She lifted her shirt to reveal a pale flat stomach and a one-inch scar just below her navel. The scar was red and puffy, a fairly recent wound.

She looked down at her stomach as she talked. "This is his. I was a Daiquiri Girl on Bourbon Street. Made great money until my boss came in and saw blood seeping through my T-shirt. He said it was bad for business and fired me on the spot. Lousy bastard. That's when I called my brother."

"Do you know anyone who was out to get Red?"

She grinned. "You a Democrat?"

"Depends," Josie said.

Winning shrugged. "Doesn't matter. You're still the enemy. Democrats, cops, government, former schoolteachers, the Pope. You were all plotting an attack on his shitty little house in the desert. You were all about to converge and demand he sacrifice his land and home to your subversive causes." She rolled her eyes and sat back down. "He told that slop to anyone who would listen. I figure more people wanted him dead than alive. Except that sick bunch of freaks he ran with."

"The Gunners."

"There are some seriously bizarre people in this world."

"Think any of them could have killed Red?"

"No clue."

"You ever hear of the members arguing with each other?"

"No clue."

"Do you know if he has any family members in the area?"

"Nope."

Josie sighed, frustrated at her lack of cooperation. "Ms. Winning, at this point, you're my best connection to Red Goff."

"Look. I'd help you if I could. But I don't know anything. He's just some weird guy that ended up dead on my couch. I'd like to know how he got there, too. Trust me." She pointed in the direction of the trailer. "But I have to sleep in that thing tonight. So, honestly, I couldn't give a rat's ass about Red Goff. The feeling was mutual once he figured out my zipper was shut. I got my own worries right now."

Red Goff's place was built into the hillside two hundred feet behind Winning's trailer. The underground dwelling consisted of a nine-foot-by-forty-foot-long wall covered in gray aluminum siding with no windows and only one entry point, a set of sliding glass doors dead center in the wall. Cactus and desert scrub had been strategically placed in front of the wall so that his house blended into the landscape.

After the coroner arrived for the body, Josie and Otto walked up the steep hill to Goff's to check out his house. Otto mopped at his forehead with a handkerchief and complained about the heat.

"What's your take on the girl?" Josie asked.

"Pegasus Winning. What kind of mother names her kid that?"

"She's pretty laid-back about it all," Josie said. "People usually try and put on a show when they're trying to hide something. Give you what they think you want."

"She couldn't care less."

Josie nodded, but her gut instinct told her Winning was innocent.

Otto pointed to the left of the house. Another structure had been built into the hillside, a one-car garage, even more carefully disguised behind a thick stand of piñon pines. "Sneaky bastard."

"He definitely wanted to hide something. Maybe he just wanted to hide himself away from the world."

"Don't you bet that son of a buck hated that trailer perched at the bottom of his driveway? I bet old Red tried like hell to buy that piece of land just for the privacy," Otto said.

"I'll call the courthouse and see who owns the land. Winning said her brother rented the land from someone, and she sends the rent payment to a P.O. box each month. The check is made out to a third-party rental agency," Josie said.

Otto asked, "You know anything about her brother? All I knew was there was someone living out here by Red."

Josie shook her head. "She showed me a picture of him, but I didn't recognize him. I think he kept a low profile. Name is Kenny Winning. Thirty years old. Tall, skinny guy. She claims she doesn't know what kind of job he had."

As they reached Red's house, Josie pointed up the hill that served as the side of his house. "Let's clear the back before we go inside."

From atop the roof, it was impossible to tell there was a house below. A half mile beyond, the land sloped into government grazing pasture and tall swaths of green native grasses, some of the prettiest country in Artemis.

"Typical Red. Builds his house on the ugliest chunk of ground on his property," Otto said.

"Facing a double-wide trailer on cement blocks." She shook her head and pointed toward a small barn with its doors wide open. "He used to raise a small herd of cattle. At least we don't have to deal with moving cows out of here. I'll check around and make sure somebody didn't run off with them."

Otto pointed to the right side of the property, where a well-tended ten-foot-by-twenty-foot garden thrived due to a drip-irrigation system on a timer. "Hard to picture Red as a gardener."

They walked back down the hill, and Josie snapped 35-millimeter pictures of the house and garage before entering. Otto set his evidence kit down and tried the sliding door with a gloved hand. It opened easily.

"Not a good sign," said Josie.

Otto slid the door all the way open and tapped on it. "I heard this is bulletproof glass shipped in from China. Cost him a pretty penny."

The two stepped into a room lit by the late afternoon sun. Several tube skylights ran approximately four feet through the dirt above the house to the ground above and provided a surprising amount of light.

"Looks like a bachelor pad," Otto said. "Couch, coffee table, and TV. Concrete floor. Not much else a man needs."

Josie winced. "Smells like Red. Musty and rank." She walked to the back wall, which was painted a deep gray. Several hundred hooks stuck out of the wall, starting at about four feet from the floor and extending to the ceiling. "What do you figure these are?" Josie asked, moving closer.

Otto stood in front of the wall and drew his finger around long, darkened shadows where something had covered the wall and kept the sun from bleaching the paint.

Otto pointed to a dark outline. They noticed the pattern at the same time.

"He had guns mounted on the wall. Dozens," Josie said. "Somebody beat us."

Gravel sprayed as a pickup truck slid to a stop outside Red's front door. A man stormed out of the truck and was about to walk in before Josie stepped up and stopped him.

"What's going on here?" the man demanded, trying to see around Josie and into the house.

"I'll ask you the same," Josie said.

She recognized him as the local pediatrician: a slightly balding middle-aged man in khaki pants and a button-down short-sleeved shirt. Average everything. He was a compact man, about five feet seven inches tall, with a soft boyish complexion and light blond hair. His lips had tightened down into an angry line; his eyes filled with unfocused anger.

"Where's Red at?" he asked, his voice shallow and nervous.

"Are you Dr. Fallow?" Josie asked.

"Yes. Paul Fallow."

"Dr. Fallow, you're interrupting a crime scene investigation. Unless you have something to share concerning the investigation, you need to leave."

The man's complexion turned gray, and he put both hands out as if searching for a chair. Josie moved backwards and allowed him entrance to Red's house. He stumbled in, and Otto and Josie grabbed his arms to lead him toward the couch, where he sat, staring up at Josie with uncomprehending eyes.

"Is it true, then, that Red's dead?"

"Where did you hear that?" Josie asked.

"I stopped at the Gun Club. Tiny was closing up for the day. I had to ask him about an order. He told me he'd heard a rumor that Red had been murdered. Is it true?"

Josie shook her head at Otto. "This has to be the gossip capital of the world."

"Looks like Lou decided to scoop the story," Otto said.

Fallow looked confused. "So, it's gossip, then—about Red?"

"No, Mr. Fallow, this time the gossip was accurate. Red was murdered. Do you have any idea why someone would want to kill him?" Josie asked.

Fallow sank back into the couch, his jaw slack. "I didn't believe it. I was sure it was just a rumor."

"Do you know anyone who was angry with Red? Anyone Red had fought with recently?" she asked.

Another pickup truck drove up the driveway, and all three of them turned to the sliding glass door to watch a large man in blue jeans, black T-shirt, and black cowboy hat climb out of his truck. Josie recognized Sheriff's Deputy Hack Bloster and met him at the door before he could enter.

"What can I do for you, Hack?"

"What the hell are you doing in Red's house?" Bloster spoke with a wad of chewing tobacco in his cheek that made it hard to separate his words. His skin had the dark, lined texture of cowhide, and he looked to be anywhere from a well-preserved fifty to a life-hardened thirty. Josie assumed it was the latter. Bloster noticed Fallow sitting on the couch and made a move to walk past Josie into the house.

She put her forearm up to block Bloster's entrance, and he flinched like he had been touched by a hot iron. "This is an investigation. You need to leave the property. If you have questions, call and make an appointment with the dispatcher. I can see you tomorrow."

"I'm a cop. I don't need an appointment. This is our jurisdiction, anyway. You're the one shouldn't be here," Bloster said.

Otto turned and grimaced at Fallow. "Is he part of your club?"

Fallow's already pale face had gone completely white. "Vice president."

Josie gestured toward Bloster's truck and attempted to maintain her patience. "Deputy, you have a conflict of interest here that wouldn't do you, or the investigation, any good. For both our sakes, I would suggest you leave until we figure out what happened here."

Bloster noticed the wall behind the couch in Red's living room. His eyes widened. "What the hell did you do with his guns?"

She considered him. The rumors would spin hard and fast, twisting the investigation into a funnel cloud of half truths and innuendo. She decided to tell Bloster the truth to gauge his reaction.

"The guns were missing when we arrived. How do you know Red didn't move them?" she asked.

Bloster pointed his index finger within an inch of Josie's chest, and she knocked it away with her forearm.

"Don't do that again. You have something to say to me, then do it with respect."

Bloster stared at her for a moment. When he spoke again, the volume was lower, but the anger just as intense. "Those guns leave the wall for one reason and one reason only."

"Which is?" she asked.

"Use." He lifted his chin in the air.

"What kind of use?" she asked.

"The kind we find necessary to keep this world running the way it ought to," Bloster said.

Fallow moaned on the couch and leaned over to put his head between his knees.

"Suck it up, Fallow," Bloster said.

"What the hell are we going to do?" Fallow said toward the floor.

"We continue to do the right thing!" Bloster said.

Josie sighed. "I need you both to leave so we can finish here. Officer Podowski or I will be in contact with you tonight or tomorrow."

She wrote Bloster's and Fallow's contact information on the small notepad she kept in her uniform shirt pocket and both men left. Otto stood at the sliding glass door and watched the cars exit the driveway, making sure they didn't stop to talk with the coroner or, worse, tamper with evidence.

After she and Otto finished a quick inventory of Red's place, they locked the sliding door with a key they had found on Red's desk and ran crime scene tape around the front of the house. Before they locked up, Josie sketched a picture of Red's desk and the location of the key. It seemed odd to her that someone as paranoid as Red would leave a key lying in the open on his desk. By the time they walked back down the lane to Winning's trailer, the county coroner, Mitchell Cowan, had finished his job and was zipping Red Goff's corpse into a black plastic body bag.

Cowan was a large man who reminded Josie of Eeyore, the sad donkey from Winnie the Pooh. His head drooped low like his gut, as if the weight of the world was dragging him down. He talked slowly, to the point of annoyance, but he was thorough and his findings were well respected in court.

Cowan lifted his balding head and waved to Josie and Otto. "Got a surprise for you."

Josie and Otto followed Cowan to the shade provided by the cedar trees. When he didn't elaborate, Josie cleared her throat, prompting him to continue, her tolerance slipping in the heat.

"That bullet exited Red's skull."

"Does that mean the shooter was up close?" Josie asked.

"Yes, ma'am. I'm guessing a pretty high-caliber gun was used. The surprise, though?" He posed the question and waited for Josie to wave him on again before he would finish. "The bullet isn't in the couch. Somebody shot him elsewhere and then arranged the body on the couch," Cowan finished with a satisfied smile.

"They either thought the police were inept, or they were telling us something," Josie said.

"Or the message was for someone else," Otto said.

With the body removed, Josie took additional pictures of the couch. They searched the trailer, looking for the ejected bullet, but there was no indication a gun was fired inside.

Otto helped Cowan get the body on the stretcher, and Josie stood outside to talk to Danny Delgado, sanitation supervisor, known locally as the Dump Man. Josie had called and asked if he would haul away the bloodstained couch to the evidence locker at the department that evening. Winning stood by the trailer door and watched as Josie and Delgado carried the couch to his pickup truck. Danny and Josie climbed inside the pickup where he helped her cover the couch with a plastic tarp before she took pictures of how it would be transported. She had a feeling the couch might play a major role in the investigation and the trial.

Danny shut the tailgate and headed for Winning like a dog after a bone. He smiled at her and rubbed his hands down the front of his blue jeans, then up and through his hair, then back down to his jeans. He had the nervous tics of a crack addict, and Josie wondered if he was really wound that tight or if drugs were the issue.

"How about I drop your couch off, then come back and take you out for a beer?" Danny ran his hands through his coarse blond hair again.

Winning scowled at him and crossed her arms over her chest but didn't speak.

"Danny. Leave her alone. A man was murdered in her home today," Josie said.

"Hey! If anybody in this town needs a beer, it's her. And I'm offering it to her free!"

Josie pointed to Danny's truck, and he winked at Winning as he turned to leave. Josie sent Otto to ride with Danny to provide validation the evidence was not tampered with before it was logged into evidence.

By the time Josie finished Red Goff's initial paperwork, she felt as if she had worked a twenty-four-hour shift. She sat in her jeep to clear up a few things before driving home. A call to the night dispatcher confirmed there was no new activity coming from across the border. She had instructed dispatch to make daily phone calls to the Artemis PD contacts in Piedra Labrada until the city calmed down. Next, she called Martínez, who told her that the Mexican prisoner from the shooting at the Trauma Center had stabilized and was ready for questioning. Martínez was working on fingerprints and hopefully a positive identification from NCIC or DACS, the National Crime Information Center or Deportable Alien Control System. Josie thanked him and told him she would be at the jail by noon the next day to interview the prisoner.

Before Josie hung up, she asked, "What's the story with your deputy, Hack Bloster, and the Gunners?"

"Bloster's too intense for his own good. He's a gun nut, but he's a good cop. He'll walk into a shit storm without a second thought. He's good with border issues."

"He showed up at Red's tonight, off duty. He threw his weight around. Wanted to know why your department wasn't conducting the investigation."

"It doesn't surprise me. I'll talk to him."

"Remind him a little professional courtesy goes a long way."

THREE

Josie pointed her jeep toward the sun, just a red bump on the darkening horizon, and drove with all four windows down, listening to Johnny Cash sing a live version of "Folsom Prison Blues." She attempted to focus her thoughts on the winding gravel road that led to her house in the foothills of the Chinati Mountains, but the image of Vie Blessings praying on the hospital floor imprinted like a watermark over everything. The wind would not clear the vision of the young surgeon, still in his blood-splattered scrubs, crying into his hands outside the clinic after it was over. And she could not erase the thought that she knew would invade every nightmare for the next month: *We are losing our town to mercenary killers.*

As Josie was cresting a hill sloping into a patchy field of prairie grass and mesquite, her eyes were drawn to her home ahead. Its pink stucco walls glowed each night at sunset. The house was a simple rectangle with a deep front porch held aloft by hand-hewn pecan timbers. Two low-slung chairs, one for her neighbor, Dell Seapus, and one for her, faced the panoramic view of the endless Chihuahuan

Desert that stretched out beyond the Rio and deep into Mexico. Behind her house, the Chimiso Peak, a rocky crag in the midst of the Chinati Mountain range, was visible.

Chester, a brown and tan bloodhound, lay on the porch in front of her door, head on his front paws, his ears draped across the floor like a head scarf. Josie knew he would not raise his head until she stood in front of him, hand outstretched to scratch behind his velvet ears. She smiled, rolled her windows up, and shut the jeep off. She'd asked Dell to stop in and feed the dog last night while she was away from home. Dell would never admit it, but he loved the dog as much as Josie did.

She unlocked the front door and followed the hound inside to a living room painted a buttery yellow and filled with rustic Southwestern furniture, Navajo Indian blankets, and more benches and chairs that Dell had carved from fallen cedar and pecan trees off his ten-thousand-acre ranch. The seventy-year-old bachelor's ranch was tucked into the foothills behind her house. Josie had come to know Dell shortly after joining the police department nine years ago. He had been robbed at gunpoint in his barn, where two horse thieves had loaded five of Dell's prized Appaloosas onto a trailer and taken off. After a four-week investigation, Josie tracked the men to New Mexico and returned the horses unharmed. Her detective work had established her as a first-rate cop in town and won her a loyal friend in Dell.

Josie had spent quite a bit of time at Dell's ranch over the course of the investigation and fell in love with the desert. Dell deeded her ten acres of land on the front end of his property, and she built her home with the trust money she had received as a child when her father was killed in a line-of-duty accident. She moved from Indiana at the age of twenty-four to escape her mother and begin a new life. A year after moving to Artemis, she moved into the first place that had ever felt like home to her. Dell claimed to always have her back, and she did not doubt him.

Josie unstrapped her uniform belt and hung it on a hook just inside her pantry door, stuck a bag of popcorn in the microwave for dinner, and walked back to the house's only bedroom, barely large enough to hold her queen-sized bed, dresser, and nightstand. She hung her uniform and bulletproof vest in the closet, then dressed in shorts and a T-shirt. She exhaled deeply, rubbing the small of her back, and looked at her empty bed, the white sheets and cotton blanket in a jumble. Her thoughts strayed to Dillon Reese, but she turned and left the room, unwilling to wander down that lonely road.

Josie laid her watch on the bathroom counter and noticed her tired eyes in the mirror. Her skin had the permanent tan of a desert dweller, and fine wrinkles radiated from the corners of her eyes from too many hours squinting into the bright afternoon light. She didn't consider herself vain, although the lines around her eyes bothered her occasionally. She wondered if she had enough to show in her life for the age that had started to accumulate on her face. When Josie was growing up, her mom had often told her she might be pretty if she would smile once in a while. She envied others who smiled often and laughed easily. She wished she could loosen up, laugh at simple things, and see the humor in life. She had tried to develop that trait in herself through the years, but she had found there were few things more uncomfortable than forced laughter.

In the kitchen, she poured a double shot of warm bourbon, dumped salt into a microwaved popcorn bag, and slumped into the couch. After two hours of CNN had done little to still her racing thoughts, she washed down two sleeping pills with another shot of bourbon and hoped her brain would grow numb by ten o'clock. She desperately needed a good night's sleep. When the phone rang and she didn't recognize the number on the caller ID, she picked it up.

"Great god a'mighty, you're a hard one to track down."

Josie knew the voice immediately, and in a split second considered begging off as a wrong number.

"How are you?" she asked.

"I'm fine, not that it means anything to you."

Josie listened to her mother inhale deeply on a cigarette, and sadness settled over her like a bad dream she couldn't shake.

"You ever planning on calling me again?"

"Our phone calls don't work out so well," Josie said.

After Josie left Indiana nine years ago, she had called her mom twice a year—once at Christmas and once for her mom's birthday—until two years ago. Their last conversation had ended in a terrible fight, and Josie quit calling. This was the first time her mother had made the call. Josie figured she needed something.

"The operator. She said this area code was Texas. You still living out there?"

"That's right."

"What city you living in?"

Josie closed her eyes and drank, thankful for the heat in her throat. She pictured her mother as she'd seen her last, the night Josie bailed her out of jail on a public intoxication charge. She had gotten drunk and physical with the bartender at the Holiday Inn lounge. Josie had paid the bond, then watched her mother stagger out from lockup, her head down, not from shame, but because she was too drunk and tired to hold it level. Her long red hair had been a wild tangled mess, and she wore a miniskirt and halter top that revealed too much sunbaked skin.

"I'm living in West Texas. You still in the old house?" Josie asked.

"It's falling in around me, but I'm still here. Nowhere else to go."

Josie's mom lived in a small bungalow with a postage stamp–sized lot. Josie figured she had done little to maintain the house, and if she didn't currently have a man around to take care of her, she was in trouble, either physically or financially.

"I've been looking for my long-lost daughter for years. I finally tracked you down, and I aim to visit. That's why I'm calling."

Her words slurred together, and Josie could only hope her mother would lose the phone number before she was sober enough to use it again.

"How about Aunt Jean? Is she still in town?"

"Nope. She got married and moved to Florida."

Beverly gave a rambling update on the few distant family members she still spoke to.

"Are you working anywhere?" Josie asked.

There was silence.

Josie's mother had no pride. She was a pro at manipulating men: neighbors, teachers, preachers, gas station attendants, anyone who could help her through her current predicament. In her prime, she had been a good-looking woman who could fabricate charm or despair at will. While Josie was growing up, life in their Indiana town was built on lies and deceit: her mother did whatever was necessary, aside from a nine-to-five job, to get food on the table and the rent paid before the eviction notice arrived in the mail. Josie wondered, with her mother turning fifty-five, if she struggled now to stay afloat.

"There's no work to be had. Jobs are all dried up. You got work out there an old woman could get?"

Josie's stomach knotted. "Unemployment's worse out here. There's no work to find."

"You going to invite me down for a visit, or do I have to invite myself?"

She hesitated, tried to come up with a decent excuse, and gave up. "Now isn't a great time."

"You don't visit in how long? Now you can't be bothered to see me when I need you?" Her words were getting louder.

"You know it will end in a fight. You might as well save yourself the money and the grief."

"You don't want to invite me? That's fine, Josie Jean. But you are my daughter, and I aim to find you. I got the area code. How hard can it be to track down a policewoman named Josie Gray in Texas?"

The line went dead.

Josie woke with a terrible headache brought on by sleeping pills that hadn't done their job and bourbon that had made the room spin. She stumbled out of bed to shut off the second alarm clock on the dresser and cursed all the way to the shower. She put her uniform on and, at the small table in her kitchen, doused a bowl of canned fruit cocktail with Tabasco sauce. An old Mexican man told her years ago that hot sauce for breakfast burned off the toxins from alcohol the night before, and she had bought into the theory. She had begun to crave the burn in the small of her stomach, and while she figured her stomach lining was disintegrating, she didn't care enough to change her habits.

The fifteen-minute drive to Artemis did not improve her mood. The traffic, normally nonexistent in the dead-end border town, was backed up at the one stoplight. A small group of people was gathered around the ten-foot-high set of bleachers in back of the courthouse. Mayor Moss had them erected when he came to office ten years ago. He liked to gather community members once a month for a Rally Round the Square. It was his opportunity to boast about his service and ensure reelection. Roughly twenty people had gathered this morning, and Josie wondered what Moss had done to gather a group so quickly and so early. She watched him approach the bleachers holding a portable microphone.

Josie parked her car in the chief's reserved spot in front of the Artemis Police Department. She started to head inside to tell Dispatcher Lou Hagerty that she would be a few minutes late until she saw Lou walking across the road to stand with the crowd.

Josie spotted Sheriff Martínez's brown sheriff's uniform standing twenty feet away from the bleachers and the gathering townspeople, and she walked over to stand beside him. "What's going on?"

He turned to face her, and she noticed a light stubble of beard on his jaw and the bags under his eyes. He had black hair and a mustache and what Josie thought of as cop's eyes.

"How the hell should I know? We're just supposed to protect this town. Why should Moss bother to fill us in?"

They turned to watch the mayor's performance. Moss wore Wrangler jeans, a plaid shirt, bolo tie, and fancy stitched cowboy boots that had cost a good seven hundred dollars and would never see a field or a cow.

For the next thirty minutes, the mayor discussed the horrors of the day prior and the fact that he was organizing an investigative team to tackle the problems on the border, as if what they were facing could be reduced to a checklist, a prioritized to-do list. Josie felt her neck and face flush hot with anger.

"You know anything about this team?" Martínez asked Josie.

"Nothing."

"In closing," Moss was saying, "I want each and every one of you to rest assured that I will do everything humanly possible to stop these criminals from further terrorizing our town. This will stop on my watch."

There was a smattering of polite applause, and then a few pockets of people formed to rehash the speech before rushing to work. Old Man Collier appeared out of nowhere, his face puckered, and planted himself in front of Josie. He craned his neck up in an awkward position and stooped so far forward that his head barely reached Josie's chest.

"My hard-earned tax dollars are paying your salaries. And what good's it doing me? I got Mexicans in my backyard shooting up my doctor's office. And the only one seems to care about this is Mayor Moss. Why's that?"

"I wasn't hired to make speeches. I was hired to fight crime.

That's exactly what the sheriff and I spent our day doing yesterday, Mr. Collier."

"You didn't do a very good job, did you?"

"We don't have much control over who comes into town. We just have to deal with the aftermath," Josie said, surprised at her patience.

"You got control." He pointed a finger to the gun at her side. "Start using that thing before they use 'em on us. Border Patrol won't stand guard, then you do it. You two candy asses need to buck up and raise a little hell's what I think." He raised a hand as if swatting at a fly and turned and left.

Josie walked into the department before Lou returned to her desk. She was not in the mood for pleasantries or small talk. In the back of the department, she took the stairs to the office she shared with Otto and Marta and unlocked the wooden door, flipped the fluorescent lights on, and listened to their familiar buzz. After filling up the coffeepot from the sink in the back of the office, she filled the coffeemaker and sat down at her desk to flip through phone messages and e-mails, prioritizing which needed an immediate response or could be saved for later, which could be forwarded on to someone else or better yet just deleted.

Josie spent the next hour online and on the phone, tracking down more details of the Medrano cartel and La Bestia. It was grim reading. The people of Mexico appeared to be cowering behind locked doors while the gangbangers skulked around the same street corners where vendors used to peddle fruit and trinkets. She'd been in law enforcement long enough to know that criminal trends were incredibly hard to reverse for the long term. How to get the control back into the hands of the authorities?

At nine o'clock, still trying to block recurring visions of the mayor from her mind, she lay a one-inch white binder in the middle of her desk. In black Magic Marker, someone had written the words THE GUNNERS, and the slogan, FORGET 911—DIAL .357. She and Otto had seized the notebook from Red's house as evidence. She had found it on top of a desk in a small, messy office just off his kitchen. The first page of the notebook read, "The policies and procedures of The Gunners: Authored by Red Goff." Approximately twenty pages followed, organized by tabs with labels: POLICY, CASE STUDIES, STATE LAW, FED. LAW, REPEALS, and INVENTORY.

Josie flipped to the first tab, titled POLICY, and read through the mission statement, ". . . to uphold the Second Amendment at all costs. To fight for *both* conceal *and* carry in the State of Texas. And, most importantly, to keep the women and children of Artemis safe in their own homes." After the mission statement were six pages of poorly written, rambling policy followed by the INVENTORY tab, which proved more interesting. It listed 263 guns, most titled to Red Goff. The guns ranged from a $250 handgun to a $4,000 Colt M4 Commando and a $5,000 shotgun from the former USSR. Each gun on the list included the owner, purchase price, date of purchase, and a serial number. It was a big break. At least they had something to work with in tracking down the guns. At first glance, she figured the collection was worth at least $175,000. Red was a forklift operator at a small manufacturing plant on the outskirts of town. His pay was probably worse than hers, so how could he afford bulletproof glass and the guns to accompany it?

A final section in the notebook was separated from the rest by a red sheet of paper with the words FRIEND OR FOE handwritten in block capital letters. A skull and crossbones had been drawn with a black marker under the title. Following were two pages labeled "Foe," with forty-seven names written in differing handwriting. Number fourteen was her name. Sheriff Martínez was nineteen. She quickly identified two other state law enforcement officers on the list and then scanned the rest. She recognized at least half the names. Most were either affiliated with government or were well-known local liberals. Josie wondered what Bloster's motivation was with the Gunners. It wasn't unusual to collect guns; it was unusual, however, to view the people who were elected and hired to protect you as the enemy. Hack Bloster's own boss was on the short list.

The last sheet in the book had the word "Friends" written across the top. She felt like she was in grade school again. Eighteen names, including Fallow's and Bloster's, were listed. She and Otto would begin interviews that afternoon.

Josie's phone buzzed and she picked it up.

"Sauly Magson called," Lou said. "Says he's found a dead cow in the Rio. Says it's hung up in a logjam outside his house."

"Tell him to call Parks and Wildlife."

"He claims its belly is packed full of cocaine."

In 1976, Macon Drench purchased Artemis, Texas, the first of three ghost towns at the end of Farm Road 170 along the Rio Grande, for ten thousand dollars. Drench was an oil baron from Houston, disillusioned with the money and excesses in the city, and in search of a place to live connected to the land. He spent twenty million dollars of his own fortune and installed sewage and water lines, bartered with the phone and electric companies to stretch lines to a town that barely existed, outfitted a police department, built one pole barn to house the first grocery store, and another to serve as the town bank. Working with a city planner from Houston, he designed a central square and laid the downtown area in a grid with main streets leading strategically to major geological formations: the Chinati Mountains north of town and the Rio Grande and Mexico a direct route south. River Road, running parallel to the Rio Grande, was the only marked road that led directly into Artemis, and that was the appeal for Drench and most of the residents.

By 1985, Artemis had more than 1,500 residents. Drench invited family and friends to settle the area, promising nothing but a new experience. Word spread and a unique group of adventurers turned land most thought uninhabitable into a thriving community. Judicious use of water and organized supply runs had made the town a home for people running away from, or running to a new, life.

Sauly Magson was one of the original founders of Artemis. He was a scrawny bald man who typically wore a blue bandanna tied around his neck, a pair of grimy jean shorts, and nothing else. Most of the businesses in town ignored the *No shirt, no shoes, no service* rule with Sauly. When he had to wear shoes, he wore a pair of leather thongs that provided no more protection than the soles of his own feet. Sauly liked the psychedelics and spent much of his time in a state of wonder at the world around him, but he was as kindhearted as anyone Josie had ever met.

Sauly grew up in northern New Mexico, near the Taos Pueblo Indians in the Sangre de Cristo Mountains. Josie knew little about him other than that he ran away from home as a teenager and roamed New Mexico until 1976, when he met Drench. Sauly helped settle the area and was known locally as one of the willful independents that turned a windblown speck along the Mexican border into a town.

Josie found him on the edge of the river, about a quarter mile from his house. He lived in a three-story, square grain elevator that he converted himself with parts and pieces he dragged home from the dump or from construction sites he worked on. It was painted a deep purple that contrasted perfectly with the blue sky and desert. A series of fifteen windows appeared to be haphazardly installed over the four sides of the structure, but the satisfying visual effect made it clear that Sauly had an artist's eye and a carpenter's skills. She thought the scene looked to be somewhere between an Edward Hopper and a Georgia O'Keeffe painting.

"What's up?" she called, smiling and waving when he realized she was walking toward him.

He rubbed his smooth head and smiled at her, revealing a handful of teeth. She noticed a small paunch in his wrinkled, dark brown belly, above his jean shorts.

"It's the dangdest thing I ever seen. I'm straight as an arrow. I swear on my grave. I stared long and hard to prove it, and I'm telling you, that old heifer's got a bellyful a coke." He pointed across the river. "I swear it. It's like some old junkie came down to the river and set up shop."

Josie's smile faded as she approached the riverbank. A small brown and white cow lay half submerged in the water, tangled in a mess of tree branches on the other side. Her abdomen had either been ripped open or torn when she got hung up in the branches, but there was definitely a gaping hole filled with something. It looked as if the organs had been removed and replaced with bags of cellophane-wrapped blocks, almost certainly cocaine.

"Did you try any?" she asked Sauly, only half-kidding.

He looked hurt. "Never touch it. Shuts your heart down. I do nothing but nature's own."

"How deep is the river here?" she asked.

"Eight feet. Want my kayak?"

Sauly disappeared into a thicket of shoulder-high grass. The area of the river around Sauly's place was thick with clumps of Carrizo cane grass, willow and cottonwood trees, rangy bushes, and soil so sandy, the banks appeared like a beach. Green patches like this one appeared along the Rio throughout Artemis and provided a welcome relief to the miles of earthy brown and gray desert.

Sauly reemerged from the grass with a small kayak balanced atop his head. He bent at the waist and laid it gently on the ground next to the river. He unclipped a paddle from the side and pulled out a fillet knife that had been duct-taped next to the oblong opening for the seat. He laid them both on the ground and told Josie to check the kayak out.

Josie gave him a wary look.

"You can't tip it. Trust me. It glides right across the top of the water." He took his hand and slowly slid it through the air.

Trust me, she thought. Josie bent to unbuckle her police boots and wondered about following the advice of a sixty-year-old stoner. She stood and saw he had taken his bandanna from around his neck and laid it out flat in the dirt beside her boots and socks while she was rolling up her uniform pant legs.

"Lay your gun and badge here. I'll guard 'em for you till you get done."

She smiled and thanked him, curled her gun belt and set it down, but kept her gun tucked into the front of her pants. She laid her radio and keys on the bandanna and tugged at her cell phone inside her shirt pocket to make sure it was secured to the Velcro.

Sauly dragged the kayak about thirty feet upstream, where a path had been cleared through the cane. He pointed the front of the boat toward the water, keeping the seat over the sandy bank, and held Josie's arm to help her climb inside. Once she settled in, he handed her the paddle and gently pushed the boat off with his foot. She glided easily into the river, then after a few shaky strokes, paddled awkwardly to the other side, about twenty feet across the slow-moving current and straight into the logjam. She didn't need to get out of the boat to get the full picture. The gaping hole in the animal's abdomen was stuffed with around ten bricks of cocaine, about twenty-five pounds' worth. Josie clipped the paddle onto the side of the kayak and then hung on to a limb of the fallen tree while she snapped pictures using her cell phone. She knew there was no reception; otherwise, she would have called Border Patrol to get them headed this way. Someone was desperate for a missing load of cocaine, and she was certain they were already scouring the river in search of the dead animal.

She maneuvered her boat next to the cow, gagging at the putrid smell and swatting flies out of her face. She struggled to reach across the carcass to pull out one of the bags without tipping into the river. Josie couldn't swim, could barely stay afloat treading water. She grabbed hold of a bag, slick with a substance she didn't want to consider, and set it in the kayak between her legs.

Sauly had already walked downstream and was waiting for her on the bank. She started to push the kayak off from the branches but noticed movement through a clump of salt cedar on the Mexican side of the river, just up and to her left. The grass wasn't as thick, and the land opened into the wide, rocky Chihuahuan Desert, but Josie couldn't see much while she was sitting low in the kayak. The salt cedar rustled again, and she spotted two male figures dressed in desert camouflage pants and short-sleeved beige shirts. Josie pushed the kayak backwards, using a limb from the tree that the cow was caught in to move herself back under the overhanging trunk for cover.

She pulled the gun out of the front of her pants and ducked her head behind the trunk. The river was approximately four feet below the bank on this side, which had eroded and caused the large tree to fall. The U.S. side of the river was a gentle slope covered in cane grass that she could have easily disappeared into for cover, but the kayak was a slow-moving target, and she couldn't risk the twenty feet to cross in open sight. She noted that Sauly had thankfully had the sense to disappear, but so had the two figures. The only noise was the water sliding past her boat and two woodpeckers knocking on trees above her. She had no doubt the men had come for the drugs. If she stayed in the kayak, she would become a target, and the number of men with guns would multiply. She flipped her cell phone open in one last attempt to catch a signal, but it was pointless. She was miles from decent reception, and she wouldn't risk Sauly's life to flag him down to go get help.

After tucking the gun back into her pants, she grabbed hold of two massive roots hanging from the tree trunk and used her arms to pull herself up and out of the kayak. She kicked the kayak back out into the river, hoping to distract the two men above her as she climbed the bank. The sandy bank gave way beneath her feet, and she was afraid she was headed down into the water. Struggling to find purchase in the dirt, she used her arms to pull herself up the massive root system and onto the bank. Sweat stung her eyes and ran down the sides of her face. The temperature was in the upper nineties, and humidity hung in the air like a wool blanket.

The kayak, along with probably twenty thousand dollars' worth of cocaine, had already floated twenty feet down the stream by the time she made it up the bank and on solid ground. The grass wasn't as thick, but there were still clumps of it for visual cover. She had no doubt the two figures had heard her movement and were hunkering down, waiting for her. She was now breaking multiple federal laws, but an armed fugitive on foreign soil was better than an employed cop dead in the water.

She scouted the area around her, and then, crouching low to the ground, she moved behind another fallen tree for cover. Fortunately she had left her vest on. Bending on one knee, she raised her hands and steadied them on the trunk, her eyes scanning for movement in the brush.

"This is Chief of Police Josie Gray!" she shouted. "Move out into the clearing. Put your hands in the air where I can see them."

No movement.

"Throw your weapons to the ground and place your hands in the air!"

A gunshot rang out and the water to her left splashed. Out of the corner of her eye, she saw Sauly running toward his house at a sprint. Josie remained still, her eyes focused on the direction the shot had come from, probably thirty feet away and slightly to her right. She heard voices and the rustling of grass and breaking branches, but the sound was moving away from her. Within ten seconds, she heard the doors of a vehicle open and a pickup engine start. Still crouching, she rushed to the edge of the thicket and looked into the clearing in time to see a twenty-year-old two-tone pickup truck take off, following the river east. The truck was too far away to get a license number, but she was betting it had come from the Altagracia Ranch: a seventy-five-thousand-acre working ranch that the Federales had been monitoring closely for ties to the Medrano drug cartel.

Sauly appeared again from the weeds like an apparition, his tanned body and bald head blending in smoothly with his surroundings. He had acquired a shotgun, which hung over his shoulder from a leather strap.

"They're gone," she called out.

"Who were they shooting at?" he yelled back.

Josie ignored the question, more worried about getting across the river and getting Border Patrol on-site before two men turned into twenty. "Can you get me back across?"

"Ten minutes!" he yelled.

True to his word, ten minutes later he had rescued the kayak downstream, dragged it back, and paddled deftly across the river, just upstream from the cow, where the bank was slightly more sloped.

"You paddle back. I'll swim. Slide on down the bank, and I'll help you in." Sauly looked up at her with a wide grin, half his teeth rotted out, his eyes bright. Josie cussed, checked that her gun and phone were secure, and started down the sandy bank, hanging on to a skinny tree to keep from sliding into the river. Sauly had already climbed out of the kayak and was waist deep, holding steady. Josie knew the river was about eight feet deep in the center.

"Let's go, Chief. Have a little faith. I won't let you get that pretty uniform wet."

With an arm on Sauly's shoulder, she managed a quick step into the boat. It rocked back and forth but held steady. Several minutes later, she was safe onshore, where Sauly smiled and handed her the cocaine she had left in the boat.

"You're a good man," she said.

While he hid his boat again in the weeds, she contacted the Marfa Border Sector on Sauly's home phone and talked with a patrol officer.

"I've got ten packages. Probably a kilo each. The cow's abdomen was sliced open. They took her organs out, stuck the coke in, and sewed her back up with what looks to be fishing line. When the cow got hung up, the fishing line snapped and her belly broke open." The sector agent took off on a cynical rant against the kind of idiots who would route their drugs across the border in a dead cow. Josie didn't recognize the agent, but he sounded fed up with the job. Josie finally broke in, "The Altagracia Ranch is about two miles upstream from here, Mexican side." She provided directions to Sauly's for the agent and said, "Shots were fired. If I hadn't had a gun pointed in their direction, they'd have been more aggressive. They'll be back."

When Josie arrived back at the police department, a city council member was sitting on the wooden bench out front under the window. Smokey Blessings, married to Nurse Vie Blessings, was thirty-five. Smokey drove a county maintenance truck, and Josie both respected and liked him. A slightly overweight father of two, he had a calm disposition and plenty of common sense. Vie was five years older than Smokey, and ran his life like she did everything else—with bossy efficiency.

He squinted up at Josie and stood as she approached. The noon sun was in his face, and he looked sweaty and nervous. "Chief."

"Smokey."

"Can we talk a few minutes?" he asked.

Walking upstairs, they talked about how Vie was handling the stress from the shooting at the Trauma Center.

"I was out at the maintenance barn, and one of the guys came running in. Told me the Trauma Center was under attack. Wanted to know if Vie was working. I said, 'Hell yes, she's working!' She'd just sent me a text saying she couldn't meet me for lunch. She didn't bother to mention she'd just lived through a gunfight."

They reached the top of the stairs, and Josie opened the office door and flipped on the lights. She pulled out chairs at the conference table as Smokey continued.

"I told Frank I was going over there. I was hell-bent on pulling my wife out of that operating room. I knew she wouldn't do it herself. She'd get herself shot before she walked out on a patient. Frank finally talked sense into me. Told me I'd get in the way. Get myself arrested, if not shot."

Josie got them both a bottle of water and turned the fan to blow straight at them. The window air conditioner took the edge off, but it didn't actually cool the room. Smokey sighed and seemed to relax a little.

"I don't know anyone who handles stress any better than Vie does. She's a perfect fit for her job. I know yesterday was over the top, but no one could have handled it any better than she did."

Smokey shook his head. "She brushes that stuff off like lint. Nothing fazes the woman." He paused and smiled. "Except Donny."

Josie laughed. Donny was their fifteen-year-old son, who took Vie's exuberance for life to the next level. Josie didn't say so, but she was fairly certain she would see Donny in the back of a police car before he graduated high school.

Smokey finally drained his water and grew quiet again, apparently thinking through what he came to say.

"I want to apologize, Josie. About the meeting that the mayor called this morning."

Josie nodded.

"I had nothing to do with that, but I should have told you and the sheriff about it. When the mayor called me this morning, the whole thing was already done. I was just told to take a seat behind him to support him. All the council was supposed to be up there. I was just the only one that could make it."

"How did he get the word out?"

"He had a group of volunteers making phone calls last night to get people there. I just figured you and the sheriff already knew about it."

Josie raised a cynical eyebrow. "The mayor does nothing without an ulterior motive. So, why didn't he invite the sheriff or me in on his show?"

Smokey shrugged and stroked his chin where the stubble of a goatee was growing in. He cleared his throat but didn't answer.

"Come on, Smokey. The snub was too obvious and too public. What was his point?"

Smokey tipped his head back and blew air out in frustration. "I asked him why you and Martínez weren't up there with us. He basically said this is his town. The law officials aren't doing enough to keep the people safe, so he's stepping in."

"I don't care about sitting on a podium. I care about this town, though. If he has ideas for how the sheriff and I can keep Artemis safer, then he needs to tell us. All he did was undermine what we do."

"It's not exactly a secret how you feel about the mayor. I'm not saying what he did was right, but I can't blame him for not wanting to talk to you about his ideas. You'd have probably shot them all to hell."

Josie stood and walked to the coffeemaker to pour a cup of burnt coffee and take a deep breath. He was right, and the heat in her face gave her away.

"Josie, I have a lot of respect for you and Martínez both, but you two aren't helping anything by antagonizing Moss."

She turned to face him. "His whole persona is designed to antagonize!"

Smokey nodded, his expression weary. "I know that. I just thought you were above it."

Josie stared, at a loss for words. Her face felt red.

"Look, Josie, you know I support you. I know Moss can be a real jackass. You're a woman, so to him you're automatically stupid. Look past that. The man wants the same thing you do. He cares about this town, and he's willing to do whatever it takes to save it. Same as you."

"I've been with this department for nine years, three as chief. I'm tired of proving myself. I need to make decisions based on what's right, not what's politically correct."

"No one's telling you any different. You have council support, and you have the community's support. Just don't jeopardize your job over a petty grudge with the mayor. We need you. Right now more than ever."

After Smokey left, she stood at the window in the back of the office and looked out onto a neighborhood of one-story ranch homes, small and shabby, cared for by people who were giving it their best against unbeatable odds. Following her initial move to get away from her mother, it was the people struggling to make it, the underdogs, who made her call Artemis home. She felt as if she'd found a place where she could make a difference to people who needed it.

She had arrived in Artemis as a twenty-four-year-old woman with a past she wanted nothing to do with, barely able to envision a future, and had applied to be an Artemis police officer. Otto had hired Josie at the end of just one forty-five–minute interview. With Josie sitting across the desk from him, he had called her former supervisor with the Indianapolis Police Department and had a brief, positive conversation.

Otto asked her what had drawn her to Artemis. Uncharacteristically, she shared personal information about her family and her desire to start over. Otto had hired her and invited her to dinner that evening to meet his wife, Delores. Aside from her neighbor, Dell, Josie privately considered Otto and Delores her closest family.

Three years ago, Delores convinced Otto he needed to forgo another term as chief in order to reduce stress in his life. Josie was honored that Otto had recommended her to take his place.

Josie heard a chair scoot across the floor and turned to see Otto sitting down at his desk.

"How's tricks?" he asked. He wore the standard blue and gray police uniform, minus the bulletproof vest that fit over his midsection only when he forced it.

Otto had just logged on for the noon-to-eight-thirty shift. Officer Marta Cruz would come on at four thirty, when Josie's shift was supposed to end but rarely did. The three worked staggered shifts, but arranged schedules so that once each week they met as a group to discuss current cases and share information. The city police coordinated schedules with the sheriff's department in an attempt to ensure at least one officer was on duty at all hours, but with vacation schedules, even that was difficult to accomplish.

Josie gave Otto a rundown on the morning. "I talked to the Assessor's Office. Drench owns the land Winnings' trailer is on. I'll go talk to him tomorrow." She pointed to the opened Gunner's policy manual that lay in the middle of her desk. "You know how many guns Red had on the inventory he kept?"

"It would appear, too many for his own good."

"Two hundred sixty-three."

"I'd think two or three would have been sufficient."

"Didn't Hack Bloster make it sound like the whole stash of guns was kept on those hooks in Red's living room?"

Otto typed in his computer log-in and turned toward Josie, his expression more interested. "That's the way I took it. But there sure weren't enough hooks to hold almost three hundred guns."

"You busy?" Josie picked up her keys.

Josie left a note on Marta's desk asking her to set up a meeting with Sergio Pando. Josie valued her personal connection with Sergio, where the intelligence exchange was based upon a friendship instead of on border regulations and politics. The law enforcement and government agencies from the two countries may as well have been from different planets. Information exchange was too often caught up in red tape and bureaucracy, wasting precious time in an investigation. Piedra Labrada had recently undergone a series of brutal assassinations that were attributed to La Bestia, and Josie was certain the assassination at the hospital was linked to them as well. While she hoped the connection between La Bestia and Artemis was only geographic, she feared the violence that had invaded their town would only intensify. She had killed a member of La Bestia at the Trauma Center, wounded another, and then placed him in the Arroyo County Jail. To compound matters, the leader of the rival cartel, Hector Medrano, had been murdered in her Trauma Center. She had no doubt there would be retribution.

Once the engine in her jeep finally turned over, Josie set the air-conditioning on high in deference to Otto. The bank's sign read eighty-nine degrees, and it was just past noon. The department uniforms were thick and held heat like insulation, a fact Otto lamented from April through October—although with an average high of 101 degrees in July, everything felt uncomfortable. He walked outside with two cans of Coke and slid into the passenger seat, griping about the heat, his aching knees, and the general decay of society.

Josie drove past the courthouse toward Farm Road 170 to follow the Rio Grande south toward Red's place, listening to Otto's running commentary about life. His dim view of the world remained balanced with optimism concerning his wife, Delores, and grown daughter, Mina, who lived in El Paso. After years of working together, Josie and Otto had formed a close friendship, one that had carried them through difficult times both in and out of the office.

Otto opened one of the cans of Coke and handed it to Josie, then pointed out his window to a large group of black buzzards circling what looked to be barren desert.

"Why would any living thing, man or animal, move to a giant blistering sandbox? Fifteen buzzards to one field mouse. Not very good odds," Otto said.

Josie smiled. "Don't be such a cynic. Don't you feel like a winner every night you make it home and realize you pulled it off again?"

"I'm the cynic?"

She pulled the jeep up to Pegasus Winning's trailer when she saw the Eldorado was parked out front. Josie rolled her window down and heard the air conditioner blowing. She put the jeep in park and jogged up to the trailer and tried the door handle. Otto stared at her as she got back in the car.

"Wondered if the trailer was locked," Josie said.

"And?"

"It was."

"There's something strange about that girl, but I can't put my finger on it."

"Might it be that she found Red Goff dead on her couch?"

"It's the way she seemed so bored with the dead body. Most women I know would have been bawling their eyes out. She was more worried about missing work."

Josie shrugged. "Bills have to get paid." She thought part of Winning's tough image was an act. She didn't have the woman figured out yet, but she would bet money she was not the killer.

The crime scene tape was still in place at Red's, and things appeared undisturbed since their last visit.

Josie put plastic gloves on and unlocked the glass door. The smell of mildew hit them both as she opened it.

Josie and Otto stood at the entrance and scanned the living room, the kitchen to the right, and the hallway to the left.

"Where's that smell coming from? It didn't smell like this yesterday," he said.

Josie flipped the light switch on and nothing happened.

"Generator's off," she said.

Otto clicked on his flashlight and walked in.

Red Goff lived off the grid, a phenomenon that could be found in pockets across the country, but was more prevalent out West. Red wasn't connected to the city utilities. He received no electricity, no city water or sewage, no phone lines. The goal was to have no connection to the outside world. It was difficult in West Texas, where growing your own crops meant costly irrigation, but Red managed it as a hobby farm. He had raised cows, which he butchered for his own meat, selling the rest off to the meat-processing plant for profit. He also maintained a garden, where he grew almost all his vegetables. He purchased nonpasteurized dairy products from a farmer in Odessa. The University of Texas used to bring out a group of Environmental Studies students each year to observe his solar operation, but the guns on his walls and the pop-up rants on government control had ended the visits several years ago. Since then, Red had practically vanished from public life, except for his status with the Gunners.

Otto called to Josie from Red's bedroom. "Look at this!"

Josie found Otto on his hands and knees, looking under a queen-sized bed with a leopard-print comforter and black satin pillows. Josie shuddered at the thought of Red slipping around on satin sheets.

Otto's voice was muffled as he pulled an area rug out from under the bed. "How many people do you know lay their rugs under the bed instead of beside them?"

Josie took the corner of the rug from Otto and pulled. Otto stood up and they moved the bed out toward the door. The room was about fifteen feet square and contained the bed and an old Scandinavian-style dresser that had been painted black. With the bed moved back against the opposite wall, a trapdoor became visible. Otto smiled.

"Nice work," Josie said, and bent down to lift the wooden door that lay recessed into the concrete floor. As she lifted the door, the smell of mildew pushed up out of the cellar and became so strong, her eyes watered. A wooden stepladder led down into a black hole.

Otto and Josie stared at each other in the flashlight's dim beam.

"Isn't this where you walk down those stairs and find ten mutilated bodies in a freezer?" Otto asked.

"Basements give me the creeps. You want to take this one?" she asked.

Otto shook his head. "I don't think that ladder will hold me."

Josie flicked on her own flashlight and shone it down the hole into standing water. "Damn."

Thirty minutes later, Josie was easing herself down the ladder wearing thigh-high rubber boots, a broom in one hand, and a miner's lamp attached to a band around her forehead. She kept the rubber boots and miner's lamp in a plastic trunk in the back of her jeep for calls that took her down along the Rio. She found the broom in Red's kitchen. Josie stood on the bottom rung of the ladder and slowly panned the light around the room. The cellar, about fifteen by twenty feet, appeared to be a supply area containing large cans of peanut butter, green beans, corn, roast beef, and lard. Sleeping bags in plastic lined the top shelf, as did various Coleman lanterns and one-burner stoves. Ten-gallon plastic containers of drinking water were almost submerged around the bottom perimeter of the room.

"It's high-dollar stuff," Josie called up to Otto. "He didn't go to Walmart and stock up. Where's ole Red getting his money?"

"I studied the list of members yesterday. I knew all the members but one, and there isn't a sugar daddy in the bunch. A few with money, but nothing significant."

She took a step off the ladder and into the room. The waders closed in around her legs, the cold water pressing against her. She poked around on the floor with the broom handle and found nothing. On the right-hand side of the room was a pipe that had apparently leaked the water. The pipe appeared to exit the back side of the building and was probably connected to a well. She could see the water pushing into the room where the pipe was submerged. Josie scanned the wall and found a shutoff valve.

She looked up toward the hole in the ceiling and saw Otto bent at the waist and squinting down at her.

"This was intentional," she said. "That valve was opened completely. I can't believe the well hasn't run dry by now."

"He had to be two feet from hell before he hit water out here," Otto said.

Josie waded across the far side of the room, where five hundred–gallon plastic trunks lined the floor. The water was just below the lip of three of the trunks. The other two were empty and floating just below the wooden shelf above them. Josie opened both and found black grease stains on the inside and the strong smell of gun oil. She wondered aloud if the missing guns had been stored in the tubs. The other three trunks were full of detonators, frag grenades, explosives, night-vision goggles, tac lights, and scopes.

"There's enough explosive here to blow up the entire town."

A small green plastic tub sat on a shoulder-high shelf in the corner. Josie pulled it down and lifted the lid. Inside were approximately a hundred photos and a 35-millimeter camera in a black leather carrying case. Josie didn't bother to examine the photos but took the tub and handed it up to Otto. She carried the remaining two trunks through the water, up the ladder, and loaded them into the jeep, and left the tubs with explosives for the Department of Public Safety to remove. Then Josie made the final climb out of the rank water and into Red's bedroom, imagining mold settling into her lungs.

Later that afternoon, Josie and Otto cataloged the six trunks into evidence and then spread the photographs out on the table in the department office upstairs. After a quick scan of the pictures, Josie sat down in disgust and shook two Tums from the bottle that she kept in her desk drawer.

Otto remained standing, hands on his hips, scowling down at the pictures. "I just never figured him for a pervert. That poor girl didn't have a clue," Otto said, pointing to a picture of Pegasus Winning in shorts, bare chested, walking across the living room in her trailer. The grainy picture appeared to have been taken by a telephoto lens.

They found around forty pictures of Winning, mostly undressed, getting ready for bed or getting out of the shower. The pictures had obviously been taken on multiple days. One picture particularly bothered Josie. Winning stood completely naked at the kitchen counter, looking toward the window as if she heard a noise, with a shot glass held just up to her lips. Her expression was distant, the look of someone trying to deaden her loneliness through a bottle. Josie wondered what she might look like through a camera lens in the privacy of her own home at night. The thought depressed the hell out of her.

Otto pulled another manila envelope out of the green tub and dumped the pictures onto the table, then laid them out in rows. The photos all appeared to be of Gunner members and various meetings and activities.

He pointed to a picture and leaned closer to the table to examine it. "Those fellas aren't Gunners. Look at the three men in the background, all wearing desert camouflage."

Josie picked up the picture and studied it. Two of the men had what appeared to be automatic machine guns strapped over their shoulders, and all three appeared to be Mexican.

"Bingo." Otto clapped Josie on the back. "Now we're getting somewhere."

FOUR

The Border Crossing at the International Bridge into Ojinaga was
backed up, typical but frustrating. Josie inched through, cursing
yet another result of budget cuts on both sides of the border. Marta
had logged on at the department at 4:30 P.M., as Josie logged off
for the night. Department-issued vehicles were not allowed out of
county, and definitely not across the border. Josie had to conduct
business in Mexico off duty and in her personal car. Marta was on
the clock, but traveling in uniform would draw unwanted attention. Josie had driven home, traded the jeep for her nondescript
ten-year-old Ford Escort, and dressed in jeans and a T-shirt. She
picked up Marta, who had changed out of her police uniform and
into a pretty blue skirt and white lacy blouse. Josie held her tongue
but smiled.

Marta left Mexico ten years ago after divorcing an abusive husband. She traveled through all the proper channels to get her green
card and a job as the night custodian at the jail. Hard work and
diligence had paid off as she worked her way up through the ranks

to police officer. She had confided in Josie that she felt ashamed for leaving her country and working in America, but her daughter's safety kept her from moving back to Piedra Labrada.

On several occasions over the past few years, Josie and Marta had met Sergio at his home, a small adobe in a barrio just south of a bend in the Rio. The stone walls were over a foot thick, with window wells that held flower boxes bursting with red geraniums. His only child, a shy teenaged girl, waved and smiled from the backyard but did not come to the front porch where they met her father. Sergio stood on the top step and smiled, threw his arms open to Marta, and wrapped her in his embrace.

Sergio and Marta had been childhood sweethearts. Marta had surprised everyone when she married a local troublemaker, and Sergio married his wife soon after. After his wife was murdered and Marta divorced her abusive husband, Sergio came calling again. Marta had resisted his advances for many years now, but she never explained her reasoning to Josie.

Josie and Marta sat on plastic chairs at a round table covered with a bright orange tablecloth and set with mismatched plates and cups. Sergio, lit up like a man tending to royalty, brought out platters of roast pork tacos and beans and a pitcher of iced tea with lemons.

Marta smiled up at Sergio. "You cook beans to melt a woman's heart."

"Ah, if only that were so; you'd have married me years ago."

Marta patted the empty seat beside her, and Sergio sat and poured drinks from the pitcher. After a delicious dinner and pleasant conversation, Josie felt she had to apologize in advance for ruining the evening with ugly police business.

Sergio frowned at Josie. "No apologies. What happened to you nearly killed me. I hear it on the radio and had to call on your safety." He paused and looked at Marta with concern. "La Bestia is responsible for the Medrano murder. Most certainly. We struggle every day. Once they infiltrate your town, they are like rats. They will multiply, getting into every corner. They will devour your city." He paused and pointed a finger at Josie. "You want to start a booming business in Mexico? Open a *funeraria.*"

Josie looked to Marta. "Funeral parlor," Marta said.

"I heard yesterday they expect Lorenzo Marín to make a full recovery," Josie said. "Is that what you hear?"

Sergio frowned deeply and nodded. "Unbelievable. He took three shots, one a centimeter from his heart. He talked to his wife yesterday, but he'll be in the hospital for another week or two. Then therapy."

"I can't believe the difference a few short years has made here. I almost don't recognize it." Marta gestured to Sergio. "We grew up running the streets at all hours. Our parents didn't give a thought to our safety."

Sergio turned to Josie. "When's the last time you drove around Piedra Labrada? More than just a trip to the restaurants downtown?"

"Probably six months or more. The crossing's too much of a hassle," Josie said.

Sergio stood and walked toward a small white car parked on the curb in front of the house. It resembled an old Volkswagen Rabbit, with rust spots and dented fenders on the front and back passenger side. "Come. Let me show you in person. Talking doesn't show the extent of the damage La Bestia has done to our city."

Sergio drove them first through the old section of Piedra, where the streets crossed one another in a maze that funneled into the central plaza. They entered a neighborhood that Marta said she knew well.

From the backseat, she scooted up between Sergio and Josie to point out a house on the right side of the street. "That's my aunt's house. We've tried to get her to move, but she refuses. Won't give up on the neighborhood."

Sergio pointed down the street. "Look at the empty houses,

Marta. People move and don't even try to sell. What would the point be? Who would buy here? I guarantee your aunt is paying protection or she would not be in the house." He gestured through his open window to a small concrete-block home spray-painted with black graffiti. The windows were broken, the front door splintered in two. A fence post that had been put into a bucket of concrete and allowed to dry lay in the yard.

"The battering ram. Clever, yes?" Sergio asked.

Marta moaned in the backseat. "So sad. This used to be such a nice, quiet area. My mother lived only a block over."

"The park, just behind your mother's old place? Gone. Nothing left but bare ground. It's so horrible, weeds even refuse to grow there."

Sergio drove them through streets that once held ramshackle shops behind sidewalks filled with people walking all hours of the day and night. Now, about half the businesses were boarded up, windows broken, filth spray-painted on the sides of buildings. He slowed his car and they watched three young boys standing on the street corner stare suspiciously at the car.

"For three centuries, we have shared trade across the river. Raised our families as one community. Since La Bestia arrived two years ago, trade has practically stopped. People like you"—he gestured to Josie in the seat next to him—"are afraid to cross. And who can blame you? A third of the officers in Piedra Labrada have already quit. Every kind of brutal crime has taken place here: beheadings, acid baths, assassinations. They are overtaking the government, the police force, businesses."

"I understand it's about the drug routes, but why terrorize the city? How does that help their cause?" Marta said in disgust.

"It's about control. La Bestia moved into Medrano's territory and had to show dominance. This is their route now, not Medrano's. It is their town and they run it. The police don't arrest them, for fear of their families' lives." He looked at Marta in his rearview mirror.

"You heard Ramón Díaz, his wife, and two children—all four of them gunned down. All he did was support the chief of police publicly at a town forum, and look what they did. They made their message clear. Since then, over two months ago, you hear no one say anything against La Bestia. The businesses pay protection. Some pay to La Bestia now, and still pay to Medrano. The cartels own us."

Josie wondered how long Artemis could hold off that kind of power. People outside the strip joining the border states of Mexico and the United States failed to realize how dangerous the situation had become. United States citizens were living next to a country facing anarchy.

The next block over was a street of small homes behind two stone pillars and a wrought iron gate with a sentry posted, dressed in a police-style uniform with an automatic weapon slung over his shoulder. Run-down brick and stucco homes lined both sides of the street, many sitting empty, none of them cared for as they were just a year ago. Sergio pointed to a home just beyond the front gate with a shrine to the Virgin Mary in a front yard that was roughly a fifty-foot-square patch of dirt. Dozens of candles burned in windows that faced the road.

"A *bajador*. He stops the runners in the desert and steals their money." He looked to Josie. "Pirates, you call them?"

She nodded.

"The good news is the routes change. Once a new route is discovered, the *bajadores* camp out. They steal guns, drugs, money. They extort money from Mexicans trying to cross the border. Life means nothing to these men. Most of those killings are never reported. Crime on crime we don't even attempt to—" He gripped the steering wheel angrily with both hands. "We put out fires."

Josie and Marta drove back to Artemis in silence that night. It had been a depressing evening: one that confirmed fears rather than relieved them. Josie knew prosecuting crimes over international borders was mired in paperwork, frustration, and pools of money her own department didn't have. Over the past year, as the border violence increased, the trust among the two cities' law enforcement agencies had deteriorated. Both countries found the other's legal system lacking. Mexico blamed the American lust for drugs and lack of gun laws, and the U.S. blamed Mexico's corrupt government and loss of control on the drug cartels. The blame was somewhere in the middle, so in a strange way, it made sense that the problems had collected and festered like an open wound in the hundred-mile strip of middle ground the locals called the Territory.

When Josie and Marta left for Mexico, Otto called Hack Bloster and Paul Fallow and asked them to meet him at the station. He'd decided to interview them together to get a feel for the dynamics of the Gunners before calling in its other members.

Fallow arrived first, still wearing his white doctor's coat over a pink polo shirt and khaki pants. His expression was grim but composed, less frantic than he had appeared at Red's place the day before. Waiting by the front desk, they discussed the slight chance of much-needed rain for the following day.

When Bloster walked in, in his brown sheriff's department uniform, the still air changed perceptibly, as if an electric current emanated from his body. Fallow made eye contact, and Bloster's back hunched up like a snarling dog's. Otto wondered if he had made a mistake calling them in together.

Gesturing toward the office upstairs, Otto walked beside Fallow, and they followed two steps behind Bloster up the dimly lit stairs. Otto glanced over and saw Fallow's eyes trained on the holstered gun hanging down Bloster's side, tapping his thigh with each step.

They took seats around the oak conference table located at the front of the office. Fallow slipped into a seat across the table from

Bloster and drew himself up like a rabbit trying to avoid notice. Bloster pulled a chair out, took his time adjusting his gun belt, and sat back in his chair with his legs apart. He took up a space that two average-sized men could have fit in. Otto thought he had the look of a man ready to explode at the slightest provocation. He had worked accidents and crime scenes with Bloster through the years and disapproved of his braggadocio. He was the kind of officer who liked to appear in charge of an investigation in front of victims, but who tried to slough off the actual paperwork and questioning to another officer.

Otto got started: "Here's the situation. We've got a body, stolen guns, and a boatload of motives. Problem is, almost no leads. Since you fellas knew him better than anyone, I need you to help me fill in some gaps."

Fallow nodded. Bloster didn't move.

"What kind of fights go on between members?"

Fallow shrugged.

"Come on. A bunch of men talking guns and politics? I know there're disagreements."

Fallow shrugged again. Bloster's nostrils flared, and Otto thought he might be getting somewhere.

"All right. Hack, we'll start with you. You're the vice president of the Gunners?"

Bloster tipped his head back slightly to acknowledge the question.

"Why don't you start with your relationship with Red," Otto said.

"My relationship?" he responded, as if the question were perverse.

"Did you think Red made a good president? Did you get along with him? That kind of thing."

"When you sign the book as a Gunner, you sign it for life. You commit to a way of life. To upholding our Second Amendment rights. We're not about getting along with each other. We're about taking care of this country, our women and children." Bloster glared at Fallow, who refused to look back and instead sipped at his coffee.

"Did you like Red as a person?" Otto asked.

"What's that got to do with anything?"

Otto sighed, already tired of Bloster's tactics. He was a cop and knew exactly what the question had to do with the investigation. "Red's dead. I need to find out who wanted him that way. I do that by asking a lot of questions to a lot of people. So, tell me. Did you like Red?"

"I loved him like a brother." Bloster sneered at Otto with the look of a defiant high school punk.

"Did you agree with the way he led the organization?" Otto said.

"Look. Red had the guns. You can't be the Gunners without guns. Get my drift? So whether I liked him or not was never the point. His sandbox. His rules."

"Who takes over the club now that Red's dead?"

Fallow cleared his throat but said nothing.

Bloster said, "I do."

"I read all through the Gunners' policy manual. I couldn't find a provision for what would happen if the president died," Otto said.

"Or was killed," Fallow said.

Otto nodded. "Correct. That wasn't in the policy manual either. So, did the members decide you would lead the group?" Otto asked.

Bloster's face turned an angry red. "What happens when the president of the United States is killed? Pretty obvious, isn't it? Why else have a vice president?"

"Who gets the guns?" Otto asked.

"It looks like you do, since we haven't seen them since you showed up," Bloster said.

"When we arrived at Red's place, about an hour after we found Red's body, the guns were gone. We searched the house and found none. You don't have them? Don't know where they are?" Otto asked, looking at him.

Bloster frowned and shook his head no.

"Dr. Fallow?" Otto asked.

"No, sir."

Otto watched Fallow for a moment and wondered if the man was going to start crying. His forehead wrinkled, and he looked as if he were holding his breath.

"Dr. Fallow, if you have any idea where those guns are, you need to tell me. This could be crucial to finding Red's killer."

Fallow slapped his hand on the table and looked at Bloster. "Why don't you ask him? He and Red were the ones who did things behind our backs."

Bloster pointed a finger like a pistol toward Fallow. "You better shut the hell up."

Fallow looked wild-eyed. "I'm tired of listening to you! You aren't the president. You aren't anyone's boss. You're just a bully. And you and Red have jeopardized everything!"

Bloster stood suddenly, knocking his chair backwards, leaned across the table, and punched Fallow in the mouth.

Otto leaped up from his chair. He pulled his gun and pointed it directly at Bloster's chest. "Back away from the table!"

Bloster took a step back, surprise registered on his face as if he couldn't believe he had just punched a man.

"Hand me your gun!" Otto yelled.

Bloster started to protest, but the fierce look Otto gave him worked. He pulled his sidearm from his holster.

Otto used his own gun to point at a folding metal chair several feet to the side of the conference table. "Sit down there and don't say another word."

Otto glared at Fallow, who was still sitting in his chair, looking like a whipped pup. Otto pointed toward the back of the room. "There's a bathroom back there. Why don't you go clean up."

Fallow walked back to the bathroom, his head hung low. Otto

turned to stand in front of Bloster, one hand on his hip, the other still holding the gun, pointed at the floor. "This the way you deal with your problems? You want to shut somebody up, so you punch them? Maybe you shoot a bullet through their forehead?"

Bloster turned his head away. "I can't stand that sissy. He had no business joining the Gunners. Only reason Red let him was money. He dropped a wad of money toward the cause so he could feel like a man." Bloster looked as if he were going to spit on the floor. "He's a joke."

Otto split the men up and interviewed them separately after Fallow refused to press charges. Bloster would not talk and said if Otto had anything more to ask, he would have to do it through a lawyer. When Bloster left, Fallow sat with Otto at the conference table again. Fallow closed his eyes and held a fist to his mouth, obviously too terrified of Hack Bloster or some other demon to come clean with Otto about what he knew.

"Talk to me about some of the other members in the Gunners," Otto said. "Who was Red closest to? Who did he have the most problems with?"

Fallow sniffed. "Hack Bloster. On both counts."

Otto was losing patience. "I got that. Who else?"

Fallow shrugged a shoulder. Otto noticed his red-rimmed eyes were a lavender color, and he wondered if the man wore tinted contacts. Otto figured he probably dyed his thin head of hair blond as well.

Fallow said, "Jimmy Johnson and Fred Grant. They're two buddies of Red's. Never missed meetings. Jimmy used to help Red with his cows. He transported them for slaughter. He and Red were pretty close." He listed several other members who attended regularly and were "true to the cause." Otto took down the names of two other men who Fallow claimed were sometimes argumentative in meetings.

"How often did the group meet?"

"Once a month. We also got together to shoot out at Red's place a few times a year. The big event was Fourth of July weekend. Red used to have a cookout and the families were invited. He'd have shooting contests for the adults and the kids. Even the wives. My wife never came, of course, but some did."

"Why didn't your wife go?'

Fallow picked up a pencil off the table and rolled it between his fingers. "Not her thing. She's not much into guns. Or socializing."

"You said he used to have a Fourth of July party. When did he quit?"

"A few years ago." Fallow stared off into space for a minute. "I don't really know why he quit. Red got a little strange the last couple of years. He quit going out. Hung out with the Gunners and that was about it. We'd even bring him supplies from town."

"Any theories on why he quit going out?"

"Not really. Just didn't like people very much."

"Red have trouble with anyone? Anyone dislike him?"

"I think a lot of people disliked him, if you want the truth. He was a blowhard. He could be mean, you know? He tried to make you look weak so he looked strong."

"Give me an example."

Fallow pursed his lips a moment in thought. He finally pointed the pencil at Otto and said, "Okay. At our last meeting, I asked a question about the guns. About storing them somewhere a little safer than Red's living room. Makes sense, right? Hack gave me grief, then Red egged him on. Wanted to know what I was afraid of. I said, 'Hey, you want someone knocking down your door to get at your guns, then fine.' Red told me I was stupid. A pansy. Didn't have the balls to be a true Gunner."

"Where do you think the guns are?"

"I have no idea. I just know they were worth a lot of money. And if they had listened to me, Red might still be living."

Back in Artemis, Josie dropped Marta off at the department. She had one more task to accomplish before heading home that night. Red's body had been found the day before, and she had not talked with his daughter, Colt Goff, an angry twenty-year-old who was known locally for her support of the liberal left. Josie had interviewed Colt for an evening dispatcher's position about a year ago, but the girl had refused to unspike her hair or remove her facial piercings. She had given up a six-dollar-an-hour raise from what she made stacking books at the public library.

Colt lived above the Family Value Store in the run-down part of town. The downtown grid of streets in Artemis was shaped like a tic-tac-toe board, with the southernmost horizontal street containing the low-rent businesses and a few apartments. City offices and the more upscale stores were located closest to the courthouse; the nicer homes were a block back, the shabbier homes and cheap apartments were three blocks back, on the fringes of the downtown area. Josie parallel-parked in front of the Family Value Store and walked up a narrow flight of stairs that led from the street to the only apartment at the top of the landing.

Colt answered the door in a pair of red plaid boxers and a man's V-neck undershirt. She looked bored, but Josie thought it was affected. Her hair was jet black and spiked, but the long spikes drooped around her head like wilted grass. Her face was pierced, with studs in her nose, eyebrows, and tongue, and black eyeliner was smudged under both eyes. She looked like a young woman in need of a good night's sleep and a bath.

"What took you so long?" the girl asked, and leaned her shoulder against the doorframe to her apartment. "I figured I'd be first on your list of suspects."

"I'm sorry about your dad, Colt."

Colt pinched her thumb and forefinger together in front of her eye, looking through the crack between them. "Honestly, I'm not even the teensiest bit sad."

"Do you mind if I come in for a minute to ask you some questions?"

"I'm good with here," Colt said.

Josie sighed. "I'm too tired to play games tonight. Let's just go inside and have a seat and talk about a few things."

The girl stared at Josie a moment, then turned away quickly, leaving Josie to follow. The small living room was littered with pizza boxes, newspapers, books, dirty dishes, and clothes. With her back to Josie, Colt opened a newspaper and covered the contents on the coffee table as if laying out a tablecloth. Josie wondered what kind of drug paraphernalia lay beneath it.

"When's the last time you talked with your dad?" Josie asked. She pulled a small notepad out of her shirt pocket and sat on the couch opposite Colt, who had pulled over a chair from the kitchen table.

"About two weeks ago. He stopped by my apartment to tell me my ex-boyfriend, Jessup Lamey, got picked up in El Paso. Thrown in the pokey for possession. It was a sweet conversation. Very loving, as you can imagine." She rolled her eyes and lifted the newspaper high enough to pull out a pack of cigarettes and a lighter.

"Do you have any idea who might have killed your dad?" Josie asked.

"Anyone with a gun and half a brain."

"A little more specific."

"It's not like we ran with the same crowd."

"You don't know of anyone specifically who would want to see your father killed?"

She cocked her head and pursed her lips with a forefinger on her temple. "Let's see. Me. My ex. The mayor. The people he called his friends. The people he called his enemies. You." She gave Josie a half smile. "Because, let's face it. You don't mind Red's gone, do you? He was a pain in the proverbial ass."

"Can you tell me where you were yesterday from about eight in the morning through dinnertime?"

"Here."

"Don't you work at the library?"

"Not yesterday. I was home sick."

"Did you go to the doctor, talk to anyone throughout the day who can verify your whereabouts?"

"Nope."

Josie stood from the couch and considered her a moment. "I'll give you some advice from someone who grew up with a difficult parent. You don't need to prove anything to anyone. It took me a long time to realize that, for the most part, people don't judge me based upon my mother's actions. I have no control over her, and I don't owe anyone an explanation for her actions."

The girl's expression faltered for the first time. "You get my name, right? He named me for a gun. What kind of father names a newborn baby after a gun?"

Josie could think of no adequate response.

"I was nothing but a nuisance to him growing up. I didn't kill my father, but I'm not going to pretend I'm sad he's dead."

FIVE

Dawn came slowly with the sun hidden behind a thick wall of clouds. The gray sky faded into the desert floor with no horizon line. Looking out her kitchen window that morning, Josie thought the day could have passed for January instead of mid-July. Clouds billowed around Chimiso Peak, causing the slow sloping mountain to appear massive. Josie let her gaze drift from the window to the small framed black-and-white photograph sitting on the kitchen counter: the only picture she had of her family. The photo was taken on a boat, with her mom and dad sitting on the backseat, Josie sitting on her father's lap, both his hands resting on her shoulders. All three smiled widely at the camera, squinting into the sun. Josie couldn't remember the day, but she loved the idea that she had once been part of a happy family.

Her father had been shot during a routine traffic stop after just five years as a trooper with the Indiana State Police. Josie had been eight. At twenty-seven, her mom had lost her protector and provider. She never took over that role herself.

Josie picked the photo up and placed it facedown in the kitchen drawer. For reasons she couldn't explain, she didn't want her mother coming to her home and seeing the picture on display. She dreaded the visit but had resigned herself to the fact that it would happen.

Josie twisted the can opener and poured out half a can of peaches into a bowl. As she ate her breakfast standing at the counter, she opened her cell phone and dialed Macon Drench, got him out of bed, and asked if she could stop by his home on her way to work.

Josie used her cell phone to clock in with Lou and drove the back roads past the mudflats, a long-ago dried-up lake bed that turned to mud during the summer monsoon season, then through the craggy Chinati Mountain pass north of town. The mountains in Arroyo County appeared larger and more imposing because the land between them was completely flat, with only spare sections of native grass and occasional patches of trees and scrub brush. The land looked to Josie as if a giant mountain range had split and separated, like the continental drift on a smaller scale.

Drench's home sat at the base of the mountains and was surrounded on either side by ponderosa and piñon pines. The steel and glass house was made up of three rectangular boxes stacked haphazardly on top of one another, extending up the side of the mountain. The excavation work alone had cost half a million dollars because of the equipment trucked in from El Paso for months on end. But the final effect was stunning, and among the pine trees, the villa could have passed for a home in Aspen, Colorado. Josie was looking forward to seeing the house. She'd heard stories but never been inside.

She parked her jeep in a spot sheltered in the pines and saw Drench standing beside the reflecting pool in front of his home. A formidable six foot five in cowboy hat and boots, often sporting leather chaps, he was dwarfed by his monstrous house.

"How do, Chief?" Drench called.

He had the ability to make a slight acquaintance feel like an old friend. Josie had talked with him on a few law-related matters through the years but had never felt intimidated by his wealth or position as the town's founder.

She made her way around the granite boulders that had been dropped along the front walkway to look like a rockslide. The reflecting pool was surrounded by smooth black granite slabs flecked with white and gold that caught the light despite the cloudy day.

"Sorry to wake you this morning," she said.

Drench waved her inside. "No worry. Come on in. Haven't even had my coffee yet."

Josie followed Drench into a vast minimalist space constructed primarily of concrete, glass, and steel. The couches were concrete slabs covered in gray and blue cushions. The space looked cold and uncomfortable, like she had fallen through a crag in an iceberg.

Drench noticed her look and smiled wryly. "Have you ever met my wife?"

"No, sir."

"This is her floor." He looked around the room with a wry smile. "She's a fine woman, but a little chilly."

Drench walked toward an angular stairway consisting of wide slabs of concrete that twisted up to a second floor; the middle box that was visible from the road. Thick floor-to-ceiling windows surrounded the room, large fur rugs were scattered about the space, and overstuffed black leather couches and armchairs encircled a bar and a fireplace on the other end of the room. Drench walked to the bar, where he poured two cups of coffee from a carafe.

"Gladys buys this stuff from the Andes. We could feed a family of four on what she spends for coffee. But it's damn good."

Josie sipped and admired it, although she thought it tasted burnt.

"What brings you to the hinterlands so early in the morning?"

"I'm sure you've heard about Red Goff?"

"That I have."

"I'm hoping for a little perspective on Red. Everyone we've interviewed hated the man. I haven't found anyone upset by his murder. Makes it a little hard to narrow the focus."

Drench squinted and looked out a wall of plate glass into the smoky sky. "Red and I go way back. He was friends with my brother, Samuel. We all went to the same grade school and high school, but he and Sam were three years older. I took off to make my fortune in Houston, and Red stayed back. He's seen some terrible things. Red's daddy was gunned down and killed by Mexican coyotes sneaking a group of illegals across. They'd stopped at his farm to camp for the night and use water from the stock pond. Red's dad confronted them, tried to run them off, and they killed him. Red never got over it."

Josie shook her head. "He never saw guns as a danger. Even though his own father was killed with a gun."

Drench raised his right hand as if swearing on a Bible. "No, ma'am. Guns don't kill. People do. Red's doctrine."

Drench pulled a barstool out for Josie and she sat. He sat on the stool beside her and sipped at his coffee.

"Red started working as a field hand the year his daddy died, and he worked hard physical labor every year after. He blamed the illegals for his family's tough life. And he blamed the government for doing nothing about the problem. Police, too. Growing up, his three sisters relied on him as a father figure. His mother died from a heart attack just after his daddy."

"No family money that you know of? No inheritance or insurance from way back to support him?" Josie asked.

"Red married an acid-tongued barmaid when he was in his thirties to help him with the farm, but she took off on him. That was Colt's mom. Red didn't have a plug nickel." Drench frowned, his gaze fixed on the desert beyond his home. "He raised his daughter in a house filled with hate. I worry about that girl quite a bit."

"So, how does a man with no money have an arsenal of several hundred guns and bulletproof glass?" she asked.

Drench leaned on an elbow and gave Josie a half smile. "I wondered that myself. None of those yahoos he ran around with has that kind of money. Bunch of men with overactive testosterone production, if you ask me. I don't know where Red got his money, but I'd imagine whoever took off with that batch of guns knows something about his murder."

"I understand you own the land in front of Red's. Is that true?"

Drench smiled. "That pissed Red off to no end."

"He ever try and buy it from you?"

He laughed. "Offered me five times what that land was worth. I wouldn't take it. He was a fun one to get mad. I never once saw him raise a hand, but he sure could cuss a blue streak. Gladys always said he had the Napoleon complex. I just think life slapped his chops one too many times."

"Do you rent out the trailer at the bottom of the property?" Josie asked.

"Yep. Kenny Winning. Although his sister's living there now. He's a nice-enough kid."

"Think Kenny had any reason to kill Red? His sister said they hated each other," Josie said.

Drench smiled again. "That was my fault. I gave that kid land to set his trailer on just to tick Red off. Kenny worked for me for a while doing odd jobs. Handyman stuff. He was a good kid, honest, dependable, but real skittish. Never stayed in one place too long, like he was being chased." He pointed a finger at Josie. "Come to think of it, that kid was dating Colt for a while. Red's daughter."

"How long did they date?"

He shrugged. "I don't know. It wasn't anything serious. Couple months, maybe."

"Think he'd have had any reason to kill Red?"

Drench bit his lip. "I can't imagine it."

"What do you know about Hack Bloster?"

Drench looked down at the bar and traced the wood grain with his finger. "This is between me and you?"

"Of course."

"I think he's a dirty cop. I had my eye on that kid ever since he moved to town. He worked for me, digging wells for about six months. I always had a hard time getting a straight answer out of him. I even told Red to steer clear of him. I told him he was insane for ever letting him join the Gunners. Red thought Bloster would give legitimacy to the group just because he's a cop. A gun and a badge don't make you legitimate."

"You have anything concrete on Bloster? Anything to back up your suspicions?" she asked.

"Nothing but a bad feeling."

Pegasus Winning sat on the picnic table under the pecan trees and stared at the tattoo on her forearm: a constant reminder of the man who had sliced her open and left her to bleed on the dirty linoleum floor in their kitchen. The tattoo had been done just a month before he sliced her, a blackbird with a ribbon dangling from its beak. The inscription on the ribbon read, *Death do us part*. The inscription was his idea, the crow hers.

She stared at the words. He had promised her that day, sitting in a chair beside the table where she lay, her arm strapped down to a rusty surgical table the shop owner had called a relic, that he would love her until "death do us part." The tattoo artist worked with a cigarette hanging out of his mouth, occasionally blowing ashes off her arm to clear the work area. She had gone into the shop for the crow and nothing else. "Sing a Song of Sixpence" had been her favorite rhyme as a kid. She had memorized it and in middle school had composed a melody that a boyfriend turned into a rock ballad. She liked that they stole shiny things but nothing of value: tinfoil scraps and screws lying in the gutter.

Her boyfriend, Brock, had told the artist to include the ribbon. He smiled, told her, "My treat." Brock had looked pleased, so proud of his offer that she smiled, too, and shrugged when the guy gave her the eye. The tattooist obviously thought it a bad idea.

She rubbed at the words, turning her wrist an ugly red, and wondered if Brock had killed Red Goff. It was eight o'clock in the morning, she had just gotten home off third shift, but her mind was restless. It bothered her about the bullet through Red's forehead. It was true what she had told the cop. Brock had been strictly knives, but he told her once that if he ever used a gun, it would be straight through the forehead. No jacking around with the heart. Too much room for error. His theory was, if you got rid of the brain, you got rid of the witness.

These were her thoughts Tuesday morning after work, sipping her breakfast, tequila hot and straight, thinking about her next move. Artemis obviously was not the end of the line for her. Every day left her skin itching like she wanted to crawl out of it; she felt like a snake must feel before it sheds. Living in a rat-hole trailer in the middle of the desert, a dead body on her couch, her brother who knows where. How much worse could it get? she wondered. Kenny had been the one constant in a life spent moving.

Then, like a mirage, a body appeared, stirring up the dust, not from the road but from the open desert behind Red's place. A dark figure growing taller with each step. She knew immediately it was Kenny. He had a lanky way of moving. His outline against the sky sloped on one side, and she could tell he carried a duffel bag on one shoulder. He stopped at one point, maybe half a mile from her, and she figured he had spotted her sitting at the table. She smiled but stayed still.

He finally closed the distance, smooth and quiet, and stood smiling before her. "Hey, sis."

Pegasus stood and wrapped her brother in a long hug and realized how terribly lonely she had grown since moving to the desert.

Chief Gray arrived downtown a little before eight Wednesday morning and drove her jeep around the courthouse toward the Artemis Police Department. She was about to pull into her reserved space when she noticed an unfamiliar car in front of Manny's, a six-room motel half a block away from the police station. The car was a low-slung Buick. A pair of fuzzy purple dice and half a dozen Mardis Gras beads hung from the rearview mirror. Josie's stomach lurched. She parked and walked down the block toward the front end of the car. The dashboard was filled with fast-food wrappers, and a deck of tarot cards lay on the front seat. There was little doubt whom the car belonged to. She walked to the back of the car and found Indiana license plates and a bumper sticker with big red lips shaped as if ready for a kiss. The caption read, GO AHEAD—MAKE MY DAY.

Once she was back at her desk, Josie ran the plate number and found the car was registered to Beverly Gray, DOB 9/9/1956, green eyes, auburn hair, five feet four inches, 120 pounds. Josie kicked the metal trash can across the room, and papers went flying. She stood from her desk and saw Lou Hagerty standing at the office door.

"That what they call pitching a fit?" Lou asked.

"What do you need, Lou?" Josie asked, failing to keep the irritation out of her voice.

"Sheriff called. Said he's got a match on your Trauma Center shooter."

The Arroyo County Jail was located east of town, just a few miles from Highway 67 in a five-year-old complex with ten holding cells and twenty beds. When Macon Drench founded Artemis, his intention had been to keep jails out of his city. He envisioned a town ruled by vigilante justice: a place where the people of Artemis took care of their own, where crime was not allowed. It was a lofty idea that didn't work. After the courthouse was built, three cells were installed in the basement, but the escalating violence along the border had made a secure and updated facility a necessity. After 9/11, money from Homeland Security was used to outfit a first-rate jail that Sheriff Martínez ran with great care, and only half the manpower he needed.

Constructed of brick and concrete block, the jail opened into a secure lobby with a visitation room and conference room for law officers through a locked door to the left, as well as a holding cell and booking desk through a secured door to the right. The hub was located directly behind the entrance and was the area where law enforcement personnel typically visited. The inmate pods and day space were located in the center of the structure. Offices were located on the outer walls, and an enclosed basketball court was located on the back side of the building. The enclosed court contained a large door that opened onto the rear lot for transport vans to allow the secure transfer of prisoners.

Josie stood outside the entrance, looked up into a small video camera, and pressed the visitor button. A second later, she was buzzed into a small unfurnished room. Josie proceeded to a second set of doors where a buzzer sounded again and the doors opened into the central hub. Maria Santiago sat behind a computer screen at a large desk. She smiled and nodded at Josie. Maria was a short, round woman with a happy disposition, able to find humor in almost anything. She was also a competent and efficient intake officer, one of Josie's favorites.

"NCIC came through with fingerprints. Sheriff's got some good information for you," Santiago said.

"How good?"

"I think he matched your shooter. He gave me a packet to give you. He got called out on a domestic about ten minutes ago," she said.

Josie smiled. "He's a saint. You have a room I can use to sort through the paperwork?"

"Interrogation room's empty. You're welcome to it."

Josie nodded thanks. "The shooter still on medical watch?"

Santiago rolled her chair away from her computer to give her full attention to Josie. "Yes, ma'am. We've had a nurse here around the clock. The sheriff's mad as a hornet. A bigwig from the hospital's already been over here twice to talk with him. Hospital says when they bill the jail for services, they expect payment in thirty days."

Josie smiled again. "Good luck with that."

Aside from the bureaucratic nightmare of submitting bills, getting signatures, receiving the appropriate supervisor and board approvals, and general passing of the buck, there was the political nightmare of working cross-border to attempt to retrieve at least some payment for services from Mexican authorities.

"Sheriff Martínez is planning on sending the nurse home tomorrow. The man's stabilized. You know Dooley Thomas? The day shift guard?"

"Yes."

"His wife is a nurse. She's offered to stop by once a day to check his bandages and get his vital signs."

Josie nodded. "Good. Anybody talked to the prisoner yet?"

"As in interviewed him?"

Josie shrugged. "I know you haven't done anything formal, but have you heard anything? Has he talked to anyone? Asked for phone calls, lawyers?"

"Nothing. He hasn't made a peep. I don't think he speaks English. Sheriff just got the fingerprint confirmation right before he called you. He was all fired up when he left."

Santiago dug around on her desk through various stacks of

envelopes and papers before handing Josie a sealed manila envelope with her name on it.

Josie settled into a typical interrogation room: a sterile, eight-foot-by-eight-foot space with one metal table and two folding chairs sitting opposite each other. She opened the packet and found the first good news of the day. Martínez had left her a handwritten note that stated he fingerprinted the prisoner and ran him through NCIC and the Deportable Alien Control System, or DACS. He found a definite match with a male Hispanic linked to a deportation case from two years ago. Miguel Ángel Gutiérrez was picked up for leaving the scene of an accident without a license. He was subsequently linked to a charge for lewd and lascivious conduct with a minor, a twelve-year-old child. He was indicted and deported, supposedly to serve time in a Mexican prison.

Josie stared at the mug shot from two years ago and recognized the man she had shot, although he was now about twenty pounds heavier, with a goatee. She was positive it was the same man. He was a member of La Bestia who had defected from the Medrano cartel. She felt her heart rate increasing and the acid burn ignite in the pit of her stomach. She remembered the case but wanted to confirm the details.

She pulled her cell phone from her pocket and dialed Lou at the police department, who gave Josie the phone number for an old friend of hers. Anthony Dixon was a detention and deportation officer with Immigration and Customs Enforcement. She had worked two deportation cases with ICE over the past several years, and Dixon was the case agent both times. Josie reached Dixon on his cell phone as he was driving down the interstate from El Paso to Houston for a federal trial. She gave him the prisoner's name and a brief summary of the murder at the trauma unit.

"I got your man, Josie. No doubt about it." Dixon spoke with a slow Western drawl, making every word sound important.

"Is he family?" she asked.

"You bet he is. He's referred to as 'Cousin' by his comrades in La Bestia. You got a nasty one. You better set up some guards outside. That bad boy belongs in maximum."

Josie laughed. "He's in the Artemis lockup. We don't do maximum security."

"Better figure something out. He's a cousin to the Bishop, who is second in command in the Medrano clan. Gutiérrez left Medrano after he caught the Bishop having sex with his wife. He killed her, then left the organization."

"So, not only has he turned his back on the most famous family in Mexico, but he has also brutally murdered the leader."

"He will be killed. It's a matter of time and opportunity."

Dixon went on to explain that Gutiérrez had a relatively short criminal history of gun and drug charges in Mexico. However, intelligence from ICE had recently linked him to La Bestia's weapons division. No surprise there. He was a suspected recruiter for U.S. cartel surrogates in El Paso and Laredo. Dixon said he would call his secretary and tell her to e-mail Josie several pictures of Gutiérrez with high-ranking gang members in both the Texas Machismo and the Tejana Guard.

Josie thanked Dixon for the information and promised to share the full case file with him at the close of the investigation. Next, she found Maria and asked to borrow a computer to pull up her e-mail account on the jail's secure server. Maria set her up on a computer that was currently not in use in the booking room. Josie logged on to her account, and as promised, Dixon's office had e-mailed her two pictures of Cousin Gutiérrez. Josie pulled a picture out of the steno pad she carried with her. It was the picture of Red Goff and the three Mexicans that she and Otto had seized from Red's basement. She held it up to the computer screen. It was a definite match for Gutiérrez. He stood in the background, just to the left of Red, dressed in a camouflage flak suit, an automatic rifle slung over his shoulder, staring intently at something beyond the photographer. Josie could tell the photograph was a few years old by the lack of gray in Red's hair. Gutiérrez had just left the family clan six months ago, so the picture had to have been taken with members of Medrano. The news was an important step forward in the investigation, but it meant trouble for the town.

The jail contained two identical pods, each with their own day space: a fifteen-foot-square room with metal tables and chairs and a TV mounted near the ceiling. Each pod housed five single-bed cells that could be turned into bunk beds, thus doubling the size of the jail when necessary. Santiago told Josie one pod was full; the other pod had two cells in use, one of them occupied by Miguel Ángel Gutiérrez. The prisoners were currently all back in their cells after breakfast.

Santiago checked Josie's weapon and put it in a locker, then escorted her back to lock up. Dooley, the six-foot-tall, three-hundred-pound day shift guard met Josie at the door with a smile.

"I want to shake your hand, Chief." Dooley smiled widely and held a hand out as Josie entered the day space. Josie smiled back, confused, and shook his hand. "You are an official legend. Took down two cartel members in one whack. Single-handed." He shook his head, still smiling widely.

"It wasn't quite like that, Dooley."

He winked and patted her gently on the back with his massive hand. "No need to be shy about it. I just want you to know the jailers got our money on you." He started walking toward the cell containing Guitiérrez, jingling his ring of keys at his side. He said over his shoulder, "You keep holding the line."

Josie assured him she would and asked about the prisoner. Dooley told Josie he had not heard a word out of Gutiérrez and that he had refused all food.

Dooley released the nurse, who was sitting in a chair outside the cell, reading a paperback book. The woman sighed heavily and thanked Josie for the break. "I was worried for my safety at first, but I'll die from boredom before anything else."

Dooley unlocked the door and rattled off a set of rules to Gutiérrez, who kept his eyes closed. It gave Josie a minute to size him up. His face was drawn, his eyes puffy and lifeless. She knew from information that Dixon had provided that he was forty-eight years old, but she would have guessed seventy. His arm was bandaged with white gauze where she had shot him, but he wasn't connected to any medical apparatus. He was still dressed in a blue hospital gown, lying on his back in bed. To the right of the bed was a toilet, a metal chair, and an empty metal shelf attached to the wall. The walls were concrete, as was the floor.

Dooley locked the door behind her, and she turned and noted that he remained close, within her line of sight. The sheriff ran a tight ship. Other than petty grievances and minor fights, there had never been a serious altercation against a prisoner or a guard since he took the reins when the jail opened five years ago. Martínez allowed very minimal contact with outside visitors, and absolutely no physical contact. Prisoners were searched daily, and metal detectors were in place throughout the facility. For a small jail, it was run very efficiently. Josie wondered what kind of firepower would be necessary to reach the prisoners.

"Mr. Gutiérrez, I'm Chief Josie Gray with the Artemis Police Department." He opened his eyes and turned his head to stare at her. "I'm your arresting officer. I have a few questions to ask you."

He said nothing, seemingly uncomprehending.

"Do you speak English?" she asked. Nothing.

She kept going nevertheless. After several minutes of Mirandizing in English, telling him who she was and telling him briefly about his situation in the U.S., Josie confronted him with his identity, his mug shots, his deportation record, and his testimony at trial. He finally broke his silence, apparently convinced it would no longer serve his purpose.

"When will I be deported?" he asked, his English good.

"You killed a man on U.S. soil. You may be deported, but only after you serve your time here for first-degree murder."

His face grew angry, his eyes suddenly bright, and the man she faced at gunpoint two days ago showed through. "This should not have been a problem for your soil! You were the ones who took a Mexican problem and made it your own. You cannot lay that on my shoulders. I was simply following my orders."

"From who?"

He turned his head from her and looked at the gray concrete wall to the right of his bed.

"Are you associated with La Bestia Cartel?"

He said nothing.

"Is the man referred to as 'the Bishop' your cousin?" she asked.

He stared at the block wall.

"Because in this jail cell, with the entire Medrano cartel ready to blow you to pieces, you are quite a target."

No response.

"Okay," Josie said, nodding. "Here's your situation: This is your second offense. You get to rot in an American jail. I will monitor your progress as you serve your life sentence. I don't like you, or what you stand for, and you will serve maximum time."

He continued to stare at the wall, saying nothing.

"I don't know how prisons in Mexico work, but here in the U.S., we despise pedophiles. They don't get treated well. In the world of prisoners, men who screw around with little kids are the bottom feeders. A guy could blow up a church full of nuns, and he'd still have the moral high ground compared to a guy like you. You can request the hole, but I hear solitaries are full up at federal penitentiary. All the filthy kiddie lovers already have those beds taken, so you'll be in with the biker boys, the skinheads. And a Mexican pedophile? The Aryans dream about guys like you."

Even with Gutiérrez partially covered under the hospital sheets, Josie could see his body was rigid, his jugular vein swollen and pulsing on his neck.

"Maybe you decide to share information, talk about La Bestia. Tell me why they want to move through Artemis so badly. What their connection here is. You might get out of jail before your family forgets you're alive."

SIX

Josie drove back to Artemis and parked one street north of the square in front of a small brick building with a sign that read OFFICE OF ABACUS. Dillon Reese, a forty-two-year-old accountant, had opened the business several years ago. A messy, very public divorce from a TV news anchor in California had caused him to seek out solitude in the smallest town he could find that would still support an accountant. He found his solitude, and Artemis gained a sorely needed financial advisor who was a sucker for pro bono jobs, including an occasional consult with the local police.

Josie had dated Dillon for six months before he got tired of waiting for her to decide if things would ever move forward. They were great friends, great lovers, but Dillon said the part that mattered most to him, the *marrow*, he had called it, was nonexistent. He told her he was done waiting and asked another woman to a Marfa art gallery opening. Josie had not spoken to him since. It hadn't ended nicely for either of them, and Josie sensed he felt as bad about the end as she did. At least she hoped he did. Now she intended to provide them both with an opportunity to at least speak again on the street, although in view of the contractions in her throat, she obviously hoped for something more. She missed him intensely.

Josie walked into the office and found Dillon's secretary on the phone. Where Josie was wiry, MS. CHRISTINA HANDLEY, as the nameplate read, was willowy and graceful. She wore a white short-sleeved shirt that brought out the deep Mediterranean glow of her skin. She had dark eyes, black hair cut in an expensive shoulder-length pageboy, and pouty lips. Her head was cocked as she talked into a headset and typed on the computer in front of her. She paused, glanced Josie's way and winked, then gave her an *I'll be with you* smile.

Christina pointed a red fingernail to a waiting area with maple furniture that matched the glossy maple floors. The office was painted in earthy shades of brown and red and yellow, each wall a different color, with black-and-white Japanese etchings grouped around the room. Josie's attention moved from the art back to the receptionist.

The woman sat back in her chair and tucked her silky hair behind an ear with a small diamond earring that glinted across the room. The secretary was a new addition to the office.

Josie's uniform pants scratched at her thighs, and the bullet-proof vest smashed her chest. She adjusted her gun belt. Never one for makeup, if she'd had lipstick in the jeep, she would have walked back outside and applied it.

The woman looked toward her suddenly, the call on her headset apparently complete, and smiled brightly. "Good morning! How can I help you?"

"I'm Chief Josie Gray. Is Mr. Reese available for a few minutes?"

The woman pressed a button on her computer and talked into the microphone near her lips. "Chief Gray is here to see you." She smiled, pressed another button, and turned to Josie. "Do you know where his office is?"

There was only one office and a storage room beyond the

secretary's desk. Josie refrained from sarcasm and just smiled. "Yes, I've been here."

"Go right on back, then."

Dillon was standing up behind his desk when she walked in. He was a little over six feet tall, slightly stooped, and wore khaki pants with a white shirt and yellow tie. He had sad eyes that turned down at the corners, but the blue was bright and intense, as if backlit. He kept his salt-and-pepper hair cut short, and Josie considered him one of the most handsome men she knew. She had never met another person so at ease with himself in the world.

He smiled warmly at her, displaying none of the awkwardness she felt. She tried to appear at ease. Looking professional, in charge, or angry were all looks she had mastered, but she could never fake relaxed.

Dillon walked around his desk and shook her hand, placed the other hand on her shoulder. "It's good to see you." He pulled back a comfortable chair in front of his desk and sat beside her rather than moving back behind his desk. "What brings you by? Social, I hope, not business."

"A little of both," she said.

"Business out of the way first, then. What do you have?"

Josie opened an accordion file she'd brought with her. It was stuffed full of paperwork, bank statements, receipts, handwritten ledgers, and outstanding bills that they had found at the house.

"I'm working on Red Goff's death."

Dillon nodded, his brow furrowed. "I heard about his murder."

"I wondered if you could take a cursory look at his files to get some sense of his debt versus income. I think most of the important information is in there. But it's just a jumbled mess. Would you have time to take a look?"

"Is this where we mix the personal with the business?" he asked, offering a crooked smile and a raised eyebrow.

"How about you bring the information to my house tomorrow, say seven o'clock? I'll provide the lasagna."

"And a bottle of merlot?"

"Absolutely."

He smiled broadly, and she restrained a ridiculous urge to stand up from her chair and kiss him.

"I'd like that," he said. "I've missed you."

At 3:30 P.M., Josie, Otto, and Marta met around the department's conference table with case files and notes to debrief on the Medrano and Goff murders. At least once each week, schedules were adjusted so they could meet and discuss current investigations and share information. This week, unfortunately, was not typical.

Josie opened the manila folder at the top of her stack. "Let's start with the murder at the Trauma Center. The man I killed has been identified through DACS as Thomas Brema, a member of the Medrano cartel."

Marta groaned. "Has the organization released a statement yet?"

Josie nodded. "What you'd expect. They released a statement in the newspaper in Piedra, saying they will get revenge. 'The Americans have blood on their hands.' That kind of garbage."

Marta covered her mouth, obviously troubled by the news.

Josie frowned. "Here's some irony: The Medranos claim we worked with La Bestia to kill Hector Medrano. We allowed La Bestia to enter our Trauma Center and shoot up our hospital in order to kill Medrano. They claim we have partnered with the devil."

"Josie, I hope you are taking this seriously. Your life is in serious jeopardy over this. Pride alone would make them go after you," Marta said.

"You might be wise to stay elsewhere for a week or two. Stay at Manny's and see what shakes out," Otto said.

Josie nodded, aware of the danger but determined to move forward. She continued, "Here's the story on the shooting: Hector Medrano, referred to as 'the Pope' in Mexico, has been confirmed as the patient who was killed at the Trauma Center. His nephew, Miguel Gutiérrez, was one of the three shooters. Gutiérrez had gotten into a feud with his cousin, the Bishop, who is Hector Medrano's son. After the feud, Gutiérrez left the family drug business about a year ago and joined La Bestia."

"You want to draw us a diagram?" Otto said.

"What caused the feud?" asked Marta.

"Gutiérrez caught his cousin, the Bishop, in the swimming pool with his wife, naked and entangled."

"Entangled?" Otto said.

"He came home early from a weekend business trip to Spain and caught them in the act. Gutiérrez shot and killed his wife in the pool but left Medrano to swim to safety. The pool boy fished her body out of the water the next morning," Josie said. "This all came from a conversation with Agent Dixon."

"Why didn't he kill his cousin?" Otto asked.

"Killing his wife allowed him to save face. Killing his cousin, who is second in command of the Medrano cartel, would have been suicide before he allied himself with La Bestia."

"Gutiérrez couldn't kill Medrano, so he defected and joined the rival gang, La Bestia?" Otto asked.

Josie nodded.

Otto said, "I'm surprised somebody from Medrano didn't pop the cousin after he left the family. You don't do that over there."

"That's exactly what I thought," Josie told him. "But they have this code of conduct. I guess the Bishop messing around with his cousin's wife was in violation of the code, so they went easy on Gutiérrez."

"Until now," Otto said. "But if Gutiérrez was willing to come over and kill Hector Medrano in our jail, then why didn't he just kill the Bishop after he was screwing around with his wife?"

Marta wagged a finger at Otto. "It's all hierarchy. His cousin having sex with his wife? That was bad, but pardonable. He left the organization because his pride required it. Now, he's in La Bestia, he's showing his allegiance to the organization by killing the leader of his former cartel. This move was designed to move him high up in the La Bestia organization."

Josie raised her eyebrows at Otto as if to ask, *Got it now?* He shook his head and shrugged.

"Here's our issue. Now that the Bishop knows that his cousin was one of his father's murderers, will he retaliate while Gutiérrez is up here? This doesn't leave this room, but I'm concerned the Arroyo County Jail is in jeopardy of attack," Josie said. "I've already talked to the mayor about getting a National Guard presence here until we can get Medrano moved."

"I say, ship the son of a bitch back to his own country and let the Mexicans deal with him," Otto said. "Leave him for fish bait or drop him on his cousin's doorstep. Just get him out of Texas."

"What message does that send? You put enough pressure, enough of a threat on the Americans, and they'll give you what you want?" Josie asked.

Marta stood from her chair and walked away, obviously shaken. Josie stood and poured three cups of coffee from the coffeemaker in the back of the room to allow her time to compose herself.

Marta sat down again at the table. "My country is imploding, and the people who care are terrified. And now we face the same terrorists here in Artemis." She shook a fist at Otto. "This is how they operate! They terrorize the good people of the city into leaving, and they fill in the voids with crime."

"Marta, we're not going anywhere," Josie said. "They will not get the best of us. This is our town. We have rules and laws that work, and we'll move forward accordingly." She paused to let her words stick. Josie had no time for philosophy or politics.

"We have questions we need answered. First, has either gang

infiltrated Artemis? Any contact with those organizations, no matter how small, is too risky. We end it now. I talked with an ICE case agent who said there's evidence the Medrano family has confirmed ties to both Houston and Atlanta. We knew they'd moved into Arizona, but they're spreading out faster than I'd thought. I don't think we're anything more than a portal into the U.S. for either group, but they're using us to get through. I hate to admit it, but Moss is right. We have to plug the hole."

"How do you plug a hole that's surrounded by a thousand guns?" Marta asked, her face still tense with worry.

"We gather information first. Marta, you make every contact you can tonight with anyone even slightly connected to the drug trade here in Artemis. Look for connections to the cartels. Otto, you concentrate on Red's guns. Start checking with pawnshops and running the serial numbers from the Gunners' policy manual."

"You think Red's death is connected to the cartels?" Otto asked. He stood from the table and stretched his back.

"Both groups are heavily involved in the gun trade, and Red had more money than a heavy equipment operator ought to have." Josie pulled the photo of Red out of her folder and pitched it into the middle of the table. "We also have the photograph with Red standing next to a confirmed member of La Bestia."

"I get he was involved, but what's their motive for shooting him?" Marta asked.

"Almost three hundred guns."

"I'd like to talk with Fallow again," Otto said. "That guy wants to squeal to someone, but Bloster has him terrified." Standing behind Josie, he reached over her shoulder and grabbed the photo of Red and the cartel members. He studied it, looking for missed details.

"Bloster is the one who has me worried," Josie said. "I haven't had a chance to talk to the sheriff yet. If he's not connected to Red's death in some way, I'll be shocked. At the least, I think he knows who killed him."

Marta pointed at Otto. "I think you're right. Fallow is the weak link. Tell him about the beheading last week in Piedra Labrada. The police officer who was doing his job and had his head cut off for not accepting the payment offered by La Bestia. Ask Fallow what he thinks will happen to him with no protection from us."

"I want all three of us back out at Winning's tonight," Josie said. "I want to reexamine the blood evidence at her trailer. I'll try luminol to see if the blood traces match up with Winning's story. Smear marks, drops of blood, shoe imprints, a fingerprint from a blood smear. I feel like we're missing something there."

Josie's cell phone vibrated on the table. She picked it up, didn't recognize the number, and set it back down again.

"Marta, I'd like you to take photos of the crime scene and look at them with a fresh eye. I'm going to take Red's nude pictures of Winning and check the angle, establish where they were taken. I can't figure why Red would keep the pictures down in the basement with his guns and ammunition. Wouldn't you keep naked pictures in your bedroom?"

Marta broke in. "Maybe they're blackmail pictures."

Josie frowned. "She's got nothing."

"So, maybe Red was blackmailing her brother." Marta winced. "With pictures of his sister."

"Otto, I want you to spend some time at Red's place, get more prints, dig through every drawer and envelope you can find. I've got Dillon going over his accounts. I'll find out tonight some preliminary information on debt and assets."

Otto grinned. "That's good," he said.

"What's good?"

"Dillon Reece going over the accounts."

"Don't start with me, Otto."

Marta put both hands in the air. "Wait a minute. Go back to Red's connection with the cartels. You think he was selling them guns? That's pretty bold. You don't connect with them easily."

"It makes sense. He got his money somehow. I'm guessing he was buying guns cheap and reselling to the Mexicans. With the feud between the Medranos and La Bestia, maybe Red got caught in the middle," Josie said. "It makes sense with Fallow, too. I think he knows about a gun deal between Red and Bloster and the Mexicans, and he's scared to death their lives are in jeopardy."

"Ole Red's guns are supporting a drug cartel south of the border. Wasn't his shtick that he wanted to protect the women and children of Texas? Sure accomplished that, now, didn't he?" Otto walked around the conference table again, scooted his chair out, and sat down grumbling about his back.

Josie looked doubtful. "Here's what I can't figure. The cartels have more guns and money than we can even imagine. Red's three hundred guns would be nice, but let's face it, not worth much effort on their part. And if they were killing him for his guns, why move the body? If they were just after the guns, wouldn't they just shoot him and leave the body where it fell? Why take him into Pegasus's trailer? I'm betting the cartels are involved, but what's their angle?"

SEVEN

"Don't look through the sights yet. Get used to raising the gun and shooting. If a lowlife draws, you think you'll have time to stop and aim? Find the sights?"

Pegasus faced the hill, sweat rolling down her neck and between her shoulder blades. It was almost six o'clock and she was irritated, hungry, and her hands were developing blisters from the awkward way she was forced to hold a pistol built for a man. Her fingers weren't strong enough to pull the carbine back and flip the locking mechanism in place in the smooth motion Kenny had demonstrated a dozen times. She could get it, but she had to hold the gun lopsided, the barrel facing up and out. If speed were an issue, she would be dead before she ever advanced a bullet into the chamber.

"You know how to load and unload the bullets. You'll never get speed with either of these guns, but they're the best I've got for you. Turn around so I can mix them up again," he said.

Pegasus turned her back to the tailgate of Kenny's pickup and faced the hill as he mixed two calibers of bullets and set out both magazines and pistols. They were on a patch of federal land miles from town, where he poached for deer. He had made a crude frame out of two-by-fours he had pulled from a trash pile behind Red's place. He duct-taped a large trash bag in the middle of the frame for her to shoot at. Masking tape outlined the shape of a man's head and chest.

After he shuffled the pieces, Kenny said, "Show me a quick load and shoot. No aiming."

Pegasus turned back to the tailgate and surveyed the guns and bullets.

"You're in the trailer, by yourself. You see a light outside the door, hear several men's voices. Talk me through what you do. Go."

She took a deep breath and surveyed the guns. "I'll use the Smith and Wesson pistol. The magazine holds ten bullets instead of six. Good if there are several people outside." She picked up the correct magazine and loaded ten .45-caliber bullets, shoving them into the spring-loaded chamber with quite a bit of effort. She popped the magazine up into the butt of the gun. "I heard the bullet advance. I'm putting my finger just above the trigger and turning to focus on the chest area of the man in front."

Pegasus pivoted, planted her feet, and brought both hands up in a smooth level motion, aimed at the target, looked over the gun sight, but did not stop to focus.

"Shoot!" Kenny yelled.

She leaned into the shot, tensing her muscles to prepare for the kickback, and pulled the trigger without thinking. The shot landed dead center of the trash bag.

Kenny smiled and patted her on the back. "Nice work, sis. Very nice."

She laughed out loud.

"How'd it feel?" he asked.

"My ears are still buzzing. The sound's caught in my head like a bee."

"And?"

"It felt good. I can do this."

"Now empty the cartridge into the hillside and watch where the bullets hit. Go."

Pegasus turned, shot until she fired one empty round. Her ears pounded. She had shot nine bullets but had little sense of where they landed in relation to her aim.

"Eject the magazine into the trunk and load up again," he said.

She rolled her eyes. "It is ninety degrees and I'm hungry. I need a supper break."

"Damn it, this isn't a joke! You think the people who stole Red's guns won't come back for you?" Kenny had the wide-eyed look that had made her nervous since they were kids. His hair was sweat-soaked, and he looked like he needed a shower. He seemed to realize he was coming on too strong and dropped his voice. "Life is seriously messed up out here. You need to move on if you aren't willing to prepare."

She wiped the sweat from her forehead with the back of both hands and sighed. "I have thirty-six dollars in my purse. Where exactly do you think I'm headed?"

"Then you better get serious. No more screwing around."

Pegasus looked up at her brother. She was five foot eight and he stood over a foot taller than her, thin, with a swagger she had always admired. She appreciated him checking on her and staying a few days, more than she could ever tell him. He refused to stay in the trailer, or tell her where he was staying, but that was fine. His presence was enough.

Ignoring his lecture, Pegasus quickly reloaded five bullets, spun, and faced the target again, discharging all five rounds. She finished, counted multiple holes within a one-foot radius of the center of the trash bag, and turned back to face Kenny with a look of triumph, her ears now completely numb, her hands tingling and sweaty.

Kenny smiled. "I'd say those son of a bitches ought to think twice before knocking on your door."

Josie sat at Winning's picnic table with a set of six photos, all taken from basically the same angle. She had started at Red's house, holding each photo up to compare the picture to the scene in front of her, but the angle was too far to the left. Josie matched up the picnic table just outside Winning's trailer, and found an exact match with her own digital camera. Red had sat at the table, probably nursing a beer, she imagined, and taken pictures of Winning through her curtainless windows.

Josie's stomach growled and she realized she had skipped lunch again. She glanced at her watch. At four o'clock, with at least another two hours' worth of work, there was no way she could pull off lasagna for Dillon by seven. She would settle for spaghetti as a backup and hope she made it to her house before he did. The image of her mother's car, parked at Manny's, crossed her mind. Josie just hoped she could hold her off one more day.

She retrieved her evidence kit and toolbox from her jeep, where they had already gotten almost too hot to handle. She was setting her equipment on the picnic table when Pegasus Winning pulled down the lane and parked beside Josie's police vehicle. The rusty car door squealed as she slammed it shut and faced Josie. Winning was wearing a white V-neck T-shirt and cut-off jean shorts. Her hair was in a ponytail behind her back, and her face was sunburned and dirty, with streaks of sweat down her cheeks and neck.

As Winning approached her, Josie lifted the photos up but didn't show them to her. "Were you aware Red had been taking pictures of you inside your trailer?"

Winning rolled her eyes. "Ask me if I'm surprised. The sick bastard."

"Had you noticed anyone hanging around outside your trailer?"
She shrugged.

"Any trash in your yard, that kind of thing?"

Pegasus shook her head no.

Josie leaned back against the picnic table and crossed her arms.
"Here's the plan, then. Officer Marta Cruz will be here shortly.
She'll be taking pictures, both inside and out. She'll help me tape
up your windows inside so we can get your trailer dark. I'll be
spraying a solution over your walls and carpet to check for bloodstains. The solution won't hurt your fabric, and it isn't harmful to
humans. We hope to finish in about an hour. Do you have somewhere you can go for an hour or so? Or you're welcome to stay in
the trailer."

She smirked. "I'll stay."

Josie shrugged. "Suit yourself. Any word from your brother?"

"No. Why?"

Josie considered her. "Well, he's your brother. He invited you
here and then left. I thought he might have found out about Red
getting killed in his trailer and come home. Doesn't seem like an
unreasonable question."

"I never said it was," Winning said. She turned from Josie and
walked toward her trailer.

Josie noted the anger in her abrupt departure, and wondered
what secrets she was hiding.

Turning away from her, Josie looked under the trees and picnic
table for evidence that Red may have left behind. As she turned, she
noticed the trees weren't uniformly green. The tips of one of the tree
branches, at eye level to her, were a deep brown. She stepped back to
view the tree from a distance. The brown coloring was primarily on
one branch, in a small area. She looked at the coloring up close and
was certain the color lay on top of the pine needles; it didn't seem
like an illness or disease that caused the branch to change color. She

gently pulled the branches apart and peered into the trunk of the tree, where she saw the bark was cut and something appeared to be protruding.

She forced herself to step back and think through the steps. If she moved ahead too quickly, she might disturb evidence that could be crucial to the investigation. She retrieved her 35-millimeter camera from her evidence case sitting under the picnic table, where it was slightly shaded.

She snapped a dozen pictures of the tree, which looked about twenty feet high with a fifteen-foot spread and deep green needles that were stiff like a bristle brush. Josie backed up twenty feet, then snapped pictures from several angles, showing the tree's relation to the house, and finally took close-up pictures of the branch and the brown covering. By now she figured it was Red's blood.

As she began to part the branches again, Marta drove up the road in her jeep and parked beside Winning's car. Josie waved and called her up. She was glad to see her; Marta's attention to detail in an investigation made her excellent in processing a crime scene.

Marta walked up with her hands on her hips. "Find anything yet?"

Josie smiled. "That I did. Give me two minutes." She pushed through the branches and dug at the trunk of the tree with a screwdriver she had pulled from her toolbox.

Josie finally emerged, cursing the sticky pine needles, and handed Marta a small plastic bag. Josie dusted the needles off her uniform as Marta smiled in sudden recognition of her discovery.

"Think this is the bullet that killed Red?" Marta asked.

"I'd lay money on it." Josie labeled the evidence bag and locked it in her jeep along with the branch from the pine tree that contained what she assumed was blood on the needles.

As they walked toward the trailer, Josie said, "I'd like you to snap pictures as I spray the luminol."

"If someone shot Red outside, then moved him immediately to the trailer, there could be traces of blood in there we didn't notice."

"I'm counting on it."

As Josie and Marta taped black plastic trash bags over the windows in the kitchen and living room, Winning sat at her kitchen table painting her finger- and toenails. After the taping was done, the trailer was dark enough to effectively use the luminol solution to test for bloodstains. Josie sat at the table across from Winning and mixed the solutions in the kit, carefully measuring, shaking, and pouring the mixture into a spray bottle. Winning turned off all the lights in the front of the trailer, and they were in almost total darkness. Marta turned on the black light and walked behind Josie as she lightly sprayed the solution on the brown carpet in front of the imprint where the couch had been. Several seconds later, two bright green dots appeared on the floor, approximately a quarter inch in diameter. Josie took a picture of the blood spots, and Marta drew a diagram in case the picture didn't develop. Josie then sprayed the solution in a swath from the couch to the trailer door. Nothing appeared in the black light until she sprayed around the door, at which point, a quarter-sized area on the threshold appeared bright green.

"Is that blood on the floor?" Winning asked from her seat at the table.

Marta held the black light closer, and there was no doubt.

Josie asked Winning to turn on the kitchen light. They stood and stared at the drop of blood, now just barely visible in the dust and dirt that had collected at the bottom of the doorway.

Josie flipped the light back off and pointed to the dollop of blood. "It's perfectly round. Imagine two men carrying Red through the door, one at his head and one at his feet. The blood would have dropped from the back of his head, straight down from the bullet wound."

Marta took additional pictures and measurements around the door, then scraped the dried blood from the threshold and collected several flakes with a cotton swab. She dropped them into a small glass vial and said she would get the blood to the laboratory drop box that night to request a DNA scan.

"So, somebody carried Red's body into the trailer and laid him down on my couch?" Winning asked.

Josie noted the surprise in her voice. She hadn't made the coroner's findings public, so no one knew the bullet had exited Red's skull, and Winning certainly didn't know Josie had just dug the bullet out of her pine tree.

"Any theories on why someone would do that?" Marta asked Winning.

"Why would the people he ran with do anything?" Winning responded.

Josie said, "Generally, when a murder victim is staged, the killer is either trying to send a message or create a diversion. Was the killer sending a message to you?"

After searching Red's house again and finding nothing new of any interest, Otto left and drove to Paul Fallow's house. He lived north of town in a small, ritzy subdivision with half a dozen stucco homes, each with three thousand to four thousand square feet of living space. By comparison to his neighbors' homes, Fallow's was a fairly modest beige-colored two story with wooden lintels and Spanish arches. Otto parked and knocked on the front door but heard no movement inside. The garage door was open to display two white midsized Acura sedans, so he walked around the back of the house, where he found Fallow in golf shorts and a light blue tank top, raking sand.

Otto stood at the corner of the house for a moment and watched Fallow walk the perimeter of a Japanese garden, about ten feet by ten feet, raking gray sand in a pattern to form concentric squares. His wife, a high school English teacher, sat on a mat at the center of the yard in the lotus position with her eyes closed. Otto wondered how in the world a guy like Fallow ended up in a group like the Gunners.

Fallow looked up and saw Otto as he approached the backyard. Fallow waved slightly, and then he tiptoed across small rocks positioned strategically to get him out of the garden without disturbing the sand.

Fallow used a bandanna tied around his neck to wipe the sweat off his face and pointed toward the front of the house. "She's deep within," he said in a whisper. "Let's not disturb her."

They went inside Fallow's home and sat in a blue room filled with puffy beige furniture. Oversized paintings of pastel geometric shapes covered most of the wall space. Otto felt his body sink a foot into the couch cushion and worried he wouldn't be able to push himself up and out. He pulled his steno pad and pen out of his shirt pocket and rested them on his knee.

"Can I get you a cold beverage?"

Otto realized he was suddenly annoyed with the man sitting across from him.

Otto ignored the question. "We received some new information about the Gunners. It's time you come clean on what you know about Red and his guns." Otto waited for a reaction—something more than the wide-eyed stare Fallow was offering. When Otto got nothing more, he pulled several pictures out of the steno pad that he carried and offered them to Fallow, who stood to retrieve them.

"That's Red in the top picture, standing next to a couple of men who are confirmed members of La Bestia. That second picture? That's Miguel Gutiérrez, a member of La Bestia. We have him locked up in the Arroyo County Jail for murdering his uncle in broad daylight at our Trauma Unit."

Fallow's face turned white and his lips curled down. He looked as if he might vomit.

"These are some bad fellows that old Red was dealing with, Dr. Fallow. I don't think you want to mess with these guys."

Fallow looked up suddenly, his eyes bright and teary. "Who says I'm messing with them! I don't know these men. That was Red's business! Go talk to Hack Bloster if you want details. I want no part of this." He clapped his hands together as if the topic were closed.

Otto didn't move. "Go ahead and look at that last photo. That's a picture of a police officer that pissed one of those other fellows off. Notice his head is gone? It's in the trash can to the right of the body. Don't think you can clap your hands and this will go away."

Fallow leaned forward and stared at the picture in his hands.

"We suspect these individuals killed Red Goff. We're taking the position that anyone associated with the Gunners is in grave danger."

"This is so unfair. I did nothing wrong."

Otto cleared his throat. "Mr. Fallow, I need to know who Red was working with."

He looked up, his eyes pleading. "I swear to you, I don't know. I'm pretty sure he and Hack were trading guns. That's all I know, and that's a guess on my part. They never allowed me into their private meetings."

At 6:35 P.M., Josie, Otto, and Marta met at the police department to discuss findings before Josie and Otto logged off. Sheriff Martínez had stopped by to ask about the prisoner's connection to La Bestia, and they all stood in the lobby area talking by the dispatcher's station. Josie was explaining to the sheriff everything they'd discovered with a worried eye on her watch. She had twenty minutes to drive home, change, and get water on to boil before Dillon arrived for dinner and a bottle of wine she had promised and not purchased. She needed a private, sit-down talk with Martínez about Deputy Bloster, but it would have to wait.

Josie's back was to the entrance door, but she heard the bell ring as they wrapped up. She turned and watched a petite woman with dyed maroon hair, red lips, and red fingernails enter the department.

"Well, if it isn't the elusive Josie Gray," the woman said. She spoke with a heavy drinker's rasp.

Josie gave the other three officers a look and said she would check in with them later. Mercifully, they apparently understood that whatever was about to transpire was personal and, most likely, humiliating. Otto and Marta turned and walked toward the up-stairs office. The sheriff walked around the woman, who turned and watched him exit the building.

"That man's got a backside worth watching, now. All these cops you run around with that good looking?" she asked, winking and smiling widely at Josie.

Josie felt her face redden. She was very aware that Lou was still at the dispatcher's desk, listening to every word and most likely taking notes.

Josie pushed the door open, and then walked behind her mom into the evening heat. She felt her hands go sweaty and her stomach seize into a knot: the same physical reaction her mother had been producing in her through years of humiliating scenes. Her body had instantly recalled and replicated the physical sensations of fifteen years ago.

With distaste, Josie watched the flex of her mother's tight back muscles through an open-back halter top and the intentional sway of her rear end. Her five-foot-five mother could paralyze her like no robber, rapist, or drug dealer she had ever encountered, and the realization depressed the hell out of her.

Her mother struck a cocky pose on the sidewalk and looked

Josie over as if assessing the damage after a car crash. "You didn't think I'd come, did you? You ought to know, if I say it, I do it."

Josie could have laughed or cried in equal measure. Her mother had never followed through on anything unless it benefited her in a significant and personal way.

"I had no idea you were coming. If I'd known, I would have set time aside. I have plans tonight. And I can't cancel," Josie said. "We can have dinner tomorrow."

"So break the plans. I drive two thousand miles, and you can't show me a little courtesy?" Her mother shook her head, her eyes wide with exaggerated shock. "You're a piece a work."

"I don't want to have this conversation streetside," said Josie. "I explained that I have plans I can't cancel. If you want to meet for lunch, stop by here tomorrow around noon and we can get a bite to eat." She pulled a business card out of her front shirt pocket and handed it to her. "Just call first in case I'm out on a call."

"Well, don't let me hold you back, darlin'." She turned from Josie and walked away, one hand in the air, the other on her hip. "It won't take me nothing to find myself some entertainment tonight."

Fifteen minutes later, Josie had left her front door open and was hurrying to the bedroom. She threw her clothes, bulletproof vest, holster, and gun into a heap on her closet floor before jumping into a cool shower. She left her hair in a clip but soaped up, rinsed the day down the drain, and toweled off before stepping out.

"Josie?"

She smiled. His voice was coming from just outside the bathroom, in her bedroom.

"Five minutes, then I'll get supper going," she called. "There's some cheese in the fridge if you're starved."

Josie swiped on concealer to cover up the dark circles under her eyes, brushed her teeth, and dressed in an ancient pair of Levi's and a gauzy sleeveless white shirt that hung loose over her thin body. She took her damp hair down, brushed it, and pulled it back up into the clip. She found Dillon propped against the couch on the living room floor with her hound dog's head in his lap.

"Chester missed me."

Dillon smiled up at her with his sad eyes, and Josie's chest tightened at the sight of him. She realized she had almost lost him. She let out a long slow breath and forced herself to relax into the moment.

She sat beside Dillon and stretched her legs out next to his. "I'm sorry about dinner. I don't even have the bottle of wine."

He reached around the dog and sat a grocery sack on his lap. "I have you covered." He pulled out a six-pack of Killian's Red and a plastic bag with whole avocados, red onions, lemons, and other ingredients she knew would turn into the best fresh guacamole in Texas.

"I heard you could use a smile," he said.

"Oh, yeah?"

"As I was leaving work tonight, Otto stopped by. He said the Queen Mother made an appearance at the department. He also said if I wanted to eat tonight, I'd better bring my own food."

Josie shook her head, not sure if she should be angry with Otto or touched that he had intervened in her behalf.

"Don't be mad at him. I asked the questions. He just told the truth."

"That would be Otto."

"How long is your mom staying?"

She shrugged. "I talked with her all of two minutes."

He stood, extended his arms out to her, and pulled her up to stand in front of him. "Let's eat. Forget work. Tell me about your life the past six months. We'll talk about Red and the Queen later."

After he mixed up a batch of guacamole in the kitchen, Josie turned up the stereo to the best of Creedence Clearwater Revival and led Dillon to the back porch. She and her neighbor, Dell, had recently built a pergola out of local wood he had dried and cured in his barn. Four large posts supported eight-foot-long limbs that stretched across the frame to make a roof to shade the area from the harsh afternoon sun.

"This is nice," he said, looking at the handiwork. "Dell build this?"

She nodded and rubbed her fingers along one of the smooth wood posts. "He's proud of the roof. It's hard to find a straight eight-foot length of wood out here that's native." She flipped a switch located by the sliding door, and a fine mist sprayed from a line that ran the length of the porch. The air cooled by ten degrees almost instantly.

Dillon sat the guacamole and chips on the redwood picnic table. "You're moving up in the world."

They ate side by side, facing several hundred acres of Dell's ranch land that ran a gentle grade up into the Chimiso Mountains. Josie pointed out two red-tailed hawks, and Dillon smiled as one of them screeched, then swooped down to the ground, most likely for a field mouse. The muted browns and grays of the scrub that dominated West Texas spread across the land behind her home, but the mountains were streaked with red and copper that intensified with the setting sun, and the pasture had clumps of deep green pine and cedar trees fenced off from his cattle. It was the kind of land she had seen as a kid watching old John Wayne movies with her father, and the rough beauty still made her throat contract at unexpected times.

Through dinner, Dillon explained what he had learned about Red's finances. Red made about forty-four thousand dollars per year as a heavy equipment operator. His expenses, purchases, as well as living expenses, debt, travel, and savings, were more in line with a man earning around eighty-five thousand per year.

"There's no question that Red was selling guns, and that's where his extra income was coming from. I counted fourteen invoices for what looked to be a wide variety of guns. Most of the transactions, though, were just referenced by a customer number. You need the file that cross-references the numbers with the customers."

"None of the receipts had customer names?" she asked.

Dillon frowned. "I recognized two local names, but most of the invoices didn't contain a name. I found one that had the city San Miguel de Allende written at the bottom of the paper. And there were three with Juárez noted on the back. There were only two invoices that raised a big red flag, though. Together, they total $3,846. Both transactions were during the month of August. And both had what appeared to be the guns' serial number as well as another number that most likely identified the customer."

"Where's the red flag?"

Dillon stood and retrieved the box from the house. He put it on the picnic table and pulled out both receipts for Josie to examine.

Her eyes widened and she looked up from the paper. "This is written out to the Arroyo County Sheriff's Department! Since when do they spend four thousand dollars on two guns? We can barely afford to pay utilities right now."

Dillon sat back down at the table. "Isn't your pal, Deputy Bloster, a member of Red's gun club?"

Josie rubbed at her temples. "How could the sheriff let this happen? He signs off on all department expenses, just like I do, before they get approved by the council. He had to approve these invoices."

"Don't rush judgment. Go talk to the sheriff tomorrow. Just watch your back."

"What's that supposed to mean?" she asked.

He folded his hands and stared at her, apparently considering his words. "You have a solid reputation, and you're well respected for the job you do."

"But?"

"But you're still a female in a male-dominated profession."

"And?"

"And I know you're friends with Martínez, but there's still plenty of good old boy vibes running through this town. If things turn ugly, you aren't in the club."

She resisted the urge to defend Martínez. He was a fellow cop, a person she had admired and trusted, sought counsel from in her role as chief, and she didn't want to believe he would sacrifice her over a piece of scum like Bloster. But she nodded agreement and let the statement go until she could think through the information later in silence.

Josie stood and began cleaning up. "Based on everything you saw, and knowing Red's history, give me your theory on what happened to him," Josie said.

"I need to get into his files a little deeper before—"

She cut him off. "Gut instinct. What do you think happened?"

He steepled his fingers and rested them against his lips as he put together his thoughts. Watching him, Josie realized how important his reactions were to her.

"I think Red was brokering guns, most likely to Mexicans. But I doubt he realized just how evil the people he was dealing with are. I imagine it was that ignorance as much as greed that killed him."

After Josie logged off for the evening, Otto conducted interviews at the police department with three additional members of the Gunners. The goal was to get a better sense of the organization and its possible ties to either Medrano or La Bestia. His first interview, with Jimmy Johnson, took place in the upstairs office at the conference table where Otto had talked with Bloster and Fallow. Johnson worked at a body shop in town and still wore his blue mechanic's uniform. Otto noted the black stains around his fingernails and on the front of his work shirt.

Otto left his stack of file folders and notes with Fallow's and Bloster's names on them in open view so that Johnson would see them. Otto also laid a file folder on the table with Johnson's name written across the tab. He placed the folder so that it faced Johnson's chair. Otto had shoved it full of paper he pulled from the recycling box so that it would look as if he already had significant information collected.

As Otto hoped, Johnson spent the first part of the interview glancing at the file folder with his name on it. He was an average-sized man with a significant potbelly and large square glasses that magnified watery blue eyes. He appeared confused and repeatedly squeezed his hands together into fists.

Johnson gave the same generic information that Otto had already heard about the Gunners. Finally, Otto pulled the Johnson folder in front of him, opened it, and rifled through the papers. Johnson asked, "So, what are you so interested in me for?"

Otto closed the folder again and took his time responding. He gave Johnson a stern look. "A good friend of yours, an associate you trade and sell guns with, has been murdered. It's come to our attention that Red may have been trading and selling guns to Mexican drug cartels. We suspect you may be doing the same."

Johnson's eyes opened even wider and his jaw dropped. "Where the hell did you get that idea? I don't even know any Mexicans to sell guns to!"

Otto smirked. "You don't know any Mexicans?"

Johnson looked even more flustered. "Well, of course I know some. I mean, I don't know anyone who I would sell guns to. I mean, I could sell guns to people. I just don't know any cartel members to trade with. That's what I meant."

Johnson's responses didn't get any better. After another fifteen minutes, Otto cut him loose. He felt sorry for the man. He looked so worried standing at the door to leave that Otto tried to reassure him.

"Mr. Johnson, just go home tonight and think about our conversation. If you think of anything that might help us find Red's killer, you give me a call. Even if it seems insignificant, call me anyway."

Fred Grant arrived shortly after Johnson left. Grant owned a small cattle ranch north of town and drove a four-wheel-drive pickup with monster-sized wheels and no muffler. He strolled into the department wearing an untucked flannel shirt with the sleeves cut off, blue jeans, and dusty boots.

When Otto turned the questioning to Red's involvement with the cartels, Grant raised his voice in anger. "I don't know who's feeding you that nonsense, but they're flat-out lying. The Mexicans killed his dad! He formed the Gunners to protect our town. He would never turn on us like that."

"Mr. Grant, I have invoices that show Red was selling guns south of the border."

"So what? There's a big difference between south of the border and selling to the cartels. I'd lay my life on the fact that Red Goff never did business with the cartels."

"What do you know about Hack Bloster and Red selling guns together?"

He gave an exaggerated shrug. "And? Big deal! They sold guns."

"We suspect they were selling guns to the Medrano cartel," Otto said.

Grant looked away as if disgusted. "They sold guns to make money for the Gunners." He looked back at Otto, his eyes squinted, shaking his head in disbelief. "Have you forgotten that Red was murdered? Don't go trying to turn him into the bad guy because you can't figure out who killed him."

"Were you selling guns with them?"

"This is ridiculous. I'm through talking to you. You got anything else to ask, do it through my lawyer."

Otto got nothing out of Grant. He suspected Grant had more to tell, but he also didn't think involving an attorney at this point would garner any new information.

The last member of the Gunners he talked with was a truck driver named Jerry Irons. Otto had known Jerry for years, and he and Delores occasionally had dinner with Jerry and his wife, Sandy. Jerry was a level-headed man with right-wing political leanings that he kept to himself unless asked. He and his wife were transplants from Vermont who moved to the desert for the warmer climate.

After several minutes of small talk about the wives and weather, Otto asked Jerry to discuss his thoughts about Red's murder.

"It's scary, Otto. What's happening to our town? I know Red had enemies. He was arrogant, and a lot of people didn't like him, but murdered? Shot in the head?"

Otto nodded. He had his own fears about the safety of his family. "Jerry, can you give me anything? Any gossip, any worries you have about various members? Bad relationships Red had with someone that might have led to his death?"

Jerry scooted his chair back, crossed one leg over the other, and rubbed at a smudge on his boot as he considered the question. "That's tough. It just doesn't look like something local. I guess that sounds naïve, but it just doesn't play out like a hate killing. Why kill him and then drag his body back inside that girl's trailer? You asked about the Gunners. I don't see anyone in the group killing him in that manner. Just doesn't work for me."

Otto finally signed off duty with the night dispatcher, feeling exhausted and frustrated. So far, it appeared the only Gunners with a connection to cartel members were Fallow, Bloster, and Red. Now one of them was dead, and the other two weren't talking. He called Delores on his cell phone to tell her what time he would be home. Fifteen minutes later, he pulled down his lane. The Podowski ranch lay about ten miles north of the river, and consisted of sixty-five acres of pasture that held a small herd of milk goats. A split-rail fence surrounded a small three-bedroom bungalow covered in white aluminum siding with a deep brick porch on the front of the house. Mangy thirty-year-old bushes lined the front of the house with little else in the way of plantings. Otto drew great satisfaction feeding and watering the goats, clearing the fence rows of brush, battling the invading prickly pear, yucca and cholla, and tinkering on a tractor that spent more hours torn down than up and running. Otherwise, landscaping didn't interest him, and Delores claimed a black thumb, but the woman could cook like no other.

Each night as he drove home from work, Otto anticipated the smells from his kitchen: sausage, apples, onions, garlic, kraut, meatballs—an endless tribute to Polish tradition. As she did most nights, Delores met him at the door, an apron over her calico-print housedress, her silver hair pulled up into a neat bun behind her head. She smiled, her blue eyes surrounded by wrinkles, and pushed the screen door open for him. After a quick peck on her lips, Otto walked through the living room and into the kitchen, dragging his briefcase. Delores followed on his heels.

"What's for supper?" he asked.

"I could feel it in my bones. I knew it was a bad one. Apple dumplings with fresh whipping cream. Sit down at the table." Delores took his briefcase from him and scooted a chair out at the kitchen table. He felt like a boy, a feeling she had nurtured in him since their first date forty years ago. He was perfectly happy letting Delores take over.

"Sit down, sit down," she said, ushering him to the chair before pouring him a glass of milk.

The smell of cinnamon and cream and butter made him dizzy. He sat at the table and watched her hovering over the stove, his perfectly capable wife, her body soft and inviting. All his life, he had seen other men chasing skinny women in high heels with hard stomachs and hard breasts, and the idea made him shudder. How could anything compare to the vision of Delores on her way to the table with a platter of steaming apple dumplings?

"So, tell me," she said.

"Not so much to tell as there should be. The man shot at the Trauma Center was killed by rival gang members from Mexico. How do we tackle that? And Josie thinks Red was killed trading guns to the Mexicans. How do we tackle that one, too?"

Delores set the platter of dumplings on the table and stood for a moment, hands on her hips. "You said, 'Josie thinks.' Does that mean you don't?"

"What's the gossip on the street about Red Goff and the Gunners?" he asked.

"The girls think the Gunners club is a drug cartel, no different from the Mexican versions," she said.

Otto smiled at her reference to the girls. It was a group of eleven old women who gathered once a week and called themselves the Homemakers. Delores was one of the younger ones at fifty-seven. They rotated homes for meetings, brought food to sample, created a craft project each week, and quilted baby blankets for foster babies. They were a nice group of ladies, but girls they were not.

"For a bunch of old women, you're on target more than you aren't."

She smiled, pleased. "Helen claims her husband buys guns off Red all the time. Claims his prices are better than Walmart."

"You said drug cartel. What do drugs have to do with it?" he asked.

Delores wove an intricate tale of he said/she said and so-and-so is related to so-and-so, who was arrested for some odd thing. When she talked gossip like this, his attention faded. He nodded and forked another dumpling into his mouth, his teeth sinking into the sweet dough, his tongue distinguishing the subtle differences among the cinnamon, nutmeg, and cloves in the rich sauce. He washed his bite down and said, "In the middle of all this mess, Josie's mother showed up today from Indiana."

Delores sat across from Otto with her own plate and glass of milk. "What did she look like?"

Otto's eyebrows knitted together. "I don't know. Like a floozy. Josie had a date with Dillon Reese tonight, and her mother showed up out of the blue, demanding attention."

"Maybe you should invite Josie and her mother over for dinner this week. Help her out a little."

Otto ignored the idea. As much as he liked Josie, he'd heard enough about Beverly Gray from her to know that he did not want to spend an evening entertaining the woman. He wiped his mouth with a napkin and asked, "No meat tonight?"

"Just dumplings. If we don't start watching our weight, you'll end up with both knees on the operating table."

At midnight, Josie walked Dillon to his car. The air was soft on her skin, and a billion stars and a fat white moon lit up the night. Dillon leaned against his car door instead of getting inside and put his arms out to her. He pulled her toward him, rested his hands on her hips, and offered a half grin that she couldn't read.

"Nothing's changed, Josie, but I can't stay away any longer."

She felt the familiarity of a fight coming on. "I've tried to explain . . ."

He put a finger up to her lips and shook his head. "That's not what I'm saying. I'm not passing judgment. I just miss you. I need to be around you. You make me smile, and I want to make you smile. You have this gigantic heart that's locked up inside you that I want to open up."

She took a step back. "Don't speak in metaphors! What does

that mean—I have a heart locked up? If I need to change, then give it to me in black and white."

He laughed at her anger and pulled her back in again, kissed her to shut her up, then kissed her again, soft and long, his hands down her back pulling goose bumps up her arms. He finally kissed her forehead and cradled her face in his hands. She had a perfect heart, he told her, that needed sleep. Then, he drove off down the dusty road toward town.

EIGHT

After a shower in an open-air bath off the main dressing area, the
Bishop sat for morning breakfast on the veranda. He watched as
two light-skinned teenage girls laid out his clothes for the day in
his room: white linen slacks and a light linen-blend white shirt,
huarache sandals and a Cuban Exo cigar. He had stopped smoking
ten years ago but found he missed the roll of the cigar between his
fingers and the taste of the tobacco on his lips more than the act of
smoking. So he had switched to carrying a fresh cigar with him
throughout the day.

He watched the girls through the glass wall that separated his
bedroom from the veranda, looking with pride as they snapped a
fresh white sheet and tucked it under the mattress. They laughed
and slipped quietly out, so unself-conscious, they never realized he
had been watching.

He had overseen every detail of the construction of his estate, and
he was proud of the outcome. The house was built five years ago to
represent his family's wealth and status, and it had achieved that goal.

Reminiscent of an M. C. Escher print, the three-story white stucco home held mysterious passageways, arches, and twisting stairs. Hand-carved teak lintels and moldings had been waxed to an ancient sheen, giving the home a substantial old-world feel that he prized. Outside the home, terraced desert landscaping wrapped all sides of the house and created quiet retreats.

The Bishop reclined slightly in his chair and breathed deeply, forcing a calm exterior that he did not feel. The damp morning air was infused with what he thought of as the smells of earth: mesquite, creosote bush, and juniper. In the midst of family or business crisis—and in fact, they were often both—he retreated outdoors. The smells, the solitude, the heat and space gave him the calm he required to make the life-and-death decisions demanded of him daily. He looked across the sprawling desert and took deep breaths to control the rage that once again was threatening to overcome him. He imagined his father's dead body, shot up beyond recognition by a man whom he had once loved as family. He wanted to destroy his cousin and every member of La Bestia: personally shove the knife through each beating heart. But he could not afford to react out of emotion or grief. Revenge was justified and expected, but revenge unplanned was inexcusable.

The Bishop's influences in life were twofold. A mother whose entire being centered on perfection: her children were fastidiously clean, neurotically prepared for life's little problems, and taught the manners of the upper class. And a father whose devotion to family and obsessive need to control had led to a dynasty feared and respected throughout Mexico. Hector Medrano gave his oldest son the nickname "the Bishop" on his twenty-fourth birthday. As the Bishop, Marco ruled the family business, organizing the leaders of the narcotics, firearms, and money-laundering divisions to carry out the missions that his own father had given him: Control the drug routes through the northern states of Mexico. A simple idea but an incredibly complex task.

The media perpetuated the myth of the Bishop as a ruthless killer with no respect for life, a fact those close to him understood was untrue, pure myth. The killings were just a necessary part of his business, no different from a priest assigning penance, a boss firing dead weight, or the *presidente* firebombing a cocaine factory: all necessary parts of the bigger picture to be undertaken with integrity and fortitude.

The Bishop smiled at the young woman who had appeared to place a carafe of fresh coffee on the table. She wore her hair in long, oiled cornrows that hung behind her back, and had a perfect chocolate-colored complexion. She stole a look at him, smiled in return, and then left, her head lowered in deference.

The Bishop watched her walk away and thought of the arrogant policewoman who had interrogated his cousin through marriage, Miguel Ángel Gutiérrez, in the American jail. After the interview with the police chief, Gutiérrez talked with an attorney provided by La Bestia. The Bishop paid a large sum of money to the rival attorney to receive the confidential details of the meeting. The attorney claimed the woman called Gutiérrez a pedophile, said he would rot in her filthy jail with the perverts and degenerates until he gave up information about the business. She had taken on a cause bigger than her abilities.

The Medranos had been collecting information on the Artemis law enforcement agencies for years as they planned and set up transportation across the border. Chief Gray had been a target of concern. He opened the manila file folder that sat on the table beside the carafe. He picked up a black-and-white photo of an attractive female dressed in a police uniform. She was in her early thirties with long hair pulled back in a tight ponytail. She was looking off in the distance, her expression proud and brooding, gauging the world through a personal lens of justice; right and wrong were hers to decide, and for that he both despised and admired her.

A second photo showed her leaning into a man bent over a car hood with his hands in cuffs behind his back. She grasped his T-shirt in a bunch with one hand, her other hand planted on the hood, and talked to him with her lips close to his ear as a larger male officer stood behind her, looking away from the scene.

The last photo was a head shot, telephoto from straight on, as she looked just to the right of the shot. She was the rare woman who wore her sexuality unself-consciously. She was stunning. Her complexion was like cream, her cheeks pronounced, almost gaunt, adding to the severity of her expression.

The Americans would use threats and intimidation, torture if necessary, to gain information about the business. He would not allow his own traitorous blood to jeopardize his family. The Bishop looked over the knee-high stone wall that surrounded the veranda, across the lap pool, and into the great Chihuahua Desert. He vowed to do whatever was necessary to bring his cousin home within the week. He would see justice served by himself, not by the Americans. Not by this woman. It was no longer business. It had become personal. *I will enjoy every detail of her death,* he thought.

Josie stopped at the bakery on the way to work that morning and bought a dozen chocolate iced doughnuts and a half gallon of milk for her and Lou and Otto. She smiled at Lou and placed three doughnuts on a napkin beside her computer. Lou thanked her, and Josie smiled all the way up the stairs to the office. She had just heard the weatherman on Lou's radio announce that the month-long heat wave was about to give way to eighty-five-degree temperatures for a few days. The rain had not materialized, but at least the heat had broken. Josie looked at her watch as she logged on to her computer. She had four hours to enjoy a good day before her mother ruined it.

Her first order of business was to study a packet of photos of missing persons mailed to her every two weeks from a Mexican human rights group supported by the U.S. Consulate in Mexico. Over the past six months, an average of thirty-three kidnappings each month took place along the border, most of them along the migrant routes. A host of cottage industry kidnapping schemes had spread throughout Mexico and into the United States, most recently into Phoenix. Thousands of virtual kidnappings were made every day; an unsuspecting parent receives a phone call demanding money be wired to an account before their family member, heard screaming in the background, is killed. The parent is too terrified to check into the claim and pays the ransom before realizing their family member is fine. The cell phone call, made from Mexico, is not traceable and goes undetected.

Another racket, express kidnappings, were popular in bigger cities. A person hails a taxi, the driver picks them up, drives a block, picks up two additional men who force the passenger to withdraw money from ATM machines all over town. The person is typically then robbed and left on the street with nothing.

But in Josie's mind, parents were the easiest target of all. She and Sheriff Martínez had led a series of town meetings on Situational Awareness to make parents more aware of their surroundings and dangers their children could be in. Josie was always surprised by how unaware most parents were of their environment, especially in terms of their kids' safety. She was certain it would be an unhealthy obsession with her when she became a parent. Although she wouldn't let herself give up on the idea of having kids, there were days when the dangers of raising a child seemed to outweigh the joys.

Josie looked through the stack of black-and-white photos of dozens of Mexican and American children, most smiling into the camera from family and school pictures, unaware of the horror they were about to endure.

She set the pictures aside after one photograph started to blend into another. She read through Marta's report from the previous night. Marta had interviewed three local drug informants about the continuing violence between La Bestia and the Medrano cartel. The general consensus was that La Bestia had moved into Piedra Labrada, where the Medranos already operated, in order to focus on a transportation route directly through Artemis.

Josie glanced up from the report and saw that Otto had silently settled in. He was sitting at his computer reading e-mail and eating a doughnut. She interrupted him and filled him in on the details from Marta's conversations.

"The international border crossing between Presidio and Ojinaga is the least used in all of Texas. And Artemis is another thirty minutes beyond the crossing. We've got desert all around us. No big cities to blend into. This area doesn't even make sense as a route," she said.

Otto shrugged. "Maybe that's the draw. No one expects it. Maybe the Beast thought the same thing. They could ease in on this little podunk town, and Medrano wouldn't notice. Didn't turn out so good, though."

She nodded. "I could see it if Medrano wasn't already a presence. But why go to battle with one of the largest crime syndicates in Mexico? There are plenty other border towns to blend into."

"I don't think these guys are into blending in. Maybe they want it known they're making a serious run on Medrano. They see Piedra Labrada and Artemis as the place to do it. We're controllable in their eyes."

Josie stood and paced the office. "We need to camp out on the watchtower for a few nights. Watch traffic just outside the city."

Otto nodded, sitting up in his seat.

"Until we figure out who is coming into Artemis, we can't know their motivation. We have to figure it out to get the connection to Red."

"I agree."

"And we have to know what they want with Artemis. We cannot allow them to win, not one round," Josie said.

"We'll get interdiction clued in to Interstate 10. That's got to be where they head once they get across the border. They're taking farm roads across the desert and up to the interstate. I'll make contact with each of the surrounding counties and let them know to involve us on any gun or narcotic stops that may involve Medrano or La Bestia."

Josie and Otto spent the next hour on the phone with the Marfa Sector Border Patrol and the Department of Public Safety Narcotics Division and Interdiction discussing their suspicions. The interdiction team was trained to look for specific signs that often signaled illegal activity: illegal crossings, drug trafficking, and so forth. BP said they would take the watchtower that night, and Josie agreed to man it the next night, on Saturday. Interdiction said they would have an undercover car watching Interstate 10, the closest interstate to Artemis. After setting up the logistics, Josie called Sheriff Martínez and asked to meet him before lunch. She sent Otto to Red's house to gather every last piece of paper, label where it came from in the house, and put it in a box for Dillon, who had agreed to sift through it all.

Josie heard the good-natured banter between the sheriff and Lou from downstairs and then the heavy booted footsteps of a large man clumping up the wooden stairs to the office.

Martínez rapped on the open door with his knuckles and entered. Josie was already carrying them both mugs of black coffee from the coffeemaker. She placed the cups on the conference table, and they small-talked the weather and the Astros, a favorite conversation topic of the sheriff's, before getting down to business.

"Have you talked to Deputy Bloster about Red Goff's death?" Josie asked.

"I have. He came in the evening after he found out about it. He'd just left Red's house after running into you and Otto."

"What was his response?" she asked.

"He was angry. Thought our office should have taken the call even though he knew we didn't have anyone available to take it. He thought you should have handed it over. I told him it was a conflict of interest, and he finally let it go. I told him to cool his jets and stay away from the investigation. I take it that hasn't happened."

She slid the Gunners' policy manual toward him. "Take a look at the section titled 'Friends and Foes.' We're on the Foes list. Bloster is a member of an organization that lists his own boss as the enemy. I haven't figured out exactly what that means yet."

Martínez barely glanced at the manual. "Bloster told me about it. Said it was nothing more than a list of people who might feel hostile toward their organization."

"That doesn't bother you? Your name on the short list?"

Martínez snorted. "We got our names on shorter lists than that one."

All right, she thought, *that's the way we're going to play this.*

"Otto interviewed Bloster yesterday, in this office, and he punched Fallow in the mouth during the interview. Otto encouraged Fallow to file charges, but he wouldn't. He's lucky Fallow is terrified of him." She paused and Martínez remained silent. "You have a time bomb on your staff."

Martínez's expression grew still. "I don't guess my employees are any of your concern."

"Let me throw one more at you." Josie handed him the two invoices that Dillon had showed her the night before. She watched Martínez study the paper, but he said nothing.

"Did you sign for those guns?" Josie asked.

"What is this? You accusing me of running a crooked department?"

"I'm just trying to figure out how you can afford guns when I can't afford soap for the bathrooms."

He didn't smile at her attempt at humor. Josie watched as he studied the invoice and the price of the guns. Finally he looked up at her, his shoulders slumped. "Bloster's been taking care of bills for the department. I don't have time to get it all done. You know how undermanned we are. I figured with his short fuse, I'd get him off the road some and put him in charge of accounts."

"How long has he been taking care of finances?"

Martínez frowned. "Since December, when Stephanie left. I can't hardly operate without a secretary. Moss wouldn't let us hire a replacement and suggested I get Bloster to help out. He just helped with some of the bills. Helped me keep things organized." He looked at Josie, his face aged ten years. "I knew nothing about these guns." He pushed his chair away from the table and stood. "You know what's even worse? You found out about these guns by accident. What else has he passed through for payment?"

Josie knew what lay behind his question. If this were more than a onetime occurrence, then Martínez's job was in serious jeopardy. Bottom line, whether Bloster was the one who'd passed off bad bills or not, it was still the sheriff's signature that went to the commissioners.

At noon, Josie walked next door to visit Mayor Moss. It was a sunny, blue-sky day with not a cloud overhead. The temperature was in the eighties, no humidity, a slight breeze—the kind of day that made her want to take off in the mountains with Chester and enjoy the outdoors. Instead, her back muscles were in knots up and down her spine as she walked down the hall to Moss's office. His door was closed, but the secretary rang in to him and Josie was allowed five minutes. It was all she needed.

"I need to know when we're getting reinforcements for the jail," she said once she was standing in front of his mammoth mahogany desk. He didn't gesture for her to sit. "The sheriff and I have other priorities. We can't take men off the road to guard it. I was serious about the jail coming under attack. We have two Mexican drug cartels with a personal interest in one of our prisoners. They'll storm it just like they did the Trauma Center."

Moss's chin jutted out. His small eyes were dark and focused. He folded his hands on the desk in front of him and stared at Josie as if trying to figure out how to explain something complicated to her. "I'm working with the governor to arrange for help from the National Guard. It takes time. You don't snap your fingers and get help. You think we're the only city with troubles?"

"What kind of time frame did they give you?" Josie asked.

"They don't give time frames, Chief Gray. When I know something, I'll call you." He turned back to his computer. "Now, if you don't mind, I'm preparing for a meeting."

"And your committee? What kind of progress has your committee made in shutting down these cartels? Do you have a time frame for your committee work?"

Moss leaned back in his desk chair and gripped the leather armrests with both hands. "I would like to think that you have more productive things to occupy your time with than harassing me. This conversation is over."

Josie walked out of his office furious not just with him but also with herself. She had sounded childish and unprofessional. She had to get a grip on her hatred toward him before it began to cloud her ability to run her office effectively. In the meantime, the safety of the officers at the jail was still a major worry.

Josie did not go back to her office. With the nauseating thought of her mother lurking around the department for lunch, she opted to ratchet up the morning with a little Hack Bloster. She called the sheriff's office and talked to the dispatcher, who said Bloster didn't come on duty until noon, but gave her his home address.

Josie drove south toward the bend in the Rio where the rock walls grew steeper with each mile. She turned onto a switchback road that zigzagged down a thirty-foot canyon. There was barely enough land to build into the rock. The three houses on the switchback looked like fishing shacks, although their inhabitants were permanent residents.

Hack Bloster's house was a thirty-foot-by-ten-foot wooden structure built into the face of the rock. To the left of the shack was a gravel area big enough for two cars to park. To the right of the house was a similarly sized garage. A twenty-foot swatch of rocky land covered with clumps of cactus and granite boulders separated the house from the road. On the road's opposite side, a twenty-foot drop led to the river below. Josie parked beside Bloster's police car and caught him by surprise when she walked into his open garage. Ted Nugent, blasting from a boom box at his feet, had kept him from hearing her car approach. A window fan on the floor blew air toward him.

He sat on a five-gallon bucket with no shirt on, wearing dusty jeans and cowboy boots. He cradled a red and black rooster in his lap with one leather gloved hand, and held a small instrument in his other hand that appeared to be sharpening the long black talons of the rooster. When he saw Josie, he stood and placed the rooster in a metal cage on a workbench behind him, then turned off the music.

"I hear those fighters run about twenty-five hundred dollars. That true?" Josie asked.

"I wouldn't know," Bloster said. He pulled a bandanna from his back pocket and wiped the sweat off his face.

"I've heard for years there were cockfights out here on Saturday nights, but I've never been able to pin one down. There's supposedly a caliche pit back in here that gets used for cockfights and dog races. You ever hear any rumors like that?" Josie asked.

"Not a one."

"Word is, it's by the windmill and water tanks." Josie gestured behind her where the top of a windmill could be seen over the trees. "Want to take a drive back there and check it out? I'm guessing you have some insider knowledge." She pointed to three metal cages along the far wall of his garage, each containing a rooster, all sitting idle in the heat of the day.

"You got a warrant to search the land, then go for it. I got no say in the matter. There's no law against having roosters, so you can take your suspicions elsewhere. You got something else to say to me?"

Josie noted the pocket holster in his front jeans' pocket and the butt of the pistol in plain view.

"You getting him ready for the fights this weekend?" she asked.

"What do you want with me?" he asked.

"Actually, I came to ask you a few questions about some expenditures you made for the sheriff's department."

He said nothing, but he picked up a beer bottle from the floor and took a long drink. He was deeply tanned, with a smooth chest ripped with muscle. Bloster was good looking in an intensely physical, imposing way; he had a dangerous quality that was both appealing and disturbing.

Josie leaned against the doorframe of his garage and took her time continuing. "In looking at Red's finances, I found some receipts for guns purchased by your department. In fact, two guns totaled almost four thousand dollars. Must be some kind of special guns."

"Seeing how you work for the city police, and that equipment is for the sheriff's department, I don't think it's any of your concern."

"Well, Hack, seeing how I'm a taxpayer and those receipts are open for public record, I think they are my concern. I think your little club is selling guns to your department. You're making a profit all over the place, aren't you?" she asked.

"You're out of your jurisdiction. You got no business out here."

"No? I thought I was doing you a professional courtesy. We can talk at the department. We can even ask the sheriff to join us if that makes you feel better."

Bloster took two steps toward her and shoved her chest. She fell back against the garage wall, and he drew his fist back as if to throw a punch. She pushed herself off the wall and bent forward, propelling her knee up into his stomach. He stumbled back from her and let his hand slide down to his front pocket toward the gun.

Josie pulled her gun and pointed it toward Bloster's chest in one swift motion.

His face registered shock. He raised both hands in the air and took a step back, bumping into the workbench.

"What the hell's wrong with you?" he asked.

"You're climbing higher on my list of suspects every day."

"Don't come on my property spouting shit you can't back up, lady." He pointed a finger directly at the barrel of the gun.

She felt the heat in her face and struggled to keep her voice level. "Then don't play games with me. You're a dirty cop, and I will expose you before this is over."

Bloster brought his hands back down to his sides. Josie kept her gun out but pointed now at the ground.

"I had nothing to do with Red's death. What purpose would it have? We were members of the same group."

"He was president of a group that you had no chance of leading while he was alive. Looks to me like there's a hell of a lot of money to be made off selling those guns. More than you're making as a deputy," Josie said.

"This is bullshit. Until you have something hard to charge me with, we're through." He turned and walked toward his house, slamming the door behind as Josie stood, breathless.

By the time Josie reached the department, she had calmed down and corralled her anger. As she passed through the lone traffic light and turned left at the courthouse, she called Lou on her cell phone and asked if anyone was waiting for her. Lou said no, her mother hadn't arrived yet. Josie spotted her mother's Buick sitting in front of Manny's Motel, and she pulled her jeep in beside it.

The motel was built like a strip mall with all six rooms opening onto the street. The office sat in the middle of the rooms, its neon light advertising ROOMS FOR RENT. At forty-something, Manny had given up a successful Holiday Inn franchise in Arizona to start his own business in Artemis. Since opening the motel twenty years ago, he had put on fifty pounds, let his hair grow into a flyaway halo about his head, shaved once a week, and claimed to smile more often than he had during all his so-called successful years in Phoenix with a bitter, anorexic wife who had spent more than he could ever make.

"Chief Gray!" Manny stood up from the recliner behind the counter and laid his book on the seat.

The office was the size of a small bedroom and painted a nicotine-stained white. There was a four-foot-long counter with a grocery store cash register on top, and a metal lockbox with the word *Keys* written in marker across the lid. Behind the counter sat a tattered leather recliner and table with a reading lamp that altogether looked like a set for an old seventies sitcom.

"Manny, those things are going to kill you." Josie gestured toward the burning cigarette under a small air purifier that sat on the table next to his chair.

Manny smiled warmly. "Chief, I am a lucky man. I have two passions in life: reading and smoking. I have the good fortune to attend to both of my passions all day long, without measure. How many men do you know that are that lucky? I will continue to enjoy my life with abandon as long as the good Lord allows."

Josie smiled. "You're doing all right, then?"

"Couldn't be better. Steady customers and fifty percent capacity for months. Gets food on the table and the electric bill paid."

"You hire a maid yet?"

He smiled and rubbed his belly. "No maid. I compromised with the doctor. I took up scrubbing toilets and changing bedsheets for exercise. I refused to go to the wretched gym, so Doc refused to see me. Said I was killing myself in my chair. He doesn't give a whit about a man's passions. So, I said fine, I'll clean the rooms every day whether they need it or not. Two hours' hard exertion. He bought it, and I got to keep my doctor."

Josie nodded. "You are definitely a lucky man."

"Now, what can I do for you? I'm sure you didn't come to rent one of my extra-clean rooms."

"Actually, I came by to see what room Beverly Gray is staying in."

Manny's smile widened. "She's a character, that mother of yours! You should bring her around more often. Life of the party, she is!" He laughed openly and pointed at the front first door to his left. "Room number one."

Josie knocked and entered after hearing her mother yell to come in. She sat on the unmade bed for ten minutes and watched her mother in front of the bathroom mirror, teasing her hair and applying makeup, a scene she had witnessed countless times growing up. It was an odd feeling, the familiarity of family combined with the uneasiness of time and distance.

Her mother chattered about neighborhood friends and classmates as if Josie had left only months before. She seemed to have forgotten any sense of bitterness over Josie's departure nine years ago. Her mother had always had an amazing ability to unconditionally love, hate, and forgive—all in the space of minutes; the problem was that she expected others to behave the same way, regardless of her own behavior.

After her mother finished primping and stopped by Manny's office to wish him a good morning, they walked half a block to the Hot Tamale for lunch. The Tamale was a popular lunch-hour diner. Small square tables and chairs were scattered everywhere and were rearranged to fit variously sized groups, depending on if they wanted a quiet corner or a hot spot in the middle to socialize. Josie chose a small table at the front window, positioning her chair with her back against the wall.

After a half hour lunch of chicken salad and chips, and more small talk dominated by her mother, Josie asked what her immediate plans were.

"I'm thinking about moving here. Thought I'd come scout it out first."

Josie was stunned. "Why?"

"All my family's gone in Indiana. Claudia got married and moved to Maine. Uncle Larry's dead."

"Are you sick?"

Her mother laughed—too loudly, Josie thought.

"No, I'm not sick. Don't you get lonely for family, living out here in the middle of nowhere?"

Josie shrugged. She didn't give it much thought. She had learned long ago that life was easier if she just let things go. She spent the holidays working overtime, read voraciously, and hiked when the walls started closing in. Dell and Otto were as close to family as she needed.

Her mother pushed her fork through a patch of uneaten chicken salad, and Josie wondered if she was seeing real emotion or yet another con. Had she been evicted, lost a job, lost her latest man?

"You got a spare bedroom I could stay in for a couple weeks? Just somewhere while I scout out the territory? I'll chip in on food."

It was Josie's turn to drag her fork around her plate. It would never work; there was no doubt in her mind. Josie had moved two thousand miles from her mother for good reason; to suddenly share a house, a bathroom in the morning, a kitchen to wash dishes. The thought of it made her sweat.

"I have only one bedroom. The house is really small." She looked up from her plate. "You better give this some thought first anyway. The only family you have in Texas is me, and it's not like we communicate very well. The heat is unbearable and you'll miss the snow and the trees. Jobs are hard to come by, too."

Her mom flipped her hand out, as if dismissing Josie's concerns. The conversation turned to banter: Josie detailing why it would not work, her mother responding why it would. Behind each of Josie's responses lay the real reason that clenched at her chest, but that she refused to speak. Her mother had not been there for her as a child. She had no rights to Josie's time, attention, or money as an adult. Josie had figured out adulthood on her own, and it was time her mother did the same.

At nine o'clock that evening, Josie threw her overnight bag over her shoulders, attached her bedroll and foam mat to straps behind her back, and began the fifty-foot climb up the watchtower. At the top, bugs scurried as she shone her flashlight around the interior room before placing her bags on the map table while she lit the two lanterns. She unfolded an army cot that had been left by some other visitor and laid her mat and sleeping bag out for the night.

She took one of the folding camp chairs and her department-issued binoculars outside on the observation deck and breathed deep. The desert had a different smell from that height. The sand and grit that permeated everything below was nonexistent, and the air was clean and dry. The silence was broken by a soft wind that curled around the deck, pushing through the rafters below to create a low whistling like a far-off train. Josie fixed her gaze on the Texas side for several minutes, away from the drama to the south, and raised her arms, allowing the breeze to lift her T-shirt off her skin. Goose bumps, a rarity in July, covered her stomach and arms. She smiled and wished Dillon were standing beside her.

She opened a package of cheese crackers and popped the top on a V8, her concession to good health. She propped her forearms on the wood railing and spilt open a cheese cracker, eating first the plain cracker, saving the best for last, then washing it all down with the vegetable juice. Marta fussed at her continually for her diet of junk food that was balanced, at least in Josie's own mind, by healthy cans and jars of vegetables and fruits. Fresh was out of the question. It spoiled in her refrigerator and wasted money. Marta gave her fruit baskets for Christmas and made vegetable casseroles for her birthday, all appreciated but largely uneaten. Of the countless ways she had seen and read about people dying, she figured a lack of fresh produce was the least of her worries.

On the back side of the observation deck, Piedra Labrada was heating up. Cars were streaming by strip clubs and bars that were lit up with neon signs flashing NO COVER CHARGE in both Spanish and English. Streetlights were visible only on the downtown streets in the newer area of town. The small industrial edge of the city was now quiet and dark, as was the old section of town, with the businesses that centered around the Central Plaza now dark and locked up for the night. Josie stood at the railing and looked through binoculars at the activity across the river and wondered at the human race, at its propensity to gather and rule, to divide and conquer. The smallness of people always struck her from atop the watchtower. Race, religion, sex, nationality: they all boiled down to the need to control, for the need to prove one man superior to another.

Josie spent several hours ruminating as she watched the traffic down below. It wasn't until one in the morning that something happened to draw her attention away from the city. Three cars trailed by a pickup truck had left Piedra Labrada and drove parallel to the Rio for about a mile west of the city. At that point, the road veered south, away from the river, but Josie watched the caravan turn right and drive through a half mile of scrub and rock to reach the river. From her distance, she couldn't identify people or even the size or make of the cars, other than the truck.

Josie thought it might be high school kids partying at first, and then suspected coyotes transporting smugglers across the river, but the scheme was more involved than that. She watched the lights of the pickup turn and face toward land as the truck backed up to the edge of the water. It was a bright night with a sky full of stars and a full moon just beginning to wane, but even through her binoculars, she was too far from the action to tell exactly what they were doing. Then a dim light appeared to travel slowly across the river, and another set of car lights appeared on a vehicle that she hadn't realized was waiting on the U.S. side of the river. She called the details in to Border Patrol but knew they couldn't get there fast enough. She had already been told they were undermanned that night.

It took about thirty minutes for the entire operation to take place. It looked to Josie as if the pickup truck unloaded its cargo, either people or contraband, onto a small boat that quickly moved across the water, unloaded, and came back again to be loaded onto the back of the truck, which quickly left the area. She watched the car on the U.S. side travel along River Road and then turn right on Scratchgravel Road, where another pair of headlights came on and followed the car north toward town. It was a smooth transaction, which Josie was certain had happened before and would likely happen again.

NINE

At noon on Friday, Pegasus stood, draining a can of off-brand tuna fish that smelled like metal into her kitchen sink. Tuna and split pea with ham soup were the only cans left in the cupboard. She planned to slip a couple cans of stew and a better-tasting soup into her purse that night at work. Shoplifting went against her moral code, such as it was, but she had to eat.

She scraped the tuna into a bowl and squeezed a fast-food package of mayonnaise on top of it. She heard cars coming up the gravel drive and stepped quickly to the window in the kitchen door to watch three black cars buzz by her trailer on their way to Red's. Through the haze of dust they left in their wake, she watched them park in front of Red's house. One man in a suit, white shirt, and tie got out and appeared to bang on Red's door, even though it was still crisscrossed with yellow police tape. Several similarly dressed men stood and faced her trailer, where she watched from her living room's back window.

She opened the coffee table drawer and pulled out the Smith &

Wesson and the fully loaded magazine lying beside it. Keeping her eyes on the men, she slid the magazine in the gun and forced a bullet into the chamber. She practiced extending her arms, raising the gun, and slipping her finger down onto the trigger, aiming at the door, where she had hung a red piece of paper at exactly five feet from the ground, the approximate height a man's chest would be if he came through her front door. She had listened to the cop and had begun locking her door at all hours, although a swift kick would gain a man entrance.

Within a few minutes, the man banging on Red's sliding glass door quit and the convoy left without stopping at her trailer. Pegasus wondered where her brother was. She had not seen him since her last gun lesson and wasn't sure if he was even still in town. Maybe this was what he was preparing her for.

Josie fed and watered Chester and let him outside to run while she caught a few hours of sleep in her own bed. She logged on for duty at noon to work a second shift with Otto. They drove a half mile past the watchtower and parked. Under a steamy noonday sun, they walked a path covered in scrub grass and salt cedar, scouting out vehicle access to the river. About a quarter mile from Josie's jeep, they spotted fresh tire tracks coming straight out of the river, near where Josie had seen the boat.

Thirty minutes later, Jimmy Dare, a twenty-year veteran with the Marfa Border Patrol, responded to Josie's call. Josie and Otto met him by the edge of the road, where he parked his white and green SUV.

"How the hell are you, darling?" Jimmy smiled wide and came at Josie with an arm thrown out for a handshake. He was a fit, five feet ten inches with a military haircut and precise movements. He wore the customary olive green cargo pants and shirt with a yellow name patch declaring him as part of Border Patrol. A .40-caliber pistol hung from a clip at his side, and he looked like a man who could use it if the situation demanded it. Josie had once watched him commandeer a van full of eight illegal aliens attempting entry, three of whom were armed. She had used him as a reliable source on border issues since she had taken the job as chief.

After they caught up on old acquaintances, Jimmy grew serious. "What are you guys doing down here to fire up the Mexicans so bad? Word is, the Bishop wants your head on a shiny platter, Chief Gray."

Josie gave Otto a grim look. She had expected that information, but hearing it spoken from another law enforcement agent was sobering.

"You do not want to make light of this. That man is scary mean, and when he levels a threat, it's usually carried out."

"Actually, the Bishop's why I called you. I have a hunch Medrano has targeted Artemis for easy access. Marfa Sector patrols what, five hundred miles of riverfront on the Rio?"

"You got it," Jimmy said.

"Your focus has never been this area. It's remote. No big cities to get lost in. Correct?"

Jimmy nodded.

"I was on the watchtower last night, looking for action, and saw four cars drive right down to the river, Mexican side." She pointed behind her to the crossing and the tire tracks in the dirt. "They launched a boat, moved the cargo, and returned the boat all within thirty minutes."

He shook his head. "We could have ten times the number of agents we have now, and they'd still find a way. What were they transporting?"

"I don't know. That's why I called you. We need help. I've got three officers, including myself. Sheriff's department is no better. We've got Gutiérrez in the county jail, on top of the La Bestia member that I fatally shot. I'm very concerned either Medrano or La Bestia are going to rip us up one night soon."

"You know who the American link is?" Jimmy asked.

"We had a local gun fanatic murdered a few nights ago. Several hundred guns were stolen from his house as well. Red Goff?"

Jimmy nodded acknowledgment. "I know him."

"I think Red was running guns with the Mexicans. Probably Medrano. I don't know if drugs were involved. I haven't made that connection. This is strictly between us, but I suspect a local sheriff's deputy may have stolen Red's guns and sold them to Medrano."

Jimmy scowled. "You got yourself a regular mess."

Josie kicked at the gravel. "It's a lot of conjecture and not much to back it up. If you can make an arrest down here, it sure would help move things along. I just don't have the manpower to make it happen."

Jimmy nodded and rubbed at the stubble on his chin. "I heard your calls for help the other night when the Trauma Center got shot up. I was working a mess myself. We stopped a van with fifteen illegals, one of the ladies in childbirth, trying to hold the baby back until they reached their destination." He shook his head at the memory. "I did everything I could to get you help that night."

Josie nodded. She didn't doubt it.

"Sanchez and I are working the watchtower tonight," Dixon said.

"Officer Marta Cruz will be working with you. I'll take the tower tomorrow night."

"I'll get the captain to commit to a week if I can. Then at least if you have trouble at the jail, we'll be close at hand. If things get bad, you call me personally."

On the way back to the department, Otto suggested they stop by Red's place.

"There are a lot of people that don't know those guns were stolen. I don't like that young Winning girl out there all by herself.

She's a sitting duck, and she doesn't seem concerned a bit about her safety."

Josie nodded, did a U-turn on River Road, and turned her car toward Scratchgravel Road. She pulled onto Winning's road and drove up the gravel lane to her trailer and stopped. "I'll check in with her."

Pegasus Winning answered the door dressed in shorts and an oversized man's T-shirt from a Harley shop. "You just missed them," she said, looking surprised to see Josie.

"Missed who?" Josie asked.

"There were three carloads of men nosing around Red's place this afternoon. I saw a couple guys get out and check his door. They snooped around the garage, in front of his house."

"Why didn't you call me?" Josie asked.

She crossed her arms over her chest and cocked her hip. It was the same body language she had used with Josie ever since she first showed up at the police department. "I didn't know it was a requirement."

"I'm not sure you realize the type of men you've got nosing around your place out here," Josie said.

Winning picked at a piece of tape on her doorframe. "They shot my neighbor in the head, broke into my trailer, and laid his dead body on my couch. I get it."

Josie and Otto took a complete description of the cars; then they drove down the lane to Red's house. After a quick sweep, they found nothing out of place. "Maybe word's out the guns are gone," Otto said.

While Otto drove them back to the department, Josie caught up with cell phone messages and made routine follow-up calls. As they reached Artemis, she discovered Sheriff Martínez was at the courthouse, guarding a witness in court for the next week. She asked to meet him on the park bench outside for a few minutes.

Otto pulled in front of the police department, and as she reached for her door handle Otto said, "Hang on." He cleared his throat and turned in his seat to face her. "You know I don't like to give you advice."

Josie smiled. "You just feel compelled."

"Exactly. I just don't think you take into account your personal well-being. Sometimes I don't think you're much better than that Winning lady."

"Come on, Otto. Just give it to me."

He smoothed his hand over his head to tame his flyaway hair. "You need to watch what you tell the sheriff. You don't know that he and Bloster weren't both in cahoots with Red and the Mexicans."

She shrugged. "I've thought of that. I don't believe it to be true, but your point is taken."

"Our fine mayor would love to see you hang from a tall branch, and I'd hate to see this give him the opportunity."

"What's that supposed to mean?"

Otto pointed over his shoulder to the sheriff, now walking across the grass in front of the courthouse toward the park bench. "If he and Bloster are cooking the books with the county, who's to say he wouldn't sell you down the river to deflect attention?"

"There's nothing to sell—I haven't done anything!"

Otto blew air out in frustration. "You aren't listening to me. Don't give me this crap about living a good life and not having anything to worry about. You're not that naïve. I don't care if they're cops or not; they're human. Odds are, if they're in trouble, they'll do whatever it takes to get out of it."

Martínez reclined back on the bench with his legs spread apart, slouched somewhat, appearing tired and angry to Josie. She sat beside him, but he said nothing.

"You need to know, straight up, if Bloster reaches for his gun in response to an altercation with me again, he is liable to catch a bullet."

Martínez still said nothing, just stared at his hands folded in his lap.

Josie wasn't sure where to take the conversation, so added, "I won't let that son of a bitch intimidate me with his fists or his gun."

"I think I'm screwed, Josie."

The flat tone of his voice raised the hair on her arms.

"I gave Bloster too much power. I couldn't keep up with the paperwork, and the bills and receipts. Running that jail takes up all my time, and I can't keep up with the department issues. I figured, Bloster's such a pain in the ass, he's always got complaints filed on him for his rough conduct, I'll just bury him in paperwork." He turned to face Josie. "That guy's got a business degree from Texas State. He's not the dumb jock he portrays himself to be. He was supposed to run his dad's trucking business, but he wanted something more physical."

"How bad is it?"

"He took over department expenditures in December. I've gone back to check, and he's been submitting false invoices since January. They've gotten more absurd each month."

"Didn't you see the expense report? Or, if not you, what about the commissioners? Didn't they question things?"

"I never submit an expenditure report. I know your office does. Sheriff's department never has, though. Since I've been in office, all I do is a monthly report. I write a one-page summary of profit and expense, and I show them a basic revenue report."

She smiled grimly and looked at the row of businesses across the street, wondering if the double standard would ever be lifted. "Otto used to do the same, but Moss requested the detailed expenditure report from me. He's never asked you for one?"

He shook his head.

"You got no worries. You're a man. Commissioners? Mayor? Come on, Martínez. You can good-old-boy your way through this."

Martínez nodded once to acknowledge her remark and then looked away.

Josie regretted her words instantly. Martínez had never played her sex against her, and he deserved the same respect.

"I'm sorry, Roy. I shouldn't have said that."

He ignored her apology and looked out across the courtyard, his expression distant. "I found receipts for several guns the department supposedly purchased from Red. There was a receipt for a contractor that doesn't exist, doing five thousand dollars' worth of repairs on the jail that never happened." Martínez looked at the ground. "I found mileage claims for Bloster driving from Texas to Florida. Two of them. He's filched twenty thousand dollars over the past six months alone."

"Where's the money coming from?" she asked.

"Homeland Security Grant. The description on the mileage claim said he went to pick up equipment for the department."

"Get the paperwork together, and I'll take it to Dillon Reese. He's discreet. Maybe we can take care of Bloster without making a community spectacle. The commissioners won't want to admit this to anyone any more than you do."

Josie stood and saw Manny step outside from his motel office and wave to her. She made arrangements with Martínez to gather all his paperwork together for Dillon by the next morning and walked across the street leaving him sitting there, staring off at nothing.

Manny was standing behind the counter bent over a ledger when she walked in the front door. Josie could tell by his meek smile that something was wrong.

"What's up, Manny?"

"I hate like anything to ask you this, but your mother left this morning without a word. She just slipped a letter under the office door. Dropped her key in my drop box. I was up and in here by seven, so she must have left at the crack of dawn." He frowned and slid her a piece of notepaper, with the words MANNY'S MOTEL in green block letters printed across the top. Under that, she recognized her mother's neatly slanted cursive.

Dear Manny,

Thank you for a sweet time. Sorry I had to miss you this morning. Places to go—people to see. Josie owes me for the bill. Just ask her to settle up with you. You take care.

Much Love,
Beverly

Josie felt her face flush and tried to keep the surprise from showing. She reached into her back uniform pocket for her money clip and pulled out her Visa card.

He held his hand up. "If you didn't know about this, then you don't owe me a dime."

"I'm happy to pay the bill." She slid the credit card across the counter and stared as her mother's signature on the note she'd written to Manny. *Much Love.*

Josie turned the radio off and rolled the windows down to listen to the wind whip the sand and grit around the floor of her jeep. She had developed a taste for bourbon on bad days, a taste that she knew was not healthy mentally or physically, but she could already imagine it sliding down her throat and heating up her belly. Some days she craved the burn more than human conversation or touch.

But at home, she bypassed the bottle of bourbon in the kitchen cabinet and changed into shorts, a T-shirt, and lightweight hiking boots and set off walking behind her house toward Dell's. The bitter smell of the sun baking the earth and trees, and the sprawling view of the brown and white Hereford cattle roaming the field made it one of her favorite places on earth.

Dell lived in a small cedar-planked house at the foot of the mountains overlooking his cattle. He got by on what he referred to as common sense rules for living. He didn't believe in charity. People either provided for themselves or they perished. "We didn't need Darwin to explain survival of the fittest. Spend a week in the desert, and you'll see it quick enough."

She found Dell's banged-up green pickup truck parked in front of the horse barn, and while it signaled he was home, he could be nearly anywhere except inside the four walls of his house.

Josie found him behind the barn with a massive cigar hanging out of his mouth, bare chested, his cowboy hat cocked back at a forty-five degree slant. He wore dusty cowboy boots and cutoff jean shorts that revealed his bowlegs. A shotgun hung from a tool belt. The tip of the shotgun almost touched the dirt as Dell bent at the waist, peering into a hole in the ground.

Dell waved as Josie walked toward him. "Go slow. Don't want to wake them till I'm ready."

Josie pointed to a mason jar filled with a translucent yellowish liquid that she recognized as gasoline sitting beside Dell. "You think you ought to put the lid on that?" she asked.

Dell pulled his hat down to shield his browned faced from the sun. "You think I'm going to blow my damn self up pouring fuel with a lit cigar?"

Josie smiled. "What's up?"

"Damn rattlers killed another calf yesterday. Found her dead in the creek. Bit in the head. Probably grazing and stuck her head down to sniff out something moving in the grass and the rattler got her. I never seen them so bad as this year. It's like the lack of rain has dried up their holes and made them crazy." He pointed to Josie's feet. "Take your boots off."

Josie gave him a wary look.

"Take your damned boots off, you pansy. I won't light up the hole until you got them back on."

Josie did as instructed, trusting Dell over common sense.

He pointed to a patch of dirt several feet from the hole. "Walk quiet and stand right there."

Josie did so, and a shiver ran the length of her body. She could feel a slight vibration under her feet.

"You're standing on top of a whole colony of rattlesnakes roiling around under your bare feet."

Dell laughed at the look on her face.

"I've seen them get to be five feet or better." He pointed at the hole, lowering his voice. "They all come out of that hole, and you'll be a dead woman in five minutes. Might be a hundred snakes or better in that den."

Josie cursed Dell, shoved her feet in her socks and boots, and walked backwards with a wary eye on the hole.

He told her to move back another thirty feet and stubbed his cigar out. He stuck a three-foot-long PVC pipe into the hole with a funnel on the top and dumped the gas down the pipe. He pulled up the pipe and backed up ten feet, hollering that the sons of bitches were madder than hell. Josie wished she'd had a camera to catch the joy on the man's face. He grabbed his shotgun from his tool belt and trained it toward the hole. As snakes twisted out of the hole, Dell blasted a dozen shells, reloading like an infantry-man.

A half hour later, they sat at a picnic table behind the cabin, looking at the twenty-five rattles he had cut off the dead snakes and cleaned up with the garden hose. While Josie checked out the bounty, Dell poured himself a glass of dark sun tea and brought

Josie a beer. A reformed alcoholic, Dell wouldn't allow the hard stuff on his property, but he kept the beer cold for Josie.

"We'll make you a dream catcher out of those rattlers. I'll show you how to stretch the sinew from a deer to make the web."

Josie smiled and slipped the bottom of her T-shirt over the beer cap and twisted. Life was so uncomplicated with Dell. She would have fallen for him years ago if he hadn't been forty years older. The man was a lifelong bachelor with seemingly no desire for intimacy.

"I saw that accountant's car parked down at your place the other night. That a good thing?" he asked.

"It's good."

"How come he's been gone so long, then?"

She sipped at her beer to consider the question and settled on the short version. "Something about my heart being in a box. I think I'm missing some key relationship gene. Things that everyone else understands make no sense to me."

"Well, I got a whole list of things wrong with me, but by god, I'm a good judge of character. And I know for a fact that you got a heart of gold, and if that accountant so much as thinks of breaking that heart of yours, he'll have to answer to me."

TEN

At 11:30 P.M. Friday night, Marta Cruz sat on the hood of her car swatting at mosquitoes. The air was damp by the river, full of life, teeming with bugs and bats, and she could smell the rank odor of decay. She preferred the dry, scorched smell of sand and rock and wind that surrounded her small adobe house in town. When Marta was a child, her mother had forbidden her and her siblings from playing in the dirty water of the river, and as she had gotten older, her mother's superstitions took root. The river was not a place for clean, decent people. Her mother said loose girls and boys who were up to no good hung out there, away from the lights of respectable homes. Down by the river was where the no-gooders partied in shanties, stayed up all hours, and earned their money through vice. Marta had never seen the sights her mother described, but the stories instilled in her a strange paranoia about the Rio. She wasn't happy about spending the night along its banks.

She had arrived two hours prior and backed her car into a thicket of scrub, then pulled additional cover around the front of her car.

Border Patrol had scouted out her position and agreed it would work. She was watching the intersection where Josie had seen the lookout car the night before from the watchtower, and waiting for any activity across the river on the Mexican side. Jimmy Dare and Tim Sanchez, another Border Patrol agent, had ATVs camouflaged and parked along the banks closer to the area where Josie had seen the exchange. Like Jimmy, Sanchez was a well-built agent who obviously took pride in his physical condition. Both agents were average height with short dark hair and muscular builds. Sanchez was bulkier, though, and obviously worked out heavily at the gym, almost to the point where Marta wondered if he supplemented with steroids. His biceps stretched the fabric on his uniform sleeves, and his chest was like a rock.

Marta slid off her hood, unclipped her flashlight from her gun belt, and began walking down to the river to wipe mud on her neck and arms to help shield her skin from the swarm of mosquitoes. As she approached the river, she saw headlights coming down the access road to the river on the Mexican side. She immediately turned the flashlight off and ran back toward her car, calling Jimmy on his cell phone as she ran.

"Looks like one car and a pickup with some kind of trailer attached," she said. She watched the headlights approach through the thick brush and struggled to see what they were driving. "They've slowed way down," she whispered.

The vehicles drove past her on the other side of the river, creeping along, apparently looking for the access point.

"They passed the turnoff we identified yesterday."

"What are they driving?" Jimmy asked. "We're down by the river, and I can't see anything."

Marta watched the lights for a moment. "It's a full-size pickup pulling a double horse trailer. The car is a lowrider. Maybe an old Mercury or Buick. They've passed you guys up. It looks like they're turning onto the Flat Rock crossing. The Rio is low enough right now, they could probably drive across it. It spreads out there and gets pretty shallow."

"As soon as they put a wheel in the river, Sanchez and I will approach on the four-wheelers," Jimmy said. "I got the driver of the truck. Sanchez will block a rear exit. You block from the front with lights and siren, exit your car, and move to the rear for cover. You let us approach the truck from the rear. Clear?"

"We're on," Marta said. "The lead car just nosed into the water, and the pickup is on his bumper." She started to pull the clumps of scrub bushes from the front of her car and got inside.

"I see them. They'll try the car first to make sure there aren't problems before they risk losing the load," Jimmy said.

Marta kept the cell phone to her ear and started her engine. She drove toward the car, leaving her headlights, flashers, and sirens off. She drove with her head out the window, listening for noise. Timing was key. If they arrived too soon, the drivers would leave on foot and run back into Mexico. They needed the car out of the river on the U.S. side without giving it time to take off. However, they hoped to keep the truck *in* the river, where the four-wheelers maneuvered easier and they would have the upper hand.

Marta inched her car up, now a hundred feet from where the vehicles had entered the river. They, too, had turned their lights off. The half moon and stars still provided enough light that she could see the truck approaching the water.

The car nosed out of the water onto the U.S. side and up the low bank. Its tires spun for several seconds before grabbing hold and lurching onto land. The truck was halfway into the river when both four-wheelers appeared out of nowhere and doused the area in spotlights. Water splashed, and the ATV's large tires slung mud and rock as they plunged into the river. Marta took advantage of the noise from the revving engines and disorienting lights. She threw on her own lights and sirens and pulled her car directly in front of what she could see now was a Buick, which was sandwiched between the pickup truck and her own car.

The front of her car faced the Buick, so Marta swung open her door immediately, crouched, but instead of running behind her own car and staying as Jimmy had instructed, she ran to the passenger side of the lead car. She wanted to take down the driver herself while the agents took care of the truck passengers. It appeared there was only the driver. No passengers. She hoped she hadn't miscalculated.

Squatting behind the window of the rear passenger door, she banged on the window and yelled for the driver to step out of the car. With the sirens blaring and the truck and both four-wheelers idling behind the lead car, she doubted the driver could hear anything.

The truck's driver threw it into reverse, gunned the engine, and hit the front of Jimmy's ATV with the horse trailer as he made a break for Mexican soil. The impact was negligible, as he had little traction in the water. She watched Jimmy give a thumbs-up to Sanchez, which Marta assumed meant he had not been hurt by the truck. She heard gunshots and ducked, then heard the hiss of the tires on the pickup being deflated.

Guns drawn, Jimmy and Sanchez both left their ATVs simultaneously. Sanchez approached the driver's side of the truck and Jimmy the passenger side. As both men yelled for the occupants to exit, the doors of the truck opened slowly. Two men wearing jeans and dark-colored T-shirts began exiting the truck and were then dragged by the agents out into the water.

While they were securing the truck, Marta turned her back on the two agents, crouched, and moved around to the driver's side of the car from the back. Her heart banged against her chest as she yelled again for the driver to step out, hands in the air. She was certain the vehicles were transporting weapons, drugs, or both and whoever was driving had a much different outlook on life and death than she did. She yelled in Spanish again for the driver to open his door, and then silently prayed to God to keep her safe for her daughter.

Marta shone her flashlight in the car with her free hand and confirmed there was only one person. Jimmy and Sanchez had both men cuffed and were shoving them noisily through the water toward her. Her main concern was that they were all targets until she secured the man in the car. Marta lifted her metal flashlight high above her head and came down hard on the driver's window, shattering the glass into the car. She slid the barrel of the gun in through the broken window and connected with the man's head. He threw his hands up and leaned toward the steering wheel.

"All right, all right!" he screamed.

Marta slowly pulled her gun back out the window, unlocked the car door, then opened it. Hearing the man use English, she shifted her response to English as well. "Slow now. Put your hands and feet out first so I can see them."

She watched as he shifted his body so his hands and then feet appeared in the opening.

"You have any weapons on you?"

She heard no response and yelled the question again, hitting one of the man's hands with her gun.

"No! No guns in here," he yelled.

"Then you ease out of the car. Slowly." As he slid out of the car with his hands and feet in front of him, it gave Marta time to look more closely into the car's interior: it was empty except for what looked like a coat or duffel bag on the backseat, too small for a person to hide under.

Within ten minutes, all three men were handcuffed and lying facedown in the dirt. Marta pulled out driver's licenses and wallets from pockets while Jimmy drove Marta's jeep and then the truck and horse trailer up out of the water and onto dry land.

A grassy opening about fifty feet wide separated the river from the road, but they needed to block vehicle access to help control the situation. While Sanchez set up flares and turned his patrol car sideways in the middle of River Road to block traffic, Jimmy used chain link cutters to break the locks on the horse trailer.

Jimmy called out to Marta. "Josie was on it. There's enough firepower in here to blow that jail to pieces. You better get ATF and request the bomb squad. Border Patrol backup is on their way, but we're going to need as much help as we can get. These guys had big plans with this kind of firepower." Jimmy walked gingerly back around the trailer. "This stuff makes me nervous as hell. I bet there's a half ton of TNT alone."

As Jimmy inventoried the truck and Marta searched the Mexicans, Sanchez rigged spotlights on top of eight-foot portable poles that he'd stowed in Marta's truck. He flipped the switch on a small generator, and it cast a surreal light over the vehicles and the men lying in the grass.

Jimmy stepped away from the trailer and approached Marta. In the bright light, Jimmy's face appeared pale and dripped with sweat. Marta thought he had the wide-eyed look of an adrenaline junkie. "We need to stand clear until ATF gets here." He pointed to the men lying on the ground. "What do you have?"

"The driver of the lead car has an American accent but no identification on him. The two men who were in the truck both have Mexican ID cards." Marta stuck her foot out and with it poked one of the men in his hip. "This one is confirmed Medrano. I know the name."

"A Medrano. Go figure. You fellas headed over to our jail?" Jimmy stood above the men who lay on their chests, their heads turned to the side. "Try and bust your kinfolk out tonight, huh? That load of explosives just might send you away for the long haul."

Sanchez left the generator and walked over to join Jimmy. "We'll need a special Medrano wing at the jailhouse."

"Look," Marta said, and pointed downstream, to the Mexican side of the river. A line of headlights were driving slowly down the gravel access road. "They're probably two miles from here."

Jimmy yelled to Sanchez to cut the lights, and he and Marta reached for two of the suspects, attempting to pull them up to a standing position to get them into Marta's jeep. Neither of them budged. All three had gone limp, their bodies dead weight. Marta placed her gun in the back of the head of the lead driver, ordering him to move, but he refused. It became obvious a contingency plan was about to be carried out, and Marta feared the three officers were seconds away from a group execution.

Jimmy pulled his gun and shot the driver of the pickup in his upper arm. "I'll shoot all three of you if you aren't up and in the back of that police car in ten seconds!"

The sound of the gunshot and their partner screaming in pain prompted the other two to scramble up on two feet and move. As the cars approached the river crossing, Jimmy was stuffing the third gunman into the backseat of Marta's squad car, a jeep barely large enough to hold four people. Marta got in and started the engine as Sanchez squeezed next to her. Jimmy placed one knee on the passenger seat, facing backwards toward the oncoming cars and hanging on to the open door frame for support.

"Go!" he shouted.

"What about the explosives?" Marta asked. Her head was pounding, and she prayed in the back of her mind as she tried to keep her focus on the approaching cars. She had heard countless stories of cartel members torturing police officers, and she felt her throat constrict in fear.

Still in four-wheel drive, she shoved the jeep into first gear and spun gravel as she pulled her car onto River Road. Sanchez's thigh was pressed against the gear stick, and she had difficulty shifting into second gear. Jimmy ducked back inside the car and faced the backseat. He pointed his gun directly at the three men and began shouting in Spanish not to move and to stay quiet or they were all dead men. Marta tried to block out the cries of the man in the middle who had been shot in the arm.

They heard gunfire from across the river.

"They're shooting at the explosives truck! Jesus, they're going to blow it up!" Jimmy yelled.

Marta pulled off the road and into the desert scrub to the north of the river to get space between their car and the horse trailer.

"Now circle around, cut your headlights, and get the car pointed back toward the river so we've got a good visual," Jimmy said. "You stay in the car and keep a gun on the prisoners. Sanchez and I will keep guns trained on that explosives truck. I just talked to Border dispatch. ETA on backup is five minutes. I talked to Josie. She's on her way with everyone she can find."

Once she'd maneuvered the jeep into place, Marta kneeled in the driver's seat and faced the three men in the backseat of the jeep, crowded in on top of one another, with one man bleeding and moaning, and all of them worried the night sky was about to light up with an explosion that might kill them all. Sanchez and Jimmy were outside the jeep, standing behind the opened driver's and passenger side doors with two .45-caliber pistols facing what appeared to be a small army of Mexicans across the river. The Mexicans had spotted them and were standing down. Marta hoped it was enough to keep them across the river until backup arrived.

A lone siren was heard coming from the north. Marta was certain it was Josie. Josie parked her car ten feet behind Marta's jeep, and Jimmy waved her car up next to theirs. She rolled down her windows to speak with them.

He yelled, "We've got three prisoners in the back of the jeep. Keep your lights and sirens on. We need a huge presence here as fast as we can get."

Josie yelled back over the sound of the sirens, "Sheriff's department is on their way. Martínez is right behind me."

Shortly after, a trail of two sheriff's deputies and two DPS cars approached from the east. Within minutes, the area was teeming with local police vehicles as well as Border Patrol and DPS, their cars pointed toward the river, sirens blaring, officers crouched behind car doors for protection. An ambulance arrived and Josie directed them to Marta's jeep.

Josie split the prisoners up, and the sheriff sent two of them to the Arroyo County Jail with a sheriff's deputy. She asked an EMT driver to get the man who'd been shot stabilized but to stay on-site and prepare the Trauma Center team. It was too soon to leave with the county's only ambulance.

After things quieted down, Josie pulled Marta into her squad car and shut the doors. Marta filled her in on the details, her voice still unsteady from the stress of the night. Josie sat in the driver's seat listening.

"How do we deal with this? How can one small town fight an army equipped with this kind of firepower?" Marta finally asked.

"The sheriff and I called several ranchers along the border and asked them to be on alert tonight. We talked to six families, all living within a half mile of the river."

Marta looked surprised. "They aren't trained for this kind of fight."

Josie pointed to the row of police cars, lights, and the similar row of cars facing them from across the river. "We're beyond training. We're just trying to hold the line. I've already called Moss and told him we've got to get National Guard presence immediately. He doesn't want to admit we can't handle this on our own, but surely he realized it tonight."

At five o'clock in the morning, the situation resolved itself when the Mexican contingent pulled back and left the explosives and trailer, apparently resolved to the fact that there was no chance of crossing into the U.S. in front of, by that point, eight police cars from five different police agencies and a helicopter guarding the trailer of explosives. By 5:30 A.M., officers from ATF were dismantling the truck, inventorying, and removing everything inside. Crime scene technicians from the Department of Public Safety were going over the area, and after preliminary paperwork was started, local law enforcement was dismissed. Marta drove home to her daughter, prayers answered yet again.

An hour later, Josie pulled onto Tower Road and saw Dillon's car parked in her driveway. He met her at the front door and pulled her into his chest when she walked inside.

She pulled back slightly and saw the exhaustion in his face. "Is everything okay?" she asked.

He closed his eyes and rested his forehead on hers. "Josie. I've been worried sick about you. Artemis has been all over the local news."

"Have you been up all night?" she asked. Invariably it caught her by surprise to find someone emotionally affected by her well-being. She wasn't sure if she should apologize for being an inconvenience.

"I couldn't sleep last night, so I got up and turned the radio on. The DJ was talking about the standoff in Artemis along the river. I called your house and then gave up and came over here to wait on you."

"Guess I should have called to check in."

"You had bigger worries. I'm not mad. I'm just glad to see you. Are you upset I came over?"

"No, of course not. I'm just exhausted. Let me take a shower and we can talk." She kissed him on the cheek and left him sitting on the couch in the living room. He looked as tired as she felt.

Standing in the shower, she let the hot water beat against her back and replayed the conversation with Dillon in her head. Second-guessing her actions and wondering if she had said or done the wrong thing; the frustrations she had wrestled with throughout their last involvement were coming back to her. Her body ached and eyes stung and she wanted nothing more than to slip between the sheets and give in to sleep. She did not want to worry about another human being's feelings.

She slipped on a light nightshirt, pulled her hair into a ponytail, and found Dillon standing at her bedroom window, tucking a comforter over the curtain rod. Although it was daylight, close to eight in the morning, the room was the color of dusk.

He pointed to the bed, his expression kind. "Take your nightshirt off, climb in, and lie on your stomach."

Dillon turned from her and she pulled her nightshirt over her head, pushed the cover and pillows away, then pulled the sheet over her bottom and lay flat on her stomach, her arms to her side. She closed her eyes and felt Dillon's weight settle onto the bed, his knees straddling her hips. She listened to his hands rub together and knew he was warming lotion between his palms, a treat she'd missed since he'd been gone. He laid his hands flat on the center of her back, applying slight pressure. He let the warmth of his hands settle into her body before moving them slowly up and down her spine, gently pushing the heels of his palms into the tauter muscles. He dug his thumbs into her neck and shoulders until she sighed with relief.

"Let me feel your skin," she whispered. "Lie beside me and hold me. I'll be asleep in minutes."

Dillon curled in behind her, slid an arm under her pillow to hold one hand, and found her other hand to hold against her chest. He pulled her into his body and tucked his bent knees into her own. He kissed her shoulder and rested his head above hers on the pillow. Her body melted into his, her attention fading with the knowledge that she was happy and safe and content.

ELEVEN

By noon, the temperature was triple digits. The two-day reprieve had made life more tolerable, but the heat was back like a furnace on full tilt. The Bishop watched the waves of heat radiating up from the desert floor and let the sun bake his skin. He stood on the back veranda of his home and listened to his elderly uncle drone on. Familial obligation dictated that he allow his uncle a place to live out his remaining days with family. His uncle had moved into his home a month ago and begun telling the Bishop how to run the family business.

"If you do not gain control of this now, the future of this family is as sure as tomorrow's sunrise. We cannot show this weakness. The Americans have slapped us into submission. Your father would never have allowed this."

The Bishop turned to face his father's older brother. He sat in a wheelchair under the awning with a light blanket covering his emaciated legs. His body tilted to one side, like a knickknack askew on a shelf, and the Bishop found himself torn between pity and revulsion.

Once king of the world, his uncle was now relegated to drool and impotence and a colostomy bag. The Bishop paid little attention to his uncle, but had already come to the same conclusion regarding the Americans. He needed no guidance. The small-town police had made a mockery of his organization.

"It is taken care of," he said.

His uncle laughed, a wet gurgle from deep in his lungs. "You lost a trailer of explosives. How is that taken care of?"

"I've sent two men to the police chief. She will pay the price for her arrogance. She will learn what happens when you don't play by our rules."

Josie woke disoriented, her head heavy with sleep. She felt Dillon's leg draped over her own and tried to figure out what day it was without opening her eyes. She lay on her back and moved her fingers lazily over his chest and allowed the drama from the night before to filter back into her thoughts as if through a deep fog. She thought she smelled a cigarette and imagined her mother sitting out in her living room, chain-smoking, and waiting on her to get out of bed.

She heard a noise and the scrape of a boot against the wood floor just before she opened her eyes. Two armed men stood at the end of the bed. Instantly awake, her body was rigid with fear. The room was dim, but she could easily distinguish that they were two males in their twenties, one stocky with a short military cut and a bushy mustache, the other taller and wearing a camouflage bandanna around his head and a long gold earring. The stocky man held his gun at his chest, removed the cigarette from his mouth, and dropped it on the floor, grinding it into the wood with his foot.

She forced breath into her lungs and pulled the sheet up, clenched it between her fists at her chest. *Take me,* she wanted to say. *Leave him be.* She wanted to stand with her hands in the air and surrender. Walk out of the bedroom with them as Dillon slept on, undisturbed.

He did nothing to deserve this. But her body was frozen, her eyes unblinking, her mind barely able to separate dream from reality.

"You made a big mistake," the man with the bandanna said, and Dillon jerked awake beside her.

"What the hell?" he said, his voice confused.

Under the sheet, Josie squeezed his forearm but kept her eyes on the two men.

"You got two choices and thirty seconds," the man in the bandanna went on. "You choose to let Gutiérrez and the other three go and you live. You keep them locked up and you die. You choose. Now. Ten seconds." He spoke with a northern Mexican accent she associated with the border towns.

She spoke with no hesitation. "They go free tonight."

"You go inside and unlock the cell and it's done, huh? They walk free to their ride home?" the other gunman said.

Terrified, Josie watched as both men raised their guns and pointed them directly at her and Dillon. She heard him gasp beside her and throw his arm over her, as if his arm could protect her from the spray of automatic gunfire facing them. Then, in tandem, both men swung their guns up toward the wall above the bed and opened fire. Wood and plaster and glass from framed pictures sprayed over them, piercing their bodies. Josie heard screaming but couldn't tell if it was coming from her or Dillon. He had rolled over on top of her, his body covering hers, his arm cupped around her head as the gunfire continued. She closed her eyes to the white fire coming from the end of the weapons. It felt as if the noise and the debris falling around their bodies lasted for hours. When they had finished, one of the men yelled above the ringing in her ears, "Tomorrow, midnight, you die if our men aren't free. You count on that."

Dillon slowly lifted off her as plaster and wood and glass fell from their bodies. Both gunmen were gone. They heard the bloodhound howling outside, and Josie leaped from the bed, running to the front door. She envisioned the dog being shot as an afterthought, but they were already in their vehicle, a black Mercedes sedan, pulling out onto the road.

Dillon came into the living room carrying her bathrobe. He wrapped her in it and tried to hold her, but she pushed him away to grab the cordless phone off the coffee table. She called in the incident to the dispatcher, then tracked down Jimmy Dixon through Border Patrol and filled him in. She called Sheriff Martínez and told him that DPS was on their way to conduct the investigation. The sheriff said he was on his way over. The mayor's number went to voice mail; she left him the details of it all on the message.

After all the calls had been made, she sat down on the couch with Dillon. He had sat in silence with the shaking dog on the seat next to him.

"Are you hurt?" she asked.

He held out his arms and showed her flecks of blood where glass from the picture frames over the bed had penetrated his skin.

"Let me see your back," she said. He hadn't spoken, and she worried he might be in shock.

They both stood and he turned away from her. A single rivulet of blood ran down the center of his back from where a larger piece of glass had lodged. She pulled the piece out with her fingernails and turned him around.

"Are you okay?" she asked.

His eyes welled up and he pulled her into his chest. "I thought we were both dead. When the noise stopped, I lay there and couldn't figure out if I had been shot or not."

"I'm so sorry, Dillon. I am so sorry you were in the middle of this. This isn't your battle."

He pushed her back and clenched his hands on her shoulders as if trying to hold her in place. "You can't keep this up, Josie. It ends today. You can't give up your life for this job. It's not your battle either. You turn in your badge, we pack, and we're out of here to-morrow. Better yet, we'll let someone else pack for us and just leave. This town, this place—none of it is worth your life or mine."

She sighed heavily. "I can't do that."

"Like hell you can't!"

"I understand you want to leave. I wouldn't ask you to stay."

The light in his eyes changed. She felt the water rising around her.

"Of course you wouldn't," he said.

"Don't play games with me. I'm too tired. You know that's not what I meant. But this has nothing to do with you and me. This is my job. It's what I get paid to do. I didn't sign a clause in my con-tract that said if things got dangerous, I could just take off. If you are afraid, then leave. I completely understand it," she said.

He leaned back angrily. "I'm not afraid for me. The woman who I—" He paused and seemed to mentally slow down. "—the woman who I care deeply about just lay in bed and negotiated with terror-ists as they shot holes in her walls. You think I should just blow this off? Just another day at the office for Josie?"

"Don't be sarcastic," she said.

"You are not trained for this kind of work. I know, I have heard, you are a great cop. Outstanding, even. But what you are dealing with is beyond cop work. It's warfare, and it's beyond your skill set!"

"My skill set?" She squinted at him in disbelief. "Could you be a little more insulting? You don't know what kind of training I re-ceived. You don't know what experiences I've dealt with to prepare for my job."

"And exactly how do they train you for men standing at the end of your bed with guns?"

She said nothing.

"What happens tonight when the Medrano clan finds out that you didn't release their prisoners like you promised? You think they won't come back and blow this house to kingdom come? You've dodged the bullet." He stopped speaking. He looked as if he wanted to say more but thought better of it.

"I'm going to see this through," Josie said. "I will not give in to these men. Look what's happened in Mexico. The government, the police force, the good people in the country have lain down and let the cartels take over. The psychopaths are running the show. I refuse to do that here. I'd like to have your support. It means more to me than you know."

He stared at her for a long moment before speaking. "I can't do this. I can't go to bed each night wondering if you'll make it home alive the next day. I want a family someday. Kids."

Josie said nothing.

Dillon stood and went outside on the front porch to wait for the police.

After Dillon was interviewed and told he could leave, Josie spent the next six hours of her Saturday with DPS and Border Patrol. The house was photographed by crime scene technicians who pored over the inside and outside, taking prints and casts. She went to the office and worked with a sketch artist for almost an hour and was pleased with the renditions. Later, Jimmy from BP showed up at the department with a boxed chicken dinner for her from the gas station. They sat together to look at pictures from the Mexican foreign nationals file. Not surprising to anyone, they got a preliminary ID on the suspect with the bandanna and earring as an infantryman for Medrano. Jimmy pulled up the man's Alien File in the DACS system and found he had been deported twice, was suspected in an armed robbery in Houston, and was wanted for a series of murders in Juárez, Mexico. Josie declined Jimmy's offer to stay at his home until things stabilized. He'd asked her out to dinner on several occasions, and she always made up an excuse. She didn't need more complications in her life at the moment, but she did agree to stay at a motel until the prisoners were transferred out of Artemis.

At seven o'clock, Josie called Moss to ask if the request to transfer prisoners had been granted by the federal penitentiary. He said he had been in contact with the warden, and they were working on a Monday-morning transfer.

"Monday? The feds don't work on the weekend? Medrano made it pretty clear today in my home that they aren't messing around. If those prisoners aren't moved by tomorrow evening, are you prepared for what's coming?"

"Do you know what makes a great man? Perseverance and determination. The willingness to tackle the problems no one else is willing to consider," Moss said, his tone pious. "Do you think this isn't weighing on my chest every minute of the day?"

"That's it, then?"

"I'm working to move the transport time up. If and when that happens, I'll let you know." He paused a moment, and his voice softened. "I'm sorry about your house. What happened to you is terrible, and I'll do what I can to make things right."

Josie heard the words but realized she was too numb to make sense of them. Usually suspect of everything he said, she was too tired to dig deeper for meaning. She thanked him, hung up, and left word with the dispatcher that she would be staying at Manny's for the night before returning home in the morning. She walked down the block and around the courthouse to the motel. Through the plate glass window, she saw Manny sitting in his recliner under the yellow glow of his reading lamp. Cigarette smoke filtered up through the light, and his attention was riveted on the book in his lap. He looked over his glasses at her when she stepped inside the door, and he stood and approached the counter. The wringing of his hands and his worry lines reminded her of Tevye from *Fiddler on the Roof*. She half expected him to break out into song.

"How are you getting along? I've listened to the radio all day long for updates. Have you caught the bastards?"

Josie glanced at the radio sitting on the counter and heard the soft classical music from the local public radio station.

"I'm doing okay. We have three new guests at the Arroyo County Jail. The feds have taken over now. They'll hopefully be moved quickly."

He reached across the counter and clasped her hand. "You need a room tonight?"

She nodded.

"You stay in room six. Right next to my apartment. You need anything tonight, you knock on the wall and I'm at your door in two seconds." He opened the key box on the counter and passed her a gold key on a smiley face key chain. "Anything else I can do?" he asked.

She paused, embarrassed, and looked down at her uniform. "I don't want to go home tonight. I can't face that house right now."

"You need clothes? You go to your room and I'll run to the store."

She closed her eyes for a moment to fight back her humiliation. She finally sighed and looked at Manny. "I can't go to the liquor store in uniform. Do you have any bourbon stocked away somewhere?"

He smiled at her warmly. "Sleep. That's what you need." He left her for a moment and returned from the back room with a fifth of bourbon, still sealed. "I get this question occasionally. On the house. The room, too, of course."

Josie turned on the lamp on the bedside table and set the air-conditioning on high. The unit hummed to life and blew musty, damp air into the hot room. The paneled walls were painted a buttery yellow, and an ancient wedding ring–pattern quilt was on the bed. Hand-embroidered pillows were piled up against a wicker headboard, and a rocking chair with a lace-covered cushion sat in the corner facing a TV. It was a cozy room that reminded her of country farmhouses back in Indiana. Josie used Manny's complimentary toothbrush and ate the cheese crackers she had brought with her from her stash at the department. She laid her uniform out across the rocker and propped herself against the pillows in bed in her underwear. She put the remote control beside her and cracked the seal on the bourbon, filling the drinking glass on the bedside table half-full. She stared into the amber liquid in the glass as if some measure of clarity might bubble up into her thoughts after the burn dissipated.

Josie wondered what her mother had done, propped up in a bed just like hers—if she had drunk her own glass of bourbon or taken pills to fall asleep. Josie had tried desperately to keep her mother's real intentions behind the mental wall she constructed, and she thought she had succeeded. She wondered now if she had been too harsh, if she should have given her mother a chance to explain things. But what good was an explanation in the end? She had been a lousy mother. The question Josie was wrestling with now was, did that give her a free pass to be a lousy daughter? And what about a girlfriend? Did her job give her a free pass to shut out a man who obviously loved her?

Josie drank, eventually straight from the bottle, until the room tilted. She closed her eyes and imagined a chalkboard with a list of solutions. She felt sure there were answers inside her and wondered: Did she want to be a good cop, a good person, a good daughter, a good wife? It was obvious she couldn't be all those to everyone, so she had to choose. She slipped down the pillows, set the bottle on the table, and fell asleep with the lights on. She dreamt about monsoons filling up the desert, the water closing in around her neck.

TWELVE

Josie sat in her squad car with the air-conditioning blowing on her face and stared at her front door for a long time. It wasn't fear so much as dread. The smell of smoke and gunpowder and the image of the guns pointed at Dillon's chest, at her face, would stay with her for many years to come. The spray of debris, the shattered glass, splintered pieces of wood trim and pockmarked walls awaited her. The sick knowledge that these men had come into her life with their guns and ruined her chance at a normal, loving relationship made her breathless and light-headed. Blood rushed to her head, and she gripped her steering wheel and let herself cry, the silent tears eventually giving way to sobs for the pathetic excuse of a life she was leading.

Eventually, cried out, she entered her house and found Chester asleep on the kitchen floor beside his dog dish. She had called Dell the night before and arranged for the dog to stay at Dell's house. Dell called her cell phone that morning and said Chester had whined all night until Dell brought him home that morning. She knelt beside Chester and buried her face in his neck and talked to him, grateful for his big, brown, nonjudgmental eyes. He'd been through hell, too, and she felt lousy for leaving him the night before. One more living being to let down, she thought.

She gave Chester a hot dog out of the refrigerator and fresh water, and then let him out to run. She gathered broom and dustpan and the large plastic garbage can from outside. As she walked down the hallway, she heard a car pull into the driveway and felt her pulse race. She dropped the broom and pulled the gun out of her ankle holster, then looked through the crack in the living room curtain to find Otto and his wife, Delores, getting out of their car and walking up the front path.

Otto and Delores were both dressed in jeans and T-shirts. Even when Otto was out of his uniform, Josie rarely saw the sixty-year-old in anything but dress pants and button-down shirt or Delores in anything but print dresses. Otto carried a large duffel bag and a home-baked pie. When Josie opened the door, Delores came at her, smiling, with both arms extended. She pulled Josie against her soft body and spoke quietly into her ear about how good it was to see her safe and how she had a bed ready with fresh sheets for her.

"We'll get your place cleaned up like new, and you can pack a bag and move in tonight. No excuses or fussing. This is the way it's going to be," Delores said.

"Dell called this morning and said he would come down this afternoon and patch the plaster in the walls from the bullet holes. It looks pretty bad right now," Josie said.

Josie took the pie into the kitchen as Delores wandered back into the bedroom with her bag of cleaning supplies. Otto motioned to the couch and Josie sat down. She noticed him staring at her and she realized how bad she must look. She hadn't showered since the day before, and her eyes and nose were still red and swollen.

"You holding up okay?" Otto asked.

She shrugged and smiled. The answer was obvious.

"Dillon called me. He said you were staying by yourself at Manny's. I told him not to worry, that I had plans to cart you home with me."

"Let me ask you something. If I were a man, would we be having this same conversation?"

"Absolutely. Except I would probably tell you to quit acting like a hero, to pack your bags, and get your ass over to the house. I can turn up the language if it makes you feel any better."

She smiled and tipped her head to acknowledge his point.

"So you'll come with us?"

"I'm worried about tonight," she said. "It's not about having a place to stay; it's about what's going to happen with the Medranos. I don't think the mayor understands the magnitude of what's happening. I've called him twice today about the prisoner transfer. He told me he was working on it the first time. When I called back, he claimed Monday is the earliest he could arrange it."

"Which probably means two days from now, once the paperwork gets jammed up some bureaucrat's hind end. Who's taking the prisoners?"

"Houston. The federal detention center takes pretrial inmates. Moss has supposedly arranged everything, but I don't know if I trust him enough to follow through on the details. At this point, I don't know if I trust him on anything."

Otto's expression was fierce. "Don't you know the warden at the detention center?"

Josie nodded. "Remi Escobedo. I worked with him a few years ago on a federal indictment. He's a good man."

"Have you talked to him?"

"Chain of command? Moss would stroke out if I went around him to check details with the warden."

"So, let him," Otto said. "You've got good instincts. You need to start there. Clean up the politics later."

After a few calls, Josie tracked down Escobedo at his home in

Presidio. As soon as he discovered it was Josie on the phone, he said he was sorry for her troubles and asked about her safety.

"I'd like to ask you a question in confidence," Josie said.

"Of course."

"It's about the prisoner transfer. You've talked to Mayor Moss about the four prisoners moving to the federal prison?" she asked.

"Yes, I spoke with him by phone this morning. You've got the shooter from the Trauma Center, and the three guys you stopped at the river with the explosives. Right?"

"That's right. Did he also explain that two more gunmen came to my house yesterday, shot up my house, and threatened me? Said that if the prisoners weren't released by tonight that I would be killed?"

Escobedo paused. "He did not."

"Is there a reason why the prisoners can't be moved today?"

"I specifically offered to set transfer up myself this morning, as soon as I heard from the mayor." His voice was measured and steely. "He told me he was working in tandem with the sheriff. The mayor did not tell me anything about the threat to your life. He explained the shooting and said we needed the prisoners moved to a more secure location. But he set up the transfer for Monday at four P.M. He chose the time. He said local law enforcement had the jail secured tonight, and a National Guard contingent was scheduled this weekend. I offered to have a transport van there by two o'clock today."

Josie rubbed the back of her neck and sat down on the couch. She stared at Otto as she spoke, trying to make some sense of what she had just heard. "It's not just my own safety; it's every officer at that jail. Medrano has a personal score to settle with his cousin, and he intends to take care of it on his own terms. This won't end until Gutiérrez is dead."

Josie heard Escobedo breathing heavily on the other end of the phone. "I don't like this. What do you know about Moss?"

"He's arrogant. He doesn't like women in authority. He's either loved or hated by everyone in Artemis, no in between. He's a control freak with designs on a senator's seat. This, though?"

"Think he's in with Medrano?"

"I don't know. There's a deputy I have my doubts about. He's scammed money from the department. Probably ten to twenty thousand from the county, and there is a fair chance it's connected to La Bestia. Gun sales."

Otto threw his hands up in the air and gave her a look that said, *Why the hell didn't I know any of this?*

"You don't suppose the mayor is playing La Bestia against Medrano, do you? There's serious cash to be had there," Escobedo said.

"La Bestia's been silent through this. I think their concern is in Piedra. It's the drug route they're after. They couldn't care less about losing Gutiérrez to a jail cell. He's a throwaway pawn. They've already got any information from him they were going to get. Now he's just leverage against Medrano and not much else."

"Do you have any other law enforcement in the county that knows what's going on? Prosecutor? Sheriff?" he asked.

"The sheriff knows some. I think he's square, but with one of his deputies possibly involved, I haven't confided much. I haven't talked to the prosecutor yet, because I don't have my facts in order. Right now, you know as much as anybody outside my own department."

"Your top priority right now has to be getting those prisoners out of town safely and immediately."

Josie sighed, frustrated, and rolled her eyes at Otto, who was staring at her intently from the couch. "I've been telling the mayor that, but I can't get him to take me seriously. Can you make that call?"

Escobedo breathed out heavily. "I don't think we want to do that just yet."

At one o'clock that afternoon, Josie and Otto met Escobedo at the Arroyo County Jail. At the suggestion of Escobedo, Josie had called Sheriff Martínez and asked if she and Otto could use the interrogation room to talk with Gutiérrez. It was Saturday, and Martínez had the day off. He agreed and told Josie to ask the intake officer to show them up to a room per his order. Josie did not mention that Warden Escobedo from the federal penitentiary would also be meeting with the prisoner in the sheriff's jail. She felt guilty about the omission, but Escobedo made it clear that Martínez was to be kept out of the loop. Escobedo viewed Martínez as an unknown at this point and didn't want to risk the chance that Martínez might blow the operation. Because Gutiérrez had already been remanded into the federal prison system, Escobedo was in the jail in his official capacity as warden.

The jailer, Maria Santiago, set the three up in an interrogation room and asked one of the guards to escort the prisoner from his cell. Ten minutes later, the jailer brought in Miguel Gutiérrez, shackled and handcuffed, wearing a bright orange jumpsuit. His arm was still in a sling from the gunshot wound at the Trauma Center, and he winced as the guard chained the handcuffs to a bar that ran the length of the metal interrogation table. Escobedo and Otto both pulled their chairs back away from the table several feet to signify that Josie was in charge.

Gutiérrez had been in custody for six days, and he appeared as if he had not eaten. His face was gaunt and ashen, his thick black hair brittle and dry. Slumped forward in his seat, he looked like an old man on the verge of dying.

"I came to fill you in on the latest bad news with your former family. As you might imagine, they want you dead. Three of them crossed the river illegally with a horse trailer filled with enough explosives to blow this jail sky high. Fortunately for you, we caught them at the river. You had a half ton of TNT designated specifically for you. Your uncle wants to blow your body parts all over West Texas," she said. "And that pisses me off to no end. That puts every employee in this jail in jeopardy every second you spend in my country."

She stood, knocking her chair over behind her, walked around the table, and punched Gutiérrez square in the jaw.

He slumped back, but the handcuffs held him in his seat. Once he'd recovered, he pulled himself upright in his chair, his expression shocked and angry, his face finally animated. He looked from Otto to Escobedo, who turned their heads in unison away from the table.

Josie hit him again, but he ducked and the punch landed across the top of his head. The handcuffs slid across the metal bar as he tried to cover himself. He screamed for a guard, and Josie scowled at him.

"Look around. See any cameras? Any two-way glass? We're soundproof and secure. The jail is made for guys like you. I could beat the life out of you and claim a pretty hefty bounty. I'd be a hero to the Bishop himself."

Gutiérrez leaned away from Josie, who stood directly over him.

"The way I see it, you have one chance at making it through this mess. You can't go back to Mexico. You'd be dead by nightfall. You can't stay here. Your only chance is a transfer to solitary maximum security."

His eyes widened, and he looked to Otto and Escobedo as if they might be ready to escort him out of the jail.

Josie pointed to Escobedo. "This is Warden Escobedo of the federal penitentiary in Houston."

Escobedo nodded. He was wearing a navy suit, white shirt, and red tie with a flag tie pin: polished, neat, and trim. He leaned back in his chair, crossed his arms over his chest, and stared at Gutiérrez. "We need a reason to get you out of here. We need an actual attempt on your life before the prison system will make the move."

His eyes wide, Gutiérrez pointed at Josie. "She just said those explosives were aimed for me!"

Escobedo rubbed at his jaw. "Trouble is, we can't prove that load was intended for you. We suspect it, but that's not the same as proof. See what I'm getting at?"

Gutiérrez looked confused and desperate. Escobedo's story was just that: a story. They had already arranged transport for all four prisoners, but they hoped to use Gutiérrez's knowledge of the Medrano cartel in the process.

"Here's what we do, then." Escobedo went on, "You work for me. I'll bend the rules to get you out of here."

Gutiérrez's expression changed. He looked expectantly to Escobedo, who now appeared to hold the keys to his life. "Tell me what you want."

Josie said, "You're going to pretend to be a Medrano today."

Hack Bloster received the cell phone call from underneath his pickup truck, where he was draining oil into a metal bucket. He continued unscrewing the bolt on the oil pan and fished his phone out from his shirt pocket with his free hand. The male voice on the other line said nothing more than, "Landline in ten minutes." Bloster flipped the phone shut and laid his head back on the concrete floor. It was the code phrase. It was the Medranos, and they wanted to deal. He had hoped the phone calls would end after Red's death.

He watched the black oil flow and remembered being stretched out with his dad under his first car. He wondered how his life had spun so far out of control. Five years ago, he had been a man with a clear sense of right and wrong: someone who acted morally, regardless the consequences. He had been proud to wear the badge, but he never allowed a rule book or code to keep him from doing the right thing. It was why he had joined the Gunners. Rules and laws were not keeping the border safe. Guns and people would see to that. He had personally vowed it.

Then Red came to him with a business proposition. He had a contact, a broker, who needed someone on the border to make a quick exchange of guns for money. Red started out as the mule, moving the guns from a contact in New Orleans to an unnamed runner

from Mexico who met him once every two weeks to receive a shipment. Eventually, Red figured out what the New Orleans dealer was
selling, and figured out he could buy off the Internet and sell even
cheaper, so Red broke from the supplier to start his own business. It
was at this point that Red involved Bloster. Red needed someone to
help him buy the weapons; he didn't have enough experience and
knowledge about the computer and Internet sales and auctions to get
the best deals. Bloster had developed the Web site for the Gunners.
He was a natural partner.

The profit was more than Hack had ever dreamed he was capable
of making, and in the beginning, the end user was nameless. He
hadn't even known Red was working with the Mexicans at first. By
the time Bloster discovered how involved Red was with Medrano, it
was too late to pull out. He was a partner, a very well paid one. But it
didn't mean that he supported the idea that the Gunners were now in
partnership with a cartel. He had never intended for Medrano to
have any association with Artemis. The cartel had been looking for a
safe route into the country, and Red had provided it right through his
front yard.

Bloster wiped his hands on a shop rag and answered the secure
phone on his kitchen counter. Bloster knew how easy it was to trace
cell phone calls, so he talked business only on a landline. His mouth
was so dry, he could barely speak.

"We got business, Mr. Bloster. You ready to do some business?"

His hands grew sweaty. "I don't owe you anything. We got all
deals squared up. You got your last shipment and we're done."

The man laughed. "You telling me we're done? You think it works
like that?"

"Red's dead."

"So what? No, we're not done until I say so. Understood?"

Bloster stared at the .38 on the kitchen table and considered
putting it to his temple. There would be no doubt in the bastard's
head that it was over then. No chance his mother and sister would

be impacted by the evil that surrounded him on all sides. Bullet to the head. Just like Red.

"Fifty thousand dollars per man, Mr. Bloster. Four prisoners? Two hundred thousand dollars. You release them, stage a breakout, lose the key, I could not care less. Tonight, before midnight. No later. I won't discuss consequences, but they won't be good if the job isn't done."

Bloster felt the acid in his stomach rising to his throat. "The jail is too secure."

"Figure it out. A white nine-passenger van will be located behind the jail by eight o'clock this evening. A driver will be in the back. It's already received clearance from the jail. You get the prisoners to that van by midnight tonight, and you're a wealthy man."

Gutiérrez was escorted back to his cell by a sheriff's deputy. Otto, Josie, and Escobedo remained in the conference room.

After the door shut, Josie leaned against the wall, bent over at the waist, and stretched her fingers toward the floor. Her back cracked and the relief was instant. She stood and unhooked her five-pound gun belt, then laid it on the table, her attention on Escobedo.

"I don't feel good about this," she said. "We're setting up a sting in the sheriff's jail without informing him. He'll be furious, and I don't blame him."

"You don't worry about Martínez," Escobedo said. "This isn't about a courtesy call; it's about saving lives. I've got two case agents on their way. From here out, I take over. It'll keep you out of hot water with the locals."

Josie narrowed her eyes at Escobedo, annoyed at his condescension. "You know me better than that. I didn't call you to get cut out of the investigation. I don't make decisions based on how much hot water I might get in. I've worked hard to see Hack Bloster in handcuffs."

"This is a federal investigation. I'm looking at a law officer who sold guns illegally across a national border. He's in serious trouble, and I suspect your mayor is culpable as well. You have too much on the line to let emotion get involved."

Josie's face flushed. She knew she could be called a lot of things; emotional was not usually one of them.

"I'm not asking to be there when you take him in, but I've got knowledge of this jail, of operating procedures."

Otto cleared his throat to cut her off, and gave her a single shake of his head. He obviously thought she was pushing too hard. She looked away and said no more, angry that she hadn't set up parameters with Escobedo when she called him. The loss of control was always the risk in calling in other agencies. Bottom line, the feds held the trump card.

Josie and Otto left the jail, basically dismissed from the investigation. They walked outside into the warm evening air, and Josie let out a long sigh. Otto said he would follow her home.

"What for?"

"So you can pack a bag. One night, Josie. Stay at our house until those prisoners are out of our jail."

Josie stood at her car and closed her eyes, so tired, she could have laid her head against the door and slept. "I'm going home. I'm tired. I'm angry, and I hate the world right now. I'm in no shape to see Delores."

"Delores doesn't care about your mental shape."

"No, Otto. Thank you, but no."

"Damn it! You're acting irrationally. Stop playing the martyr! Does this really prove you're tougher than them? That you can't be bullied?"

"It doesn't prove anything! They have invaded my home, shot up my bedroom, and could have killed the man I love. If I don't fight back now, I lose all self-respect." She lowered her voice, the fight gone out of her. "And at this point, that's about all I have left."

At sunset, Josie left her house to walk Chester back to Dell's place. Following the dog's meandering path, she watched him sniff and ignore a hundred different scents. She searched the sky, hoping to catch a glimpse of a pair of aplomado falcons Dell claimed were nesting on the property. She'd been searching unsuccessfully for several months. She tried to turn her focus outward, to get out of her own head, but the tension and anger that pulled at her muscles did not ease on the walk.

Dell immediately recognized the look on her face when she approached him outside his barn. "Trouble?" he asked.

"I need you to keep Chester tonight."

"You staying at your cop friend's house tonight?"

"Most likely."

"Liars go the same place as thieves."

She smiled. "For a person who has no family around here, I sure have a lot of people giving me advice on what I need to do." Dell said nothing, just stared at her patiently and waited for her to come clean. "I'm going to the watchtower. I'll be able to see our houses as well as the crossing the Medranos have been using across the river. If they so much as approach my house . . ." She let the thought hang in the air.

A strong gust of wind blew dirt around their feet, and a layer of dust she had heard called sand-flour coated her skin and the inside of her nose. Dell covered his nose with the crook of his arm and closed his eyes for a few seconds until it passed. The blistering heat of the day had mixed with a dry border wind from the south. The southern winds stirred up occasional dust storms in West Texas that would reduce visibility to nothing. The monsoon season, which usually ran from June 15 through September 30, still had not materialized, and the threat of dust storms was a weekly occurrence. The July wind was capable of stirring up fine sand particles that hung in the air and formed whirlwinds that tore across the desert, infiltrating every crack and crevice.

Josie looked at the strip of orange and red that spread across the horizon. "I want my town back," she said. "I want my life back to normal. I want to clock off at four and take a hike in the evening with Chester. I want to quit worrying all the time about men who slink around our land at night with AK-47s slung over their shoulders."

Dell snapped his fingers. "Give me ten minutes. I got a brisket in the fridge from last night. I'll pack us a sandwich and grab my guns and my bedroll."

After a halfhearted argument, Josie finally agreed to put the dog in Dell's house and set up observation at the tower with Dell. Technically, she wasn't on duty, and she could use the company. And she knew what *grab my guns* meant; he had a small arsenal he kept packed and at the ready in an old duffel bag that remained by his nightstand. He also smoked the best brisket in all of West Texas.

Josie changed into a pair of jeans and a black T-shirt and her uniform boots. Her badge was in her back pocket, and her ankle holster was strapped into place. Like Dell, she had packed her own arsenal in an Eddie Bauer duffel bag that Dillon had bought her for her birthday last year. They'd used it for camping gear during a weeklong hike through Big Bend National Park, a trip that was a buried memory for now, one she refused to dig up.

At about six o'clock, Josie and Dell loaded up her jeep and drove the three-mile stretch of gravel road to the watchtower. Josie evened out her backpack, bedroll, and duffel bag on her shoulders and back and started the climb. She kept an eye over her shoulder at Dell, who kept up with no problem, in better shape than most men she knew. Once on the observation deck, they both dropped their loads and leaned over the railing outside, enjoying the view as the burn in their legs subsided.

Josie opened two folding chairs on the deck while Dell carved up the brisket onto tin camping plates from his duffel bag. She contributed a pull-top can of fruit cocktail and convinced Dell to give it a heavy dollop of Tabasco sauce. Leaned back in their chairs, feet propped on the deck rail, they ate the brisket with chewy pieces of French bread they used to wipe up the leftover sauce on their plates. Glad for Dell's quiet company, she checked for messages and put her cell phone on vibrate in her pocket. Otto had called earlier to ask her one more time to spend the evening with them and had seemed genuinely happy that she was outside the house with Dell for the night.

Josie had set her cell phone's alarm clock for five in the morning to give her time to get home and shower before her morning shift. Warden Escobedo had promised to call when something broke loose at the jail, but she wasn't sure how much longer she could wait before placing the call herself. He had said he wanted the transport ready by 8 P.M., another hour. She felt the heavy thump of her heart pressing against her chest.

After she and Dell finished dinner and laid out their bedrolls on cots in the lookout room, they settled back into their chairs on the observation deck to watch for movement along the Rio to the south. Josie filled Dell in on the current drama, including the threat by Medrano to blow her house up if she didn't release the prisoners by tonight at midnight, and the probable gun connection with Red, Bloster, and the Gunners.

"It's guys like Bloster and Red you have to keep an eye on. Any man that has to join a club to protect his house or prove his manhood is a weak imitation. I don't need a club to keep people off my land."

"Who do you think killed Red?" Josie asked.

"That's just the problem. Those gun nuts get so paranoid, they think the whole world is out to get them, when in reality, ninety-nine percent of us couldn't give a rat hole less what they do in their little meetings. In the end, usually turns out to be one of their own that punches their clock, leaving the rest of us shaking our heads."

Dell had turned his chair to face north and was sighting down the barrel of his shotgun toward Josie's house. He tapped her on the thigh with the gun barrel to make a point he had made a hundred times.

"A man loses his common sense, his ability to think rationally, he loses his ability to survive. And, what's the number one rule of the desert?" he asked.

"Survival of the fittest."

"That's why the good guys will always have the advantage."

THIRTEEN

Pegasus Winning stood in the stockroom in the back of Value Gas, sneaking a cigarette. She was the only employee on duty, and the store and lot were currently empty. From her vantage point, looking out the square window in the stockroom door, she had a clear shot to the front entrance. It wasn't even eight o'clock, and she didn't get off until two in the morning. She was bored out of her mind and had already restocked the chips, her only chore for the night, outside of running the register and locking up. Sundays were torture.

She had time to finish two cigarettes before she heard the buzz of the front door and saw her brother lope inside. He scoped out the aisles and walked the perimeter of the store, looking for either Pegasus or trouble, probably both.

"Hey," she called, stubbing out her cigarette on the stockroom floor.

"You here by yourself?" he asked.

She nodded and walked to the front of the store to stand behind the register. He followed and threw a bag of cookies and a pack of gum on the counter. She thought he looked tense.

"I'm taking off soon. I'll try and stop by tomorrow. Just in case, though, I wanted to let you know. Tell you to watch your back. Be safe. Remember to knock the safety off if you have to use it." He smiled, a half grin, and chucked her on the chin. "Be careful, sis."

She didn't speak. She could not force the words out, so she just smiled and nodded her head at his back as he turned from her. He didn't do good-byes, and his effort to see her now made her nervous. She usually found out he was leaving through a note or phone call after the fact. She watched his car pull out of the lot, and the loneliness felt like a thousand pinpricks through her heart.

The tears had just begun to roll when a sheriff's deputy walked into the store. He glanced at her and then gave her a second look as if assessing the situation. She wiped her tears off with the backs of her hands and sniffed to stifle the flow. The cop walked quickly around the store, as if he wanted something specific but couldn't find it. He didn't bother to ask questions, and she didn't offer to help. He finally grabbed a Mountain Dew and set it on the counter.

He pulled his wallet out of his back pocket and stared down as if he couldn't believe what he saw. "Son of a bitch."

"No money?" she asked.

"What a day."

"What a life," she said.

He shook his head and smirked as if understanding completely.

"Just take it," she said. "Pay me back another day."

He started to protest, but she scooted the Mountain Dew across the counter toward him. "You're good for it, right?"

Hack Bloster sat in his squad car and twisted the plastic cap. He stared at the girl behind the counter through the window. He had almost refused a dollar-and-fifty-cent soft drink because it felt too much like stealing, yet he was headed to work to break four murderers out of jail in exchange for money. What had happened to him? He stared at the girl, remembering the tears running down her face when he walked into the gas station, and he wondered if it was too late to change things.

Warden Escobedo had called Sheriff Martínez and filled him in on the setup at his jail. Josie had been right about Martínez: he needed to know what was happening at his jail, not because of misguided interoffice courtesy, but because he could make an off-duty stop at the jail and blow the entire operation wide open. At this point, if Martínez did anything to sabotage the operation, he effectively implicated himself as well as Bloster. Martínez was instructed to remain at home and talk to no one until he received further notice. Escobedo knew the sheriff was furious at being ordered to stay away from his own jail, but he was respectful and agreed to the terms.

Two local employees, jailers Maria Santiago and Dooley Thomas, were on duty inside the jail that night. Escobedo had already briefed both of them on their roles, the confidential nature of the prisoner transfer, and the volatile, life-threatening situation they were facing that night. After talking with them, he felt confident that both would handle their roles professionally.

Escobedo was sitting in the white prisoner transport van waiting on Bloster to make contact. Escobedo had changed out of his suit and dressed in a jailer's uniform from the federal prison in Houston. When the National Guard caravan drove past the jail and continued on another mile to Main Street, he pulled binoculars out of the glove compartment and watched a man dressed in black jeans, cowboy boots, and a denim-style shirt riding a white Harley Davidson Super Glide escort the unit around the courthouse square. Escobedo watched in amazement as the caravan of four Humvees and two covered trucks wrapped the block twice like a parade route with the man waving to the pedestrians like a grand marshal.

He hadn't planned on the addition of the National Guard to the equation and had no idea how they would fit into the scenario, or if they were staying around the courthouse or moving in around the jail. Escobedo called Sheriff Martínez's cell phone.

"Why didn't you tell me you had National Guard troops arriving tonight?" Escobedo yelled.

"What are you talking about?" Martínez asked.

"It's like a city parade around the courthouse. Some crackpot on a white Harley is leading them around the block, waving."

"That's Mayor Moss."

"The streets are filling up. People are cheering on the guardsmen," Escobedo said, reaffirming his hatred for small towns, confirming his love for Houston. "Do they not realize the guard is here to protect them from mass murder?"

"Last word I heard from the mayor was that the guard was on hold until further notice. Let me give him a call and—"

Escobedo cut him off. "You don't call anyone. The only phone call you answer is from this cell phone. Understood?"

Escobedo noticed the hesitation before Martínez answered, "Yes, sir."

Bloster parked his cruiser behind the jail as a white transport van pulled in the back lot and drove toward the prisoner transport area. All the pieces were fitting together, which did nothing to calm his nerves.

He watched the continuing parade of National Guard trucks file around the courthouse. They added yet another variable to a night full of them. He worried some of the guard members might fan out to check the area and question him about his purpose, but as a deputy, he should be in the clear.

He shut his car door and felt as if every eye in Artemis were trained on him, his hypocrisy laid bare for the world to witness. He had reached the lowest point in his life, and he imagined his deceit and dishonor glowed from his skin like radiation.

After being buzzed into the jail, he signed his name on the sign-in clipboard Maria handed him and asked how she was doing.

"Not bad," she said. "You doing okay?"

"Not so good. I had a shift change. Wasn't supposed to work tonight."

"It's no good coming in on a day off," she said, and turned back to her paperwork.

"I got assigned the prisoners. I'll be organizing transport later this evening. The sheriff asked if I'd take care of this. I'll get the paperwork all filled out and get it back to you before I go." With his nerve endings on fire, he shut his mouth, aware he was explaining too much.

"No problem. We're down a man tonight, and I'm stuck here at the desk." Usually cheerful and talkative, she seemed busy and pre-occupied.

He looked down at the clipboard in his hand. "What's going on with the National Guard?"

"I'm not sure. I guess the mayor organized it."

"Are they stationed outside, or are they coming inside the jail?" he asked.

"No one told me anything," she said.

Bloster nodded and wondered at her attitude. She was usually one of the friendliest employees at the jail. He hoped he was just being paranoid.

"Can you buzz me back? I need to check in with the guard about the transport."

Maria buzzed him through to the center of the jail, where the inmate pods were located. As the door locked behind him, Bloster slowed his breathing and took measured steps down the short hallway. He pressed a red button on the wall, and Maria buzzed him into the day space.

Just inside the door, Dooley, the day-shift guard, sat at a desk, watching three inmates who were lounging at a metal table, watching a TV on the wall. Dooley was a giant man who barely fit into the folding chair he sat in.

Seeing Dooley at the guard desk caught Bloster by surprise. "How come they have you working night shift?"

"Sheriff called me in tonight."

Bloster broke out into a cold sweat. He had told Maria the sheriff had also called him in, which was a lie. What if Dooley and Maria talked and decided to call the sheriff to check on the schedule mix-up? If everyone remained quiet tonight, Bloster knew he could cover his schedule with the sheriff and explain it as a mistake.

"You here to cover me for supper break?" Dooley asked.

Bloster was starting to panic. He needed time to sit down and work through his plan again. He had to check in with the transport driver first and make sure it was set up as a legitimate prisoner transfer.

"Give me ten minutes to run an errand," Bloster said. "I'll be right back." He pressed the intercom. "Maria? I need back through again. Then I'll relieve Dooley for supper break."

The door buzzed and the lock clicked loudly. Bloster maneuvered through the series of locked doors, with each step expecting disaster.

Once outside, he felt a rush of adrenaline and a tinge of hope that he might actually accomplish the prisoner exchange without becoming one himself. He avoided eye contact with the guardsmen, now standing outside their trucks and talking in small groups in front of the jail. Bloster took the sidewalk beside the brick building to the back parking area, where the van and his own patrol car were parked.

The driver of the van wasn't in the driver's seat, but his head appeared after Bloster knocked on the window. The van was running and the driver lowered the window. He was a middle-aged man dressed in the uniform worn by jailers at the federal penitentiary. Bloster had never been to the jail, but he recognized the federal patch below the man's name on his pocket.

"You here for the prisoner transport?" Bloster asked, his blood pounding like a hammer in his head.

"You got four for me to take back?"

"Yes, sir."

The driver passed Bloster paperwork through the window, and he was shocked to see that it appeared legitimate, with signatures and times and the names of the prisoners. With the paperwork in his hand, Bloster realized he was making what would look like a legitimate transfer. He couldn't believe the Mexicans had that kind of access to the inner workings of their prison system, but at that point, he was glad they did.

"You need help with the prisoners?" the driver asked.

Bloster said no, that he would bring them out to the loading dock on the basketball court. He had started to walk away when the driver called him back to the van.

"Let's do this now before the prisoners are out here," the man said. He reached down between the driver and passenger seats and picked up a briefcase, which he laid on his lap. He flipped the latch and opened the case to reveal stacks of twenty-, fifty-, and hundred-dollar bills.

"You want to count these?" the driver asked.

Bloster shook his head and attempted to keep his paranoia in check, forcing himself to face the driver and not look over his shoulder.

"You get all four prisoners in the van, I give you the case, and I'm out of here. I don't like that convoy of National Guard sitting out front. The faster we get out of here, the better."

"What happens to me when it's discovered these prisoners were never received in Houston?"

"The paperwork is done. As far as your jail is concerned, the prisoners were taken as planned. These men get erased from the system, and you made a good day's wages."

Bloster directed the driver to pull the van to the gym entrance, where a large garage door would open via Maria in the central hub. The van entered, the door was shut again, and the basketball court was secure now for a prisoner exchange. The van turned around and backed up to the only entrance to the jail from the court while Bloster went back around the front. Maria buzzed him in, and he moved directly to the pod of prisoners again. Dooley, who was supposed to get off for supper, grumbled, but he helped Bloster handcuff the first three prisoners.

Dooley asked Bloster, "Does that driver know he'll be taking rival gang members?"

Bloster looked at him blankly. He felt as if his brain could not process any new information.

"These three are from the Medrano cartel. They were the three that crossed the border to blow this one out of jail." Dooley turned and pointed to a prison cell behind him, where Gutiérrez stood watching from behind the bars. "I figured they'd send two vans. One for these three, and one for the La Bestia dirtbag behind us."

Bloster could think of nothing to say. He just knew he needed all four prisoners out of the jail by midnight. "Let's get these three loaded. We'll get their hands and feet locked into the bars on the van. They should be safe enough."

Dooley raised an eyebrow and shook his head. "Whatever."

Each of the three prisoners' hands was handcuffed separately to a bar behind their lower backs. Each of their feet was shackled in a similar manner to the floor of the van, and a chain was wrapped around their waists like a belt and attached to another hook behind their backs. Under some circumstances, Bloster would have thought the setup was overkill. Tonight, he thought it was a good idea. Bloster didn't know what might be in store for the four prisoners, but he suspected Gutiérrez was in trouble.

Back at the cell, Dooley held his nightstick in one hand and the handcuffs in another as Bloster unlocked the cell door. Dooley rocked back on his heels, jutting his large stomach out farther and tapped his nightstick on his palm, letting the handcuffs dangle from his finger.

As the door opened, Gutiérrez moved to the back of his cell, his face stricken. "You can't take me with them! They'll kill me!"

Dooley smiled at Bloster. "Get a load a this. This guy thinks it's okay for him to kill people, but it's not okay for people to kill *him*. He didn't watch *Sesame Street* when he was little."

Bloster ignored Dooley and turned Gutiérrez around, twisting his arm in the sling until he cried out in pain. Bloster gritted his teeth and snapped the cuffs on. Finally in enough pain, Gutiérrez submitted to Bloster and Dooley and made the trek to the transport van, walking between the two of them.

The driver was standing at the back of the van, guarding the three prisoners when Bloster opened the side door and pushed Gutiérrez in, locking his hands and feet to the bars. He faced forward, and the three prisoners behind him immediately started with barbs, spoken in Spanish, but the intent was clear. It would be a long ride for all of them.

Bloster had no idea who the driver of the van was or how he had obtained federal papers, but the way Bloster saw it, he was in the clear. If he was questioned by Sheriff Martínez, he would say the feds called him, stating he needed to come into work to take care of the prisoners, the paperwork was in order, and he had followed orders. The whole transaction took less than an hour, and aside from the suitcase of money, it felt like a dozen other transports he had worked over the past few years. He could not believe his luck.

By eight thirty, Josie had paced around the perimeter of the observation deck a dozen times. There had been no movement toward her house, and Scratchgravel Road was empty. Dell had asked Josie if she'd considered what kind of retaliation she might receive when Medrano discovered the prisoners were released but moved to a maximum-security prison. She had no answer, though she thought of little else.

At 8:45 P.M., Josie noticed a line of four cars on the Mexican side heading westbound toward the access road along the Rio. She pointed them out to Dell, who was already standing up from his chair.

"They're headed toward Flat Rock," Josie said.

"Can they get those cars through the river?"

"It's wide and shallow enough. That's how they've been crossing."

"Wouldn't you think they'd realize police and Border Patrol use this tower to watch them?" he asked.

"Imagine how many times they've crossed unnoticed. We use this only when we have confirmed suspicions. We don't have enough manpower to make good use of it."

They watched the first car make a turn at the river, and there was no doubt about their intent.

"That's it. Let's head out before we lose them," she said.

Dell's duffel bag was already packed back up, and he slung it over his shoulder and took off down the steps. Josie threw both guns in her bag and followed Dell. About twenty feet from the bottom, her cell phone vibrated. She slowed, fished it out of her shirt pocket, and answered, hanging on to the stair railing with her other hand and feeling for the dark steps below with her foot.

"This is Escobedo. Everything is in place. Bloster's in the jail preparing the prisoners. We should be on the road within fifteen minutes. He's seen the money. I've got two agents outside ready to make the arrest once he takes possession."

Josie blew air out. "We have trouble. I'm at the watchtower. I just watched one of four cars cross the access point they've been using on the river." Josie heard a string of profanity and went on. "I'm just getting off the tower. I've lost the visual, but I hear them. They're northbound on River Road, headed toward town."

"So they're either illegals, or Medrano's clan come to break the prisoners free," Escobedo said. "Call me back when you're on the road and have a visual."

"This isn't a transport of illegals. They don't work this way. Not out in the open with this many cars together. We need to prepare for the worst."

"Bloster's coming out the door now. How far away are you from the jail?"

"Fifteen minutes."

"Get DPS and Border Patrol on the phone to work with local dispatch. I've got to square up with Bloster and get on the road. I don't want a shoot-out at the jail. I want as many patrol units as you can find to escort this van out of town and stop those cars. Just keep the sheriff's department out of it."

Within minutes, Josie had caught up with the four cars and made visual contact. Dell was sitting quietly in the passenger seat beside her, but she knew he was watching for anything that could cause them problems.

She called Escobedo back to confirm she had them in her sights; his phone went to voice mail. They were driving the speed limit, and Josie hung back a safe distance with the headlights on her car still off. The moon and a sky full of stars provided just enough light for her to see the road.

Josie and Dell both rolled their windows up as dust started to fill the car. Josie's eyes had begun to water and her throat felt caked with dirt.

Dell pointed out the front windshield. "Look how much the wind has picked up just since we were on the tower. I can see the dust swirls on the highway even in the dark."

Josie said, "I think Escobedo is making a big mistake, Dell. There's no way you and I can pull over four cars, but if we called in the sheriff's department right now, we might get lucky. We need these cars stopped before they reach that van. We just don't have enough manpower."

"Was that a direct order?" Dell asked. "Can you call the Sheriff's men in yourself?"

Josie gripped the steering wheel, realizing every second counted against them. "It was an order. I can't even call the Guard out, because I can't reach Moss. We better get some help soon or we'll all end up dead."

Bloster locked the last prisoner's handcuffs to the handrail in front of his seat in the transport van. He was sweating, his heart racing. He was about to accept two hundred thousand dollars and had to make the decision to trust the process the driver had explained, or to leave his home tonight and start a new life in Mexico.

The driver called Bloster to the front of the van, where the man once again presented the briefcase. Bloster nodded, took the case, and walked toward his patrol car in the back of the employee parking lot, trying to keep from running.

As he reached his car, two men in navy suits exited a dark gray Crown Victoria parked three cars away from his patrol car.

The taller man stopped walking and pointed a gun directly at him. "I'm Detective Marcus Hammond with the Federal Bureau of Investigation. This is my partner, Bill Smithers. You are under arrest. Set the case on the ground and raise both hands in the air."

The shorter of the two men wore a grim expression and continued toward Bloster with his badge held up for Bloster to inspect. Bloster saw the driver of the van standing in the parking lot, taking pictures.

Bloster looked back at the agent.

"Put the case on the ground and raise your hands in the air. Now!"

His hands were numb, his body in shock. He slowly sat the case down beside him. What he had taken for luck was a setup by the feds. He noticed several National Guardsmen across the street watching his arrest and feared he might vomit.

The shorter agent took the case and walked away while the taller man cuffed Bloster and turned him around toward the van. The agent read the list of crimes he was being charged with and mirandized him as he watched the driver enter the van with the prisoners and drive off. Bloster realized he had just prepared an actual transport for the feds. That was why it had looked legitimate. Because it was.

Josie was driving sixty miles per hour in the dark with her lights off on a road that was paved but pockmarked and washed out down to gravel in some areas. She was three miles from the courthouse in Artemis when Escobedo reached her on his cell phone and said he had just pulled out from the jail.

"The four cars are probably five minutes from you. They have to have a lookout posted next to the jail, watching for the transport van," she said.

"I just hope it wasn't someone in the sheriff's department."

Josie blew air out in frustration. She thought he was wrong about Sheriff Martínez being involved.

"I think we need the sheriff's men out here. We can't handle four cars," Josie said.

"Absolutely not. There's too many unknowns with him. You've got DPS and Border Patrol on their way. Correct?"

"I'm afraid they won't make it in time. If you stay on River Road, you're about thirty minutes from Highway 67. We need to get these cars stopped before we reach the highway. Are you familiar with the Arroyo Pass?"

"I've taken it a few times," he said.

"You think your van could make it?"

The Arroyo Pass was a dry gully that could flow like the Nile during heavy rains and flash flooding. It led from River Road in Artemis to Highway 67, and cut off about ten minutes of drive time. The dirt road was no problem for the locals, but it was rough without four-wheel drive, and the blowing dust would make it harder to navigate at night.

"I don't know. These vans are about worthless on anything but paved road."

"The arroyo has quite a bit of rock in the bottom of it," Josie said. "I think you'd be okay. And it might throw the Mexicans off your trail."

"Might be worth the risk," he said, his tone doubtful.

"We'd be isolated if things turn bad. If you made it all the way to the highway before Medrano's men caught up to you, we'd be home free," Josie said.

"I can make it. Get dispatch to set up a roadblock before we reach 67. Call Presidio PD and see if they can send officers. We need every car they can find. I've got only one deputy with me in the back with the prisoners. Any idea how many people are in the cars?" he asked.

"I can't tell. I'm about a half mile from them. When we drive through Artemis, I'll catch up and scope them out under the street-lights in town."

She shut her cell phone and gave Dell the phone number to the police station.

"Call Lou and have her tell Otto and Marta we need them at the Arroyo immediately."

Josie called Don Steele, the Presidio chief of police. He said he had one car already on 67. He promised two more units within ten minutes. Lou, over at dispatch, signaled Josie on her portable radio and said DPS and Border Patrol were en route to destination, but she couldn't tell Josie how many cars or how soon.

River Road passed through the center of Artemis, directly past the jail, and connected with the Arroyo two miles out. Escobedo called and said he had turned off, and the dust and wind were causing poor visibility. He was worried about staying on the road.

Josie pulled behind the four vehicles at the lone red light in downtown Artemis. Under the streetlights, she discovered each of the cars appeared to carry at least four men.

She told Escobedo, "We're talking at least sixteen men, most likely armed, coming up against three officers," she said.

"I hope we didn't make a mistake coming down this pass. I'll check back in. I need to focus on the road. The wind is really picking up." Escobedo, clearly unnerved, disconnected again.

Dell unzipped the duffel bag on his lap. "Count me in as a fourth, Josie."

"You can't use those guns. You'll end up in jail over a fight that's not yours. Just stay in the car and cover me if things go wrong."

Josie could feel Dell staring at her from the passenger seat. "The last standoff with the explosives? They lost that round. Those boys don't intend to lose this one. You better use every resource you have."

Josie's stomach was on fire. It would kill her if something happened to Dell. She never should have brought him with her.

Once through Artemis, the four cars picked up speed dramatically until they reached Arroyo Pass, then slowed down abruptly, trying to decide which route the van had taken.

The dust was blowing so heavily now that the van's tracks had vanished. Arroyo Pass was visible only because of the green sign that designated it a road. The pass was approximately twenty feet wide, and it ranged from three feet to about five feet deep, making it very hard to drive up and out of the arroyo once a car was in it. The bottom was covered with small rocks and sand, which Josie hoped would be easier for the larger van to navigate than the cars the Mexicans were driving.

Apparently familiar with the area, the two lead cars headed straight into the Arroyo and the two behind them veered off down Highway 67. Josie followed the cars down into the Arroyo, but within minutes, the other two cars had turned around and were behind her.

Josie was starting to panic. The red lights were barely visible in front of her now, and the white headlights were directly behind her. It was a terrible position to be in, sandwiched between the four cars. She had miscalculated.

"Hang on, Dell. None of them have four-wheel drive. I'm going to peel off and circle back behind them."

Josie heard Dell cock the gun he held. "Just give it plenty of gas or you'll slide backwards."

Josie cut a sharp right into the desert just ahead of where the arroyo cut deep into the earth. She shut her headlights off so the other cars wouldn't know her location. She knew the area well but inched forward, driving in complete darkness, turning her car to follow the brake lights of the others, barely visible in the blowing dust. The lights of the cars stopped, but she knew without four-wheel drive they could never make it up the embankment as she had. She wouldn't be followed, and for a moment felt relieved. Then she heard the gunfire.

"Get down!" she yelled to Dell.

Dell leaned below the dashboard, his hands covering his head.

Josie bent down as well and focused her attention on getting her tires to grab hold of something. She didn't dare drive straight into the desert, where the sand was hilly and treacherous. Without lights, she could easily flip her jeep. The gunfire faded as the cars took off again, struggling to keep up with Escobedo's van. They were obviously more interested in the prisoners than in her.

"Call Lou and find out where Otto and Marta are."

Josie turned her headlights back on and slowly drove over the edge of the embankment and down into the arroyo, the jeep rocking from side to side as it bottomed out. The red taillights were about fifty feet in front of her, and she turned on her flashing lights and turned her headlights on bright to disorient the driver in front of her. "This time, *they* made the mistake," she said.

Dell used his own cell phone to call Lou, who said Otto and Marta were both driving their jeeps and were both just entering the pass behind them.

"Let me talk to her."

Dell handed his phone to Josie.

"Lou, I need you to get the National Guard contacted. Tell them we need backup ASAP. We've got big problems. I tried to reach Moss several times, and he isn't answering. I can't wait on him to be the contact. You call and get them here now."

Her cell phone rang. It was Escobedo. "I can see their lights. They can't be more than half a mile from me."

Hearing the worry in his voice, she hesitated, and then explained they had already fired at her.

"Whatever you do, don't let them stop your van. You'll be a dead man. Lou just called and said Otto and Marta are both right behind us. In four-wheel drive, they ought to be up with us in three or four minutes," Josie said.

"I figure I've got about two miles before I'm at the highway. Presidio called and said they have four cars set in a roadblock with DPS and Border Patrol ETA in five minutes. Their cars are on Highway 67 headed south. The wind is blowing so bad, though; I can't even tell if I'm on the road or not anymore."

Josie heard gunshots, and Escobedo cried out. "They're hitting the back of the van!"

She tried to ignore his panic. "You have to stay in the pass no matter what! Keep pushing through. You'll be able to tell if you're veering off the pass. From where you are, there's about a three-foot incline on either side until you reach the highway."

He began to reply, but the gunshots were so loud, they distorted his voice. All she could hear was static. The line went dead.

Headlights appeared in her rearview mirror, and she called Otto. He confirmed he was behind her.

"They're shooting at Escobedo," she said. "I'm going to try and get up top and catch up to the lead car. I'll try and shoot out their tires. Be prepared if I do, though. They could come out shooting. Escobedo said he's only about two miles out, then we've got help from Presidio PD and hopefully Border Patrol."

"Get up top. I'll call Marta and tell her we've got the back two cars. Think you can take out both the lead and the second car?"

"I'll give it my best."

She put the jeep into low four-wheel drive and attempted the embankment to her right, having to take it at an angle instead of straight on, which would have been safer. Her front right tire spun and spit dirt. She stopped and backed up a few feet, taking the bank head-on. From behind her, Otto's headlights lit up the sandy bank, and she gunned her engine. The front tires lost contact with the bank and almost flipped the jeep backwards. Josie gave it full gas, and the back tires propelled them forward. She and Dell instinctively leaned toward the dash, trying to push the jeep up out of the pass by sheer will. The tail of the jeep spun left, then caught on a rock and spun them up onto the desert floor. The ground wasn't as sandy as the dunes, but it was strewn with rocks and boulders.

"Are you okay with using a gun as we drive?" she asked Dell.

"You bet," he said. He held a semiautomatic Luger up to show her.

Josie called Escobedo and was relieved to hear his voice. He said the lead car had slowed behind him, bogged down by the sand, but was still pushing forward.

She explained the plan to Escobedo as she drove around a boulder that was now surrounded by swells of dirt moving like ocean waves.

Escobedo yelled into the cell phone, "They've shot up the back of the van!"

Josie listened to static and commotion in the background for over a minute. Finally Escobedo came back on the line. "An officer in the back of the van said one of the prisoners was hit but he's alive. They don't dare stop me. They'd never get a car around the van. The road's not big enough. They're waiting for the Highway. You call me back when the lead car is stopped. I'll let you know as soon as we see the roadblock. I have to be close now."

Josie had turned her flashing lights off and was now making better time on top of the arroyo than the cars below her, which were bogged down in sand. She spotted the headlights of the lead car and second car as they bounced and swerved along the arroyo below her. Dell was a good shot, but the odds of him hitting the tires from a hundred feet in near brownout conditions were slim. Driving five miles per hour, Josie had about thirty feet of visibility.

Dell climbed into the backseat to use the driver's-side back window. The lead car was just in front of them to the left. It gave him a cleaner shot than sitting in the front passenger seat. Josie was worried about return gunfire and the possibility of the back two cars catching up with them.

"Are you set up yet?" she called back to Dell.

"I'm ready."

Her cell phone buzzed against her chest, and she answered. Otto said, "We got number three and four cars stopped! I got one tire on the number three, but it was enough to get them buried in the dirt. Marta left her jeep with her lights and siren on directly behind them. The National Guard knows her position. They're just a couple minutes behind but will provide backup. Marta is with me. We're coming on top of the arroyo, headed—" His voice cut out, and the call was dropped.

Josie shut her phone and hollered back to Dell. "The third and fourth cars are dead. Two left. Otto is coming up top." Her car was full of dirt and dust, and the wind howled through the window in the backseat, making conversation almost impossible.

She tried to steady her driving as much as possible. She was now five feet behind the lead car and about the same distance above it. The car was a dark brown lowrider Mercury. The second car was within ten feet of the first. She could see Escobedo's brake lights just ahead. Her fear was that once Dell started shooting and the Mexicans discovered her location, they would fire back and it would escalate into full-on war.

Within a half-dozen shots, Dell had taken out the right rear tire and then shortly after hit the front window on the passenger side, blowing out the glass. Once the car stopped, the driver immediately turned his headlights off. The second car did the same.

"Way to go, Dell!" Josie shouted.

Her excitement was short lived as her right front tire got hung up on a large rock. Josie felt her jeep lurch forward and then stop. Gunshots were fired, and they felt bullets ring the back end of the jeep.

"We have to get out of here," Josie said. She shut the engine off, and she and Dell got out of the jeep and ran to the back for cover. It was pitch black except for the headlights of the car in the arroyo. Behind the jeep, Dell placed his duffel bag between them and they both huddled together, trying to block the sand from their faces.

"They could be circling around our car right now." Josie pointed into the darkness. "I don't want to get out in that dust storm, but we can't sit here."

Dell dug through his duffel bag and handed her a pair of goggles. He found another pair for himself. "I knew the way that wind was blowing earlier, this was coming. At least you'll keep the dirt out of your eyes."

Josie pointed behind Dell. "We passed a large boulder before the jeep got hung up. It's about fifteen feet back. Stay behind that boulder until backup gets here. I'll take cover on the other side of the jeep, where I can see their car."

Dell reached over and squeezed Josie's arm before she stood up. "You be careful out there."

Twenty feet away from the car, Josie crouched behind a large rock. From there, she could see both her police car and the car below in the arroyo. The second and third cars were both stopped now, unable to move between the car that Otto shot out and the car that Dell had disabled. Marta was parked in the pass. Josie and Otto were both parked on top. In order to keep from drawing fire, all the officers and Dell were now taking cover in the desert until the Guard arrived to light up the area. All four of the Medrano cars were empty. The cartel members were either hunkered down in the desert as well, possibly waiting for reinforcements, or had already taken off on foot. The standoff had reached a critical impasse.

FOURTEEN

By choice, Dell lived a solitary life. He wanted no part of the wives and kids and friends that settled over middle-aged men like a shroud. He was mostly a silent man who preferred his own thoughts to those of the people around him. It wasn't that he found women mysterious or unapproachable; he thought they were a pain in the ass. They worried about handbags and fabric colors. Of late, he had noticed the disease spreading to the male species as well. And then Josie Gray, a kindred spirit, came along and he had let his guard down. She was the daughter he had never wanted; she was his friend. He was terrified for her safety and where she might be at that moment.

These thoughts cluttered up his mind and kept him from focusing on the pain in his knees as he crouched behind a boulder in the dark. The wind had grown fierce, and sand and debris pelted his face and arms, stinging like fire ants. His head was tucked down into his chest, and he felt guilty he wasn't guarding the car or keeping an eye out for the men who might have been circling around him in the dark while he hunkered down, Josie left unprotected.

But the exhaustion that had suddenly overtaken him was like nothing he had ever experienced. He lost track of time, not sure if it had been minutes or hours he had spent crouching in the dark, and eventually his thoughts whittled down to nothing more than the wind roaring through his brain and the endless whine of police sirens in the distance.

The surprise of being pulled to his feet was soon replaced with an intense, stabbing pain in his knees and feet as blood began to flow again to his extremities. His arms were wrenched behind his back, his hands tied roughly with rope. His goggles were covered with a thick layer of dust, so he couldn't see who had grabbed him, but he could hear at least two men speaking Spanish, hissing instructions at him that he couldn't understand.

Dell was shoved forward, and walked blindly with a man grasping his arm. He knew they were headed back toward the jeep because he could still sense the headlights from the Mexican car in the arroyo below him. The man holding his arm pulled Dell into his chest as if he might try to run and then stood motionless. Dell was certain they were taking him as a hostage in Josie's four-wheel-drive police car. He feared she had been killed.

Dell felt as if the air had been released from his lungs like a balloon deflating. His muscles felt limp and unresponsive, his resolve numbed. He had never been a man prone to fear; he prided himself on his ability to power through anything, but he no longer knew where he was. He had lost contact with Josie. He felt as if he was within moments of dying.

The gunshot paralyzed him when it came. Unable to move, he tried to feel where the shot had struck him, tried to feel the pain somewhere on his body. Then he felt movement down his back, felt something slide down his backside, and he realized that the man who had been holding him was slipping to the dirt. Two more shots fired, and Dell ducked to the ground himself, unhurt but trying to avoid the gunfire. He had no idea where the bullets were coming from, or whom they were intended for. As he waited for something to begin making sense again, an unbearable weariness overtook him and he dropped to the sand.

Dell woke to hands on him. He felt them pulling at his shirt, slapping at his cheeks, and then he felt the warmth of a face next to his own. Josie was calling his name. He sensed lights through his eyelids and tried to remember how to open his eyes, but he could not find the strength. He squeezed a hand he hoped was Josie's and blacked out.

Josie and four National Guard soldiers leaned across a backboard and held flashlights for the medic. The wind had died down to thirty-mile-an-hour gusts, but it still made viewing the equipment difficult. The medic and the soldiers strapped Dell onto the backboard and loaded him into the back of an EMS Humvee outfitted for desert travel.

Josie had known Dell's location and had looked in his direction frequently. When she saw the two Mexicans circling toward the car, she had intended to shoot before they ever reached Dell, but they moved too quickly, and she couldn't get off a shot. As the gunman stood with Dell clutched to his chest, waiting on the other man to turn the lights and sirens off, Josie had a clear shot to the man's head. Luckily, Dell had been slumped forward, weak from what the medic said was almost certainly a heart attack. It had been the most terrifying shot she had ever taken, but it hit her target. She then shot and killed the second man, too, as he exited her car. Otto and Marta were able to take another man into custody and wounded a second, but two others fled on foot.

Three of the National Guard units had made quick time down Arroyo Pass and caught up with Marta and Otto to help them stabilize their prisoners, then arrived at Josie's car as Josie fired her first shot. At the end of the pass, Presidio Police met Escobedo and the transport van and followed him to the interstate, where they escorted him to Houston. Four Border Patrol units arrived and made their way down the pass to where the lead car was located. They found six men hiding just outside the cars, who gave up without a fight. The Mexicans were clearly outnumbered at that point. A total of ten men were in custody, two were dead, one was injured, and it was suspected three additional men were at large on foot.

It was dawn before the wind died down enough for the Border Patrol helicopter to safely fly the area in search of the men who ran. After an hour in the air, the helicopter was called off for another emergency in El Paso. Josie sent Otto and Marta home at 4 A.M. and stayed until almost six, working out the messy details of an investigation among multiple agencies, determining with DPS, Border Patrol, and the Presidio Sheriff's Department who was responsible for the myriad details that could make or break a case against the men at trial.

Josie left the crime scene and drove straight to the Trauma Center. Vie Blessings was the ER nurse on duty and pulled Josie in for a hug. She whispered in Josie's ear, "Sweetheart, you deserve a big old bonus check after the week you've had."

Josie smiled and asked about Dell.

Vie took Josie's hand and led her down the hall. "It's best if I show you."

Josie followed Vie into one of the two overnight rooms and found Dell propped up in bed, scowling at a TV set hung on the wall across from his bed.

"You wonder why young people can't think anymore? Flip through this trash. Biggest bunch of drivel. It's a wonder people even got the common sense to get out of bed in the morning, watching this all day long."

Josie, wondering how nurses put up with old men like him, smiled as she approached his bed. "How you doing?" she asked.

"Are you serious? That old biddy Blessings thinks she can keep me in bed by locking up my pants and underwear, but she don't know me too well, does she?"

Josie winked. "I think you have a crush on Nurse Blessings."

"Don't give me any smart mouth."

"What did the doctor tell you?" she asked, bumping his feet over on the bed with her hip so she could sit at the end.

"You look like hell, girl. You need to go home and go to bed. I'm fine. Heart attack. No big surprise. They want to ship me to Houston for tests, but I put an end to that. No one's going to plug me into a machine to keep my ticker charged. If it runs out of juice, so be it."

She didn't even attempt getting into that pointless argument. "How long do they want to keep you?"

"I didn't listen. Go talk to that old prune. See if you can't work me a deal. I need to feed the horses."

At ten o'clock in the morning, Josie slumped on the couch and stared at Chester, who lay sleeping at her feet. She sipped at a tumbler of warm bourbon, her solace for a night that would keep her from sleeping for months to come. She had taken a shower and dressed in a nightshirt, but she knew sleep was a distant hope as she stared at the blank TV screen. She leaned her head back and felt the steady numbing of her body, her brain, the slowing of her senses, the heaviness of her eyelids, and she prayed for the deep uninterrupted sleep of the guiltless. She wanted to sleep like those uninitiated few who still believed in the inherent good of people. She stared at a long hairline crack in the ceiling above her that was lit by the harsh morning sunlight. She wondered if she believed in the inherent good of anyone anymore. Dillon was good, but she couldn't factor him in just now.

The hurt was too fresh. Otto and Delores were as good as any two people she knew, but she could tick off twelve others who were equally as bad, who given the choice would rather shoot you than shake your hand. Dillon had done nothing to deserve the dangers of the lifestyle she had chosen. He was a good man, and she had no right to drag him down the garbage-strewn path she had chosen to call a career.

Josie stood up and set the empty glass on the coffee table, the tumbler clicking too hard. The noise raised Chester's head from the floor in front of the front door. The old dog looked suddenly alert and ready to protect. She sat on the floor beside him and picked up the cell phone from the coffee table. The dog laid his head on her lap and fell back asleep within seconds. With a stomach sick with guilt and shame, she flipped her phone open and dialed Dillon's cell phone. After three rings, it went to voice mail. She hesitated and almost hung the phone up, but knew he would see the missed call anyway.

"Dillon, it's Josie. Hope you're doing okay. I know you're at work. I'm sorry to call you like this. I know I don't have the right. I just need you. I need a sane person to talk to."

Thirty minutes later, Josie had moved from the floor up to the couch again, unable to face her bedroom. Otto and Delores had cleaned it, swept the remnants of the attack from her room. Dell had come in and patched the holes in the walls while she was at work. But the white hot flash of the bullets, the flying debris, the threats, and the deafening sound of the guns played in a repeating loop in her mind. She could still smell cigarette smoke lingering in the air, and she wasn't sure she would ever be able to sleep in her bed again. Then she heard a car in front of her house. She didn't reach for the gun lying on the coffee table. She knew with certainty that Dillon, good caring man that he was, had come.

She held the door open for him and they stood awkwardly inside the living room for a moment. Dillon wore his office clothes, a navy suit and red tie, and stood with his hands in his front pants pockets.

"I appreciate you coming over like this," she said.

"I heard about the mess last night."

"I don't even know where to begin," she said. "It's like my brain has shut down on me."

"Come in the kitchen, and I'll make you a cup of hot tea," he said.

Several minutes later, he sat down across from her at the kitchen table with two hot mugs and tea bags.

"I want to do this job," she said, staring into her mug, "but I don't know if I have what it takes. I feel like the floodgates of Mexico are leaking and all their violence and chaos is about to flow into our country. And we're in the direct path. And by some bizarre twist of fate, I'm the one that's supposed to repair the crack. I know this is absurd, but in some ways, I feel like the security of this nation rests on my shoulders."

"Josie, the Mexican and United States governments can't figure out how to solve the problem. What in the world makes you think you can?"

"That's just it, though! No one gets it. It's like looking at those sad pictures of starving kids in Africa. They're disturbing to look at, the problem seems too big, but it's not in people's neighborhood, so they turn the page. They watch a thirty-second news blip on TV and figure they're informed. Unless you live with this fear every day, how can you know how serious it is?"

"So what now?"

She scowled and rubbed her temples. "I don't know. I care so much about this town and about this damned job, but it's destroying my life. I'm scared to sleep in my own bed. I can't walk my dog outside without worrying I'll be gunned down by some Mexican cartel. I feel like my life has spun completely out of control." She took a deep breath and folded her hands in front of her on the table. "Mostly, what bothers me is how much I need you, and I am so sorry that I've lost you."

He took a minute and seemed to be considering her words. She wondered if she had said too much.

"I've always been guarded with you because I didn't want to scare you off, or make you think I was pushing you into something you weren't ready for. I'm too tired for that anymore," he said.

She nodded, and he seemed to take it as the okay to continue.

"I love you, Josie. I've fallen in love with a cop. I didn't realize until the last couple of days just what that means to you. The day those gunmen came into your home and shot up your bedroom, I just couldn't wrap my head around the idea that you would willingly step back into that kind of danger again. It seemed like utter suicide to me, and I resented that. I resented that you cared more about your career than your life with me."

He paused, his eyes tired. He reached a hand across the table and placed it over both of hers. "I would have turned in my badge if I were you. But I thought about it. I'm an accountant; I'm not a cop. This is what you do, and I have to trust you can handle the job. That you'll be as safe as possible so you can come home at the end of the day."

She took one of her hands from under his and rubbed at her eyes. "I'm terrible at this. I don't even think I know what love is. I know I want it, and I know I've never cared for anyone like I care for you. Maybe that's what love is. I just feel like I don't deserve what you give me, and I have so little to give you in return. I felt lousy calling you this morning after what you've been through."

He smiled and leaned wearily back in his chair, rubbing both his hands over the top of his head, a move she had long ago recognized as a sign of frustration in him. "Your phone call was what I've been waiting on for months. Before today, you've never admitted you need anyone. It's not easy dating Superwoman. I have an ego, too."

She felt the air change as if a wire had snapped, releasing the tension in the room. "How many times can we start over?" she asked.

"I guess until we get it right."

After Dillon left, Josie slept on the couch for four dreamless hours and then dragged herself off the couch into a hot shower. She drove to town, forcing her eyes to stay open, and logged on for the four-thirty-to-midnight shift with Otto. She was at her desk when he entered the office. He looked as if he had gotten less sleep than she had.

"We're too old for this," he said, sitting down in his chair but facing Josie's desk rather than his own. "You get any sleep?"

"Couple hours. You?"

He tilted his head, noncommittal. "You staying at your place?"

"Yep."

"You need to set up some counseling for those shootings."

Josie gave her own noncommittal shrug.

"You can't kill three men, I don't care how justified they were, and not get some kind of mental issues from it. Delores said one of her friends has a son in Odessa who's supposed to be some kind of super shrink. Give him a call. Charge the bill to the mayor."

"If I need to talk, I'll talk to you. I don't want to talk about it with a stranger."

"I'm not going to let up on this one," he said.

"I have no doubt."

"You going to call the sheriff?" Otto asked, still facing Josie.

"About what?"

He didn't answer, just looked at her.

"What is this? Since when did you turn into my mother?"

"You'd feel better if you got the call over with. Put it out of your mind that way."

"Otto! Give me a break!" Josie faced her desk and turned her computer on to end the conversation. She knew she needed to make things right with Martínez. She hoped that he understood the position she had been in, but truth was, she'd be furious if roles had been reversed. He'd been refused access to his own jail while the city police and the feds took down one of his employees. She promised herself that she'd call later.

They both began the process of slogging through the phone calls and e-mails required of any major investigation with DPS and Border Patrol. The paperwork and documentation, especially with two homicides, would take days to complete. At five thirty, Lou buzzed Josie and told her Mayor Moss was on his way up to see her.

Otto smirked. "Think he's here to apologize for hanging you out to dry? Probably here to save his hind end before word gets out to his voters."

Moss flung the door open, knocking it against the wall, then faced Josie and Otto, hands on his hips. "I had the National Guard here! I had everything taken care of! You didn't have to lift a wretched finger, but you go and get the warden from the federal penitentiary involved. It was a complete embarrassment!"

Josie stared, too shocked to respond.

He pointed a finger at her. "This wasn't any of his concern. And who the hell gave you the authority to contact him behind my back?"

"You are way out of line," she said, her voice controlled.

His face grew redder, and he kicked the side of her metal desk. "I'll have your badge for this. You've got us plastered all over the news—again! Farmers sitting on top of their barns with shotguns one day. You killing Mexicans the next. It looks like I don't have any control over my own damned town!"

Josie took a deep breath and willed her blood flow to slow. "Let me tell you the way I see it."

Moss ignored her. "How do you expect me to keep this town afloat with this kind of publicity? I got the Town Council on my ass preaching about public relations, and I got you going behind my back starting a war with the Mexican cartels!"

"You had no business arranging security for this town without first consulting the sheriff and me. If you don't like us, then fire us, but don't sabotage the job we're trying to do. Not right now."

He kicked her desk again, leaving a sizable dent this time, and pointed a finger inches from her face. "Don't tell me how to run my office!"

Otto stood up from his desk. "You either lower your voice and speak in a respectful manner or you leave this office immediately. Chief Gray doesn't deserve that kind of talk."

Moss's face puckered. He looked ready to throw a punch at Otto, but instead turned and walked to the back of the office and looked out the picture window at the small subdivision and gray desert beyond.

Josie talked to the mayor's back. "Here's the way I see it: Two assassins broke into my home while I was asleep and nearly killed me. They destroyed my bedroom and threatened my life. They made it very clear that they were going to kill me if their men weren't set free. And you knew all this! You knew the danger I was in and yet you allowed these prisoners to stay in our jail even though transport was available through Escobedo."

He turned from the window and faced her, his expression incredulous. "I had it taken care of! That's what the Guard was for!"

"We didn't need to wait for the Guard. We had a better solution available!" Josie said.

"I wasn't going to request that a National Guard unit come all the way to our town, then turn around and send them away because you got a better deal somewhere else. We needed to at least make use of them for a day," Moss said. "What happens next time we call for their help? They'd laugh us off."

Otto looked at Josie and shook his head slowly, trying to signal her to keep her temper in check.

Josie's voice dropped. She was so angry, her hands were shaking.

"You're telling me that you left four known assassins in our jail as a public relations move? You left them there so you wouldn't look bad?"

Moss said nothing, but he stared at her as if turning her words over in his mind.

She went on. "It wasn't just my life at stake. It was every one of the employees walking through that jail yesterday. You saw the catastrophe they sent down on that transport van yesterday. If we hadn't moved those prisoners when we did, it's hard telling what kind of disaster you'd be dealing with today."

Moss shook his head and walked by Otto and Josie without a word. He slammed the door behind him, rattling the glass. They looked at each other, listening to his cowboy boots banging down the stairs.

"What do you do with information like that?" Otto said finally. "The people of this town ought to know the kind of yahoo they elected into office."

"He operates inside the margins, but just barely."

"You think he's mixed up with Red's death? With Medrano?"

"I don't know." Josie shook her head. "Here's what bothers me, though. We know Deputy Bloster was cooking the books. He was submitting a vague expense summary directly to the commissioners. The sheriff provided Dillon a whole box of receipts and paperwork that Bloster had cooked, but before that, all those doctored receipts never left his own office. They didn't have to. The commissioners never asked for them. The city police? We have to submit a detailed expense report with receipts attached. Is it that Moss hates me and wants to make my life miserable? He figures a good ole boy like Martínez would never screw the city? Or is Moss in on the scheme?"

FIFTEEN

Standing at the bathroom sink, putting on mascara, Pegasus was thinking about her brother. She wondered if he had left town and was thinking he was a son of a bitch for not calling her first, when she heard banging on the outside of the trailer by the living room door. She put her makeup down and grabbed the pistol she kept by her bedside table. She popped the magazine into the gun and advanced a bullet, then leaned against the wall in the kitchen to peer out the side of the curtains. She saw a man flattened against the side of the trailer beside the door and grinned. Kenny was checking out her response.

She yelled, "Step away from the door before I shoot a bullet through your head!" She unlocked the dead bolt, swung the door open, and pointed the gun toward Kenny's head in one fluid motion.

He smiled widely. "Nice. Very nice. You win this round."

He followed her inside the trailer. The air-conditioning had been running all day, and the temperature was almost cold. Kenny sighed and flopped on the recliner, staring at the empty space where the couch used to be.

"They have a Goodwill downtown. Stop by and tell them you're looking for a couch. Tell Marie you're my sister. She's got connections around town. She'd probably get it delivered, knowing her."

She nodded and threw an old bed pillow on the floor and sat on it, leaning her back against the living room wall. "So what's the plan?" she asked.

"I want to take you out for lessons one more time before I hit the road. I think you'll be okay. I got the word around town that you're a badass. Somebody'll think twice before coming out here and screwing with you."

"Why do you want to draw attention to me? Nobody even knows I exist here."

He laughed. "Red Goff laid out on your couch like a mortuary? Trust me. Everybody knows who you are and where you live. You're either the joker's right-hand girl, or they want to take you out for killing the desert's last messiah. No in between out here in the sticks."

"I don't ask for this. This stuff just follows me around. You're quick enough to stay two steps in front of it. Not me, though. I'm always knee deep in the sewage."

"You hang out here where I know where you are. I got some guys keeping an eye on you, watching the trailer and the gas station." He leaned to one side in the recliner and pulled his wallet out of his back jeans pocket. He took out a wad of cash. "There's five hundred bucks there. I paid Drench your rent for the next six months. That ought to keep you floating until I get things settled."

"What things?"

"Don't worry about it."

"So, take me with you. Let me help."

He stood. "Hide your money. Let's go shoot."

Josie paced the office after Moss left, thinking through the mayor's actions and his response to her subterfuge, trying to determine if he was an idiot or a criminal. Otto got annoyed with her and left to buy a snack. She considered his remark about counseling and knew he was right. She had always thought a line-of-duty killing would be something she would attack rationally, break it down into pieces like any other problem. Once she examined the events leading up to the shooting, the act itself, and her actions afterwards, she would determine if the killing was justified. She would answer questions such as, Was it was necessary? Did it save another person's life? Would she do it again in the same situation?

But that wasn't how things were turning out. There would be an investigation by DPS into the shootings. She needed to get the details and facts straight in her mind. But she found herself numb to the details, as if she couldn't feel anything. She wanted to feel guilt or anger or even shame, but she just felt empty.

She called Escobedo to check on the details of the prisoner transfer, and he said it was complete. Three of the prisoners had been housed in solitary confinement until their status could be evaluated. Gutiérrez was in the infirmary but would most likely be transferred out the next day.

She stood at the window, looking at the clear blue sky and wished she were outside, walking through the hills up into the ponderosa pine behind Dell's place. She imagined the smell of mesquite and baked earth and could feel the heat on her skin. The intensity of the last week was catching up with her. She was exhausted and having a hard time maintaining focus. She walked to the back of the office for another cup of coffee.

After Otto returned, they sat at the conference table and ate packages of mini chocolate-covered doughnuts. To Josie, they tasted as if they were dipped in paraffin, but Otto loved them. He finished his own package and started on hers.

"Someone killed Red and laid him out on Winning's couch. Why didn't they just drop him in the dirt? What's the connection to her?" she asked. "It's gnawing away at me, and I can't get past it."

Otto dipped the last doughnut in a cup of steaming coffee, swearing as half of it dropped to the bottom of the cup. "If Medrano is the connection, who knows? Those people have a flair for the dramatic. You ever notice that? Beheadings, dead bodies hung off overpasses, body parts run up flagpoles. Maybe laying out Red's body in her trailer was some kind of artsy statement."

She looked at her watch. "It's after six. Winning ought to be at work. I'm going to drive over there again."

"You want me to ride along?"

"No. I just need to get a feel for it again. Someone shot Red, stole his guns, flooded his basement, and moved his body to look as if he'd been shot in Winning's living room. The only thing that makes any sense to me concerning motive is someone wanted his route. Somebody wanted the connection to the Mexicans. Bloster makes more sense than anyone else, but he's got an alibi. And I don't see him moving the body."

"You ever get his work schedule confirmed?" Otto asked.

"Winning came home at eight thirty in the morning. She went to bed, woke up at five P.M., and found Red dead on her couch. Hack Bloster worked day shift that day. I've read the transcript for his radio contact with the dispatcher throughout the day. There were brief periods of time that he could have shot Red, but it seems unlikely. He'd have to have killed him, carried his dead body through the yard, and then positioned him in the trailer by himself, all while in uniform. It doesn't feel right. Even if Hack killed Red, someone else was involved, too."

Josie drove slowly down Winning's lane, scoping out the deserted area. Other than Red's place and Winning's trailer, there wasn't another house for miles. She pulled her jeep beside Winning's black Eldorado and killed the engine. She scanned the area and saw no movement. The curtains were drawn on the trailer, and it appeared dark inside. Josie got out of her car and walked up to the trailer, tried the handle, found it locked, and was pleased Winning was taking precautions, although Josie couldn't imagine whom the woman would leave with. She knew basically no one and was supposed to be at work.

She heard gunshots. A single, then three quick fires. Josie ran for her car, taking cover behind the front bumper. The shots were coming from Red's place. Thirty seconds later, more shots in quick succession. Josie radioed Otto for backup, and then decided she would be less a target on foot than in the car. She ran down the line of pine trees that bordered the east side of the driveway. The shots were coming from behind the mound of dirt and bushes that covered the top of Red's house. Easing slowly up the hill, her gun aimed and ready, the shots started again, two singles, then rapid fire. She had counted a total of ten shots, and assumed a magazine had been emptied.

Behind the thick stand of bushes she heard voices, a male and a female, laughing.

Inching closer, she found Pegasus Winning and the man she assumed was her brother, Kenny, target-shooting at paper plates duct-taped to a pile of scrap wood. Josie stood unnoticed for a few minutes, watching the two interact. It became obvious there was a shooting lesson being given. Kenny was taking the experience more seriously than Pegasus was.

Josie holstered her gun, approached them from behind, and yelled hello. Kenny Winning turned around in surprise tinged with something else: anger or panic, she couldn't be sure.

"I'm Chief Josie Gray. And you are?"

He introduced himself but didn't offer a handshake.

"So, you're the elusive brother. How long have you been in town?" Josie asked.

"Couple days."

"How long is a couple?"

"Two or three," he said, shoving his pistol in his back pocket.

"Let's narrow it down to an exact date. When did you arrive in Artemis?"

"What is this?" he asked.

"It's a question, and I'd like an answer."

"I don't know. Tuesday, I think."

"That's funny. I talked to someone who saw you on Monday."

He glared at her and pulled a bandanna from his back pocket to wipe the sweat out of his eyes. "Why'd you ask the question if you already had the answer?" he asked.

Winning rolled her eyes. "She's talking smack, Kenny. She's been looking for you all week. Don't listen to this."

Josie noticed the difference in her demeanor. She was tougher in front of her brother; she had always acted more bored with Josie.

Josie addressed Pegasus. "I think it's the other way around. I've asked you about your brother several times. Each time you've denied he was here. Now it sounds like he's been here since Monday. Why didn't you just tell me if you weren't trying to hide something?"

Pegasus took her ponytail down and angrily pulled her hair back again, getting the sweaty strands off her face. She started to speak, but Kenny interrupted her.

"You people kill me. Cops automatically assume the world should bare their collective soul to you at the asking. I got news: People aren't aching to talk to you. That takes a little more trust than most people can give."

"I really couldn't care less about your soul, bared or otherwise. I've got a murder to solve and one awfully evasive suspect."

"So, I'm a suspect now?"

"Until you can convince me otherwise."

"What happened to—?"

Josie interrupted. "Innocent until proven guilty? I've heard it too many times to count. You give me an honest, straight-up answer, and I won't have any reason to question your guilt."

He stared at her and didn't say a word.

She nodded, her face flushed with anger. "I'll try this one more time. If you don't want to be polite, I'll handcuff you and take you down to the station, where I don't have to be polite either. Puts us on a level playing field that way. So, here's what I want from you." She held a hand up in the air to tick each point off on a finger. "When did you arrive? What are you doing here? When are you leaving?"

"Tuesday. Visiting my sister. Tuesday." He held his thumb up for the first answer, his first finger up for the second, and his middle finger up for the third. He smiled as he stood there, flipping her off.

"What was your relationship with Red Goff?"

"He was a cretin."

"And?"

"He was a jerk. A pervert. I hated Pegasus living back here by him, and I'm glad he's not around to harass her anymore."

"Where were you last Sunday, the day Red was killed?" Josie asked.

"I was driving from New Orleans. I went down and stayed with friends for a while. I got a friend who can vouch I was still in New Orleans Sunday morning."

"If you thought Red was so awful, why did you tell your sister to come up here, then leave her with no word on your whereabouts?"

"I got to make money. Can't make it around this hellhole."

"I thought you went to New Orleans to visit."

"I went to N.O. for a lot of reasons. Pegasus is capable."

"Is that why you're out here teaching her how to shoot?"

"You bet it is. You got to be prepared."

Kenny provided plenty of banter but no information, and Josie left. He had said he planned to leave the next morning. Josie didn't like him, but she had no reason to keep him from leaving. As she walked down the hill that ran beside Red's house toward Winning's trailer, she saw a black stretch sedan with tinted windows coming down the road, traveling fast. It appeared to be an Infiniti or some other foreign luxury car. All the windows were up, and the car was throwing a wake of dust behind it. Even at a dead run, she couldn't make it to her car before the sedan reached her. With images of the gunmen from her bedroom in her mind and her adrenaline surging, she pulled her gun and clicked the safety off. Sweat beaded on her upper lip as she considered her next move. She had already called Lou and canceled the call for backup. She remembered she had the key to Red's house still in her pants' pocket and fished it out as she ran the rest of the way down the hill beside Red's and put the key into the sliding door. Bulletproof glass, she thought. The car was heading down the driveway toward Red's place as she pushed the door open, entered, and locked it again. She stepped back away from the door and knew she could not be seen through the tinted glass.

The car pulled to a stop directly in front of the door as she radioed Lou again to ask Otto's location. Lou said he had stopped for a stranded motorist, and Josie requested immediate backup from anyone in the area. She told Lou to call Border Patrol and request immediate assistance.

The feeling she'd had at the trauma unit, trapped inside the operating room with gunmen prowling outside, was back.

The driver of the sedan, a muscular white male dressed in a black suit, opened his door and didn't even bother a glance toward the house before opening the back door. A large well-dressed man with a barrel chest, a dark pockmarked face, and a long, neatly trimmed mustache exited the car. He wore white linen pants and a pale blue linen shirt with a cigar in the pocket. His face was heavily lined below his tinted sunglasses, and his hair was jet black and oiled back in a manner she associated with trouble. Josie figured he was about six foot two and 250 pounds. Two other men, both wearing dark suits, white shirts, and sunglasses, exited after him and converged behind him next to the driver.

Josie spread her feet slightly in a shooter position and held her pistol firmly in her right hand.

The large man smiled and bowed slightly, dipping his head toward her, even though she was certain she couldn't be seen. She had seen pictures of the Bishop, and she had no doubt it was him.

"Chief Gray? Please, let us have a civil conversation, man to woman. Please." He spoke loudly, and she could hear his muffled voice through the glass. "Please, you offend me. Your safety is assured. I would never dream of hurting a lady as lovely as you."

Josie kept her attention focused on the men in front of her and hoped Pegasus and Kenny wouldn't walk down the driveway into the middle of it.

Josie moved to the right of the door, where she was still protected but could talk more easily. "What are you doing on Red Goff's property?" she yelled.

"Mr. Goff and I were acquainted. I came to pay my respects."

"To who?"

He tilted his head, gave a dismissive gesture. "To the place. To the spirit of Mr. Goff."

The sun was setting, but it was still over ninety degrees. The Bishop looked cool and unfazed in his sunglasses.

"Maybe I was looking for you," he said.

She felt the familiar burn in her stomach. "I'm listening."

The Bishop turned from her and faced one of his men. Several seconds later, the cell phone in her pocket rang. She pulled it out of her pocket as he retrieved a cell phone from his bodyguard. It was her police number, a restricted number, and he had access. She opened her phone in spite of her fury.

"Let's be civil, Ms. Gray. You won't come out here and talk with me? We'll talk by phone. You run a nice town here. Good people. You want to keep the town safe. I have no problem with that. Your little town has no interest to me, no—" He stopped, struggling to find the right words. "I want no more than a road into Texas. A simple access, uncomplicated. You and I, we can have a mutually acceptable agreement. I provide you with security, with the tools to keep your town safe. You need guns and weapons, a new jail? I provide that. You need a house with security, a place where you go home at night and feel secure? I provide that. Everyone benefits."

Josie stared at him and wondered how easily Hack Bloster had sacrificed his principles for this man. How long had it taken Bloster to sign away his career for a pile of blood money?

"Mr. Medrano, you may have bargained with others in my town, but you won't bargain with me. I abide by the rules, and I enforce them. I won't negotiate with you. You can cross the border legally in Presidio, just like all the other Mexicans."

He smiled with condescension and wiped a handkerchief across his forehead. "You give up your town's security, just like that? No thought to what this could mean to your citizens? Life can be a very dangerous proposition when you have no protection."

"This may work in Mexico, the veiled threats and intimidation, but it doesn't work here. I have the United States government, the Border Patrol, the Department of Public Safety, ICE, ATF, and every law enforcement agency along the border ready to provide us protection. How many of your clan did you lose this past week to us? Two killed, how many in jail? A dozen now?" She paused and stared at him through the glass. "Turn your car around and head south. We don't want you here."

He tensed. The men flanking him seemed to recognize the insult and shuffled their feet, all taking a step forward. It was like watching a pack of dogs react to the alpha male.

Medrano leaned to one side and spit on the ground. "To see your animal go missing, your man friend disappear. To watch your house in flames. These would be tragedies for you to experience like you have already cursed my family. You killed my father in your hospital— allowed a man to shoot his body to unrecognizable pieces of meat as you personally watched and did nothing. You killed a friend. Shot him in cold blood in your hospital."

She lowered her voice to little more than a whisper as she tried to calm the anger in her throat. "I want you out of here. Now." Josie knew she could do little in response to his threats. Lou had told her Border Patrol was thirty minutes away, Otto another five to ten minutes. She was outnumbered.

"You are a beautiful woman. You are wasting yourself on this small drama. You have eyes made for bigger dreams than this." His expression had tightened; his words didn't match the vicious look on his face.

She closed the phone.

The Bishop turned from her and raised both arms in the air to the men standing behind him and walked toward the car. Josie turned, tripped over a stool by the door, and ducked as gunfire exploded onto the door. After several seconds, it stopped. The glass, unbelievably, was still intact.

From the kitchen, Josie could still see the men outside. Medrano said something in Spanish and laughed. The men behind him laughed as well and shouted something toward the house that she was glad she couldn't interpret.

Medrano pointed a finger at her and yelled, "You will regret this day, Ms. Gray. Have no doubt about your mistake."

SIXTEEN

After the latest threat from the Medrano clan, Otto convinced Josie to take an early supper break at the Hot Tamale to cool off and re-group. Border Patrol had met her and Otto at Red's house, and they were writing up the report and processing the scene. Otto stopped to talk with a retired schoolteacher who wanted to gripe about a parking ticket while Josie ordered and found a table in the corner. If she had laid her head down on the table, she would have been asleep within minutes.

Vie Blessings sat down across from Josie, squinted her eyes, and winced. "You don't look so good."

Josie shrugged.

"Things calmed down any?"

Josie found that everywhere she went lately, people asked for an update, which usually translated to a request for assurance that the violence was over.

She shrugged again. "Not enough."

Vie leaned into the table, and Josie could tell something else was on her mind. "I hate to ask this. I know how busy you all are right now, but someone has set up a camper back behind our place. Smokey told me to mind my own business, but I wondered if you couldn't drive by sometime and check it out?"

"Is the camper on your land?"

"No. It's on government property. You know where we live? Out behind the mudflats?"

Josie nodded.

"There's maybe half a dozen houses back in there, but the land across from us is all federal grazing. I don't want some squatter setting up camp for good. Now there's a trailer set up there, too."

"Doesn't your land bump up against Red Goff's place?"

Vie pursed her lips and squinted. "Sort of. There are a couple miles of federal land that separate our place from Red's land. Smokey always said we were either the safest people in Texas, or the stupidest for living next to that guy."

"Do you know if the person is a local?"

Vie squinted, her expression uncertain. "No clue. I've never actually seen the person staying back there. I don't know if someone's living there or just storing something."

Otto finally walked over to the table, and Vie stood.

"You two be careful out there."

Otto took her place at the table and reached into his shirt pocket. He pulled out a little plastic bottle of Visine and pushed it across the table. "Better take a shot," he said.

Josie let the drops fill her eyes and sighed, wiping the tears from her face with a napkin. She filled Otto in on her conversation with Vie.

"Let's run out there after supper and check it out," Otto said.

She also told Otto about her visit with Kenny Winning.

"You think he might be the camper?" he asked.

"It would put him right behind his own trailer and Pegasus. He could make it through there with four-wheel drive easy. If he were walking, I'm guessing it's a little over a mile from where Vie was talking about."

"Why not stay at his own trailer, then?"

She shrugged. "He's been here for a week and we didn't know it. Sounds like a pretty good plan. There wasn't a vehicle at the trailer today, other than Pegasus's Eldorado. I wish I'd thought to ask him where he was staying, and where his car was, but it didn't click with me until just now."

After a massive burrito, coffee, Coke, and two doses of Visine, Josie felt as if she might survive the shift. The waitress cleared the plates away and Otto paid the bill while Josie started the jeep to get the air conditioner blowing cool. Otto finally got into the passenger seat carrying chocolate chip cookies for dessert.

The mudflats were located north of Sauly Magson's property about three miles from the river. The land around Sauly's and up into the mudflats was the greenest area in Artemis. Prairie grasses covered the ground, not just in clumps as in the rest of Artemis, but in thick swaths of green that rustled in the never-ending wind. Natural springs and mountain runoff kept the area green most of the year, a nice change of pace in the desert. Vie and Smokey's place was located on a road that wound through the hills and the grass. A house dotted the road every half mile or so. Red's place and Winning's trailer were north of the mudflats by another mile, where the land turned suddenly barren and bereft of color.

Josie pulled her jeep along the edge of the road and looked across the field. Otto pointed out a camper set up a half mile away, barely noticeable down the slight embankment. Viewed from a distance, the grass was silken and feathery and moved in gentle waves in response to the breeze. But walking through the three-foot-high blades of grass left thin cuts along any exposed skin, which burned for hours. Josie knew that fact was moving through Otto's brain at that very moment.

She pointed toward the camper. "No tire tracks. If the owner of the camper approached from this road, the grass would still be mashed down in places. He had to have come in from behind Red's place." Josie looked over and found Otto staring out his side window, drumming his fingers on his thighs. "Feel like taking a walk?"

"Not really." Otto opened his car door and affixed his radio to his gun belt. "You owe me a Coke when we're done."

"Deal," she said, and got out to follow him.

The temperature had dropped into the eighties, and while Josie thought the light breeze and temperature were ideal, she knew Otto would be sweating. The sunset to their right was still high, but the reds and oranges were already spreading out like spilled paint.

After a five-minute walk through a field, they came upon a campsite with a ten-foot pop-up camper facing toward them. The camper was fully extended, its closed door facing a small fire pit with a coffeepot lying on the ground beside it. A ten-foot pull-behind U-Haul trailer, most likely hauled by a pickup truck or SUV, was to the right of the camper. Otto pointed out the bumper sticker on the back of it that identified a local rental company. Josie pulled her cell phone out and dialed the number.

"Loan to Own. This is Cammie speaking."

"Hi, Cammie. This is Chief Josie Gray with the Artemis Police. How are you today?"

The young girl was chirpy and helpful. Last year, Josie had stopped her three times for a blown headlight and finally followed her to a local auto parts store, where she helped the girl change the broken light. Cammie recognized Josie and thanked her again for helping her with the light, then said she would be happy to look up the plate number.

After several minutes of waiting on hold, Cammie came back on the line and said she'd found the number Josie gave her from the back of the storage unit. Josie wrote down the specific rental information, then thanked her and asked her to keep the information confidential.

"Dr. Fallow," she told Otto after she'd hung up.

Otto raised his eyebrows. "Why would Paul Fallow need to set up a camper, rent a trailer, and then hide them both out here?"

Josie smiled. "Here's the kicker. He rented the trailer the same day Red Goff was killed."

Otto pointed a finger at her. "The same day Red's guns were stolen." He shook his head. "That little bastard."

Otto approached the trailer door, and Josie called him back. "I don't trust this guy. He may have traps set. We need to get back and cook up a warrant and open this trailer up."

They walked around the perimeter of the campsite, looking for something else that might tie the area to Fallow but without finding anything useful. Once back in the jeep on the side of the road, Josie stared out the window, thinking through the day.

"Why is Medrano spending so much time here? Coming in person? Pegasus saw the car at Red's place several days ago. They know there's nothing in Red's house. They know the guns are gone."

"Unless there's something there we didn't discover."

"We've been through that house, thoroughly, three different times. Marta went out again and walked the property and searched the garage. Nothing."

"What's the draw, then, if it's not Red's place?"

"What if it's Fallow?" she asked. "Maybe Medrano came to meet with him today, and I got in his way. Maybe Medrano wasn't going to Red's place at all. Maybe he was headed back the lane to meet up with Fallow."

"He's buying the guns Fallow stole from Red's place." Otto smoothed the flyaway hair down on his head. "That guy's got more gumption than I gave him credit for."

"Fallow is taking over Red's business. Could be that Medrano was here for a lot more than Red's guns." She pointed past the camper toward the direction of Red's house.

"You think Fallow could have killed Red, manipulated Bloster?" Otto asked.

Josie pulled out onto the gravel road with no answer, but she was positive they were getting close. She called the Loan to Own office and asked Cammie to notify her immediately if Fallow tried to return the storage unit.

The shift from 4:30 P.M. to 1:00 A.M. was Josie's favorite time to work. Life did not really begin until the nine-to-five workday ended. It was when people fought and made up. After sunset, people let their guard down and said things that were not appropriate during the day. The dark gave people something to hide behind. Even as a kid, she had liked nighttime. Her mom would take off for whatever scheme she had cooked up, and Josie would have the house to herself—a relief from the tension of living with her mother's mood swings.

She walked to the back of the office and pushed open the large windows to allow a warm, fresh breeze into the office. Otto would complain later that she had let out all the cool air, but it was worth his grumbling. She could hear the faint street sounds from below, the occasional laugh or yell from a kid riding by on a bicycle. Even with the past week's hell, she would not trade her small town for the big city. She had lived in Indianapolis for two years and worked as a patrol officer in the downtown division. Too many people in too small an area.

Otto had been called out on a domestic dispute, and Josie had stayed back to catch up on the stacks of paperwork and phone messages that had gone unanswered the past few days. She had made the warrant request from the judge for the storage trailer and then settled in to wait for the response. She hoped to have an answer within an hour. She sat at her desk and sorted the stacks of paper into a top-ten to-do list for the night and felt her anxiety over the pileup begin to subside.

In the middle of replying to an e-mail from Jimmy Dixon from Border Patrol, Lou buzzed her on the intercom and said Sheriff Martínez was on his way up to see her. Josie felt sick. She had dreaded talking with him since the arrest of Bloster at the jail, and she had put off calling him despite her resolutions. She had no idea how Martínez might view the events that took place in his own jail.

Martínez walked into the office in uniform, looking pale and tired. He was a large-framed man who typically carried himself at his full height. He walked in the room slump shouldered, his black hair unkempt.

Josie stood from her desk and pulled out two chairs at the big wooden conference table. "Can I get you coffee?" she asked, hoping to gauge his mood.

He shook his head and sat, crossed a leg, and gave her his complete attention. "I came to apologize. Hack Bloster should never have treated you the way he did and got away with it. You were dead right with him, and if I'd responded correctly, some of what happened this past week would have been avoided."

She was surprised at the apology. "I hope you understood my position. I hated to call Escobedo, not because of Moss, but because of you. I just didn't know where else to turn."

"You should have been able to turn to me, but I had my head stuck up my back end."

She started to speak, and Martínez interrupted her with a hand.

"Dillon brought the paperwork to me this morning. I appreciate him bringing it directly to me. He sat down and explained everything. Bloster scammed close to twenty thousand dollars over the past six months right under my nose. Our budget can't take that kind of hit. I just finished a meeting with the mayor. I gave him everything."

Josie winced. "What was his response?"

"Typical Moss. His first instinct was cover it up, keep it from the voters, what's done is done. I asked him, How do you cover up sewage? Bloster's already in jail. What's the point in covering up at this point? You could see his shifty little eyes calculate. Pretty soon he'd flipped. He decided he was the one who ferreted out the dirty cop and closed the connection with the cartels. Saved our town from anarchy. No doubt, you'll see the headlines in the paper this week."

Josie's jaw dropped before she laughed, the first good laugh she'd had all day. "Our hero."

"At this point, I'd let about anyone take the credit."

"Have you talked to Bloster since his arrest?"

"Briefly. I had some questions for my own piece of mind. I couldn't figure out why Red, a guy who hates Mexicans, goes into business selling them guns."

"You don't think Red would sell his principles for a profit?"

"Bloster claims he sold the cartels guns so they'd kill each other off. So, yeah, his so-called principles were a joke."

"What happens now?"

He closed his eyes and rubbed them with his thumb and forefinger. The silence stretched for some time before he finally looked up, his cheeks sagging and eyes bloodshot. "It won't matter what happens. Hack Bloster has ruined my standing in this community. There will be people who can't wait to see me fired, guilty or not."

"Come on, Martínez, buck up. You don't let those people get to you on a normal day. Why now? There's always buzzards waiting for the carnage. Just like there are people that support you every day." She paused and reached across the table to tap him on the forearm. "We'll still support you. The people who hated you before will hate you still."

"Except now I've given them reason."

Josie banged a fist on the table. "Listen to yourself! You sound like one of those women who won't accuse a rapist because she thinks it's her fault somehow! Bloster scammed the system. He scammed you, the commissioners, the mayor, the whole town for his own selfish gain."

"If the sheriff can't control his own department, how can he control the town? That's the question people will ask."

She lowered her voice. "You aren't the criminal," she said. "You're trying to run a twenty-bed jail and the department on your own. You need help."

He tipped his head to concede the point. "You're in no better spot either. We can't keep this pace up. We're both undermanned by fifty percent."

"We need a reserve force," she said. "We need people on the border with guns to hold the line. At least for the next few months. We have good people in this town who can help us. We don't need to do this alone."

The phone on her desk buzzed and Martínez stood to leave. He waved and thanked her for listening and walked out of the office. Josie buzzed Lou back. She said Judge Lewis was on the line.

"Chief Gray?"

"Yes, Judge. Thank you for getting back with me so quickly this evening."

"From everything I've heard, you people are doing an excellent job down there, considering what you're up against. You're fighting the good fight. Just keep that in mind."

"Yes, sir. I appreciate that."

Lewis had been a judge in Arroyo County for thirty years. He was a gray-haired, stooped man who pulled no punches with anyone. She appreciated his faith in her.

"Paul Fallow is trespassing on federal property. No need for a warrant from me. His belongings can be seized immediately."

SEVENTEEN

Josie and Otto drove separately and met in the parking lot of the Loan to Own at 11 P.M. The business was located in a white cinder block building surrounded by a large paved parking lot and half a dozen trailers and storage units. Cammie Brown, the owner's daughter, pulled into the lot after them, driving a bright blue Mustang and got out of the car wearing flannel pajama pants imprinted with big red hearts and a matching sweatshirt, her hair in a ponytail tied neatly with a white ribbon.

Josie shook Cammie's hand and introduced Otto.

"Did you notice my lights? Everything is working perfect. And I just got my license plate renewed." She flashed a bright smile and bounced into the store to retrieve the paperwork and the keys to the unit. She gave everything to Josie, who thanked her and said she could leave.

"Why don't you let me go back out to the field and check the trailer out? That way you can talk with Fallow and we can be sure he won't show up. Tell him we're confiscating his belongings and see what he gives you. If I find the guns in the trailer, I'll call you," Josie said.

After leaving the rental store, Otto stopped by the police station and grabbed the policy manual for the Gunners. He pulled into Paul Fallow's driveway at midnight. All the lights in the house were off. He rang the doorbell, hoping to wake Mrs. Fallow as well. Otto had not talked with her yet, and he was curious what she would say about her husband's trailer rental. After ringing the doorbell a second time, he watched through the side window beside the front door as both Fallow and his wife walked down the stairway together wearing two-piece burgundy-colored pajamas. Mrs. Fallow was cinching a matching floor-length robe around her waist as Fallow looked through the window. He recognized Otto under the porch light, deprogrammed the alarm, and unlocked the door.

"What is it? What's happened?" Fallow asked.

"Dr. Fallow, I apologize for waking you, but I have police business I need to discuss with you."

"It can't wait until morning?" he asked.

"I'm afraid not."

He stepped back, his eyebrows knit together in worry, and introduced Otto to his wife, Karen. Otto nodded hello. Scowling, Mrs. Fallow wrapped her hands around her arms as if she were cold and walked into the formal living room. Otto followed her and sank into a puffy beige couch facing her. Otto leaned forward and set the Gunners' binder on the glass coffee table.

"What's this about?" Fallow asked.

"I'm sure you've heard that Hack Bloster was arrested."

He nodded. Karen sneered.

"That puts you in a special place," Otto said.

Fallow wrinkled his forehead, looking confused.

"With Red out of the picture, and Hack in jail, that means you take over the business."

"I have no desire to take over the Gunners." He glanced at his wife. "I'm through with the Gunners."

"He should have never joined them to begin with. Bunch of grown men acting like animals." Karen squeezed her arms tighter.

"It's not the organization or the men's club I'm referring to. It's the business."

Fallow looked to his wife, then Otto, his expression still confused.

Otto sighed. "Dr. Fallow, we found the trailer you rented behind Goff's house. Your belongings are being confiscated as we speak. Parking the trailer on federal land wasn't a good idea."

His eyes were wide now, and he sat down on the couch by his wife as if his legs had given out from under him. "What in the world are you talking about?"

Otto looked between the two of them. Karen's expression turned from confusion to anger. Her lips were thin, pressed tightly together. "So help me, if you bought more guns, or gave more money to that group without my knowledge, we are through. Finished, Paul."

He looked at his wife but pointed at Otto. "I don't know what he's talking about!"

Otto opened the binder on the coffee table and handed a piece of paper that lay on top over to Fallow. "Here's a copy of the rental agreement for the U-Haul trailer. There's your name."

Fallow grabbed the paper and studied it, his face turning pale.

"You son of a bitch." Karen's voice was low and steady. Her eyes were filled with rage, and it made Otto remember her serene expression during her yoga pose.

Otto pointed to a list on the front page of the binder. "Here's the hierarchy, Mr. Fallow, right in your manual. Number one, Red's gone. Number two, Hack's gone. You're next. Number three man on the totem pole. That gun-trading business with the Medrano cartel?

You take the reins, now the others are out of the way. I'd say that's pretty good motive for murder."

Fallow stared at Otto, then down at the manual, then back at Otto. "Where did you get this?"

"This is the Gunners' manual we confiscated from Red's house."

"No! That's not right!" His look of confusion had turned frantic. Fallow stood and walked quickly from the room.

"Dr. Fallow. Fallow!" Otto yelled after him. He and Karen both stood and ran after him. Otto pulled his gun. He'd misjudged Fallow. Accusing a murderer at night alone? He suddenly felt stupid.

The doctor walked down the hall and into a small office area, where he pulled a binder off a bookshelf that sat next to a messy desk.

Fallow's eyes were wide and unfocused. He opened the binder to the front page and held it up to Otto. "See! This is the hierarchy you're talking about! That manual you have is wrong. We never changed it after Kenny left. Bloster refused to move me up the list."

Otto leaned in and read. It was a typed list, not the handwritten one they had. The list read:

1. Red Goff
2. Hack Bloster
3. Kenny Winning
4. Paul Fallow

Otto felt his pulse begin to race. "Why didn't you tell me Kenny was a member of the Gunners?"

Fallow's mouth opened. "You didn't ask! Why would I tell you that? He's not participated for the past few months because he moved out of town. He and Red got into it over something."

Otto grabbed the manual from Fallow, ran down the hall, and picked up the manual he brought with him, then left the house, making a run for his car. When he got inside, he called Josie's cell. She didn't pick up. It was probably silenced. He had to reach her before she connected with Kenny.

Josie parked her car at Vie and Smokey Blessings's house and walked toward Fallow's campsite. She could see the dim light from one lantern, and the thuds and bangs convinced Josie he was packing up camp. She had hoped he would be home and the campsite empty. Josie wondered if Fallow hadn't been thrown out of the house and taken up residence at the campsite. She figured Otto could talk with Mrs. Fallow while she confronted the doctor at the campsite.

Moving cautiously through the grass, Josie spotted someone removing armloads of guns from the storage unit and putting them into the pop-up camper. But it wasn't Fallow. It was Kenny Winning. He was moving quickly, not worrying about careful packaging, obviously trying to make a quick escape. After Winning dumped a load of guns onto the camper floor and started making his way back over to the trailer for another load, Josie took several quick steps into the dim light of the campsite.

"Stop right there, and put your hands in the air where I can see them!"

Kenny didn't even turn to look at her. He ran half a dozen steps to the trailer and jumped through the open door. Fortunately, the door was held open with a chain and he couldn't pull it shut, but he moved to the right of the door, inside the trailer and out of her line of sight.

"Kenny, this is Chief Gray. You need to give it up and come out of the trailer with your hands held in the air. You won't get out of this one." She stopped talking and heard nothing from inside the trailer. "I don't want to see you get hurt. Step slowly outside the trailer." Josie stood with both feet planted firmly, her arms extended, gun aimed on the trailer. The amount of ammunition in the campsite was staggering to consider, and it reminded her of the rattlesnakes roiling around under her feet at Dell's place, waiting to strike if provoked.

A hand extended about twelve inches into the open doorframe, and Josie realized Winning was holding an explosive device.

"I want you out of here now!" he said, his voice loud and angry. "I want your gun and gun belt on the ground as well as your cell phone. Throw them down now or I'll throw this and six others just like it! I will blow you to pieces!"

Josie moved just outside of the lantern's light and opened her cell phone, noting that she'd missed several calls from Otto. She found Pegasus Winning's cell phone number in her contacts and was surprised when Winning answered.

Josie whispered who she was and asked if Winning knew where her brother's campsite was located.

"He has a trailer set up straight back from Red's place. You need to get down here. He's got a trailer full of guns and he's talking crazy. Drive down here and talk sense into him before we all get blown up." Josie hung up without waiting for a reply.

"Kenny, you know we aren't going to do that. You're outnumbered here."

"Bullshit! You can't come near me without getting blown to pieces, so don't tell me I'm outnumbered!"

She tried to reason with him, trying to stall. "Kenny, you can't do this to your sister. You're all the family she's got."

"Don't bring her into this! She has nothing to do with this!"

"Kenny, if you're thrown in jail for killing a police officer, you'll never see her again. Whatever has happened to this point, we can work through it. Just come out here so we can talk."

Josie noticed the Eldorado driving through the grass toward the campsite.

Pegasus parked and jumped out of the car, shouting Kenny's name. Josie put her hands up in the air to slow her down. She pointed toward the trailer.

Pegasus called her brother's name, softer now, and approached the trailer. He said nothing. She stopped just outside the door.

"Kenny? What are you thinking?"

Pegasus tentatively looked inside and found him sitting on the floor, his legs stretched out in front of him, each hand holding a grenade. Kenny's head was leaned back against the wall, his eyes closed.

She stepped inside quietly, not wanting to startle him, terrified by what she saw. The dim light from the lantern cast angular shadows across the guns piled three and four deep on the floor in the back of the trailer, most of them large, most likely automatic. A box of explosives lay to Kenny's right side. She winced at the smell of gun oil and sweat.

"Kenny," she whispered, and sat beside him, careful not to touch him yet. "What are you doing, buddy?"

He turned his head toward her and opened bloodshot eyes. "It's all turned to shit."

"Are these the missing guns from Red's place?"

"I wanted to get us out of this wasteland. Just enough to get a start somewhere else. Vermont or Montana. Start a bait-and-tackle shop. Anything but this." He threw his hands into the air as if this was what his life had become.

Pegasus wiped sweat off her forehead and tried to stall the feeling of desperation that was starting to take over. "Did you steal Red's guns from his house?"

Kenny had always been in charge; now he looked at her as if she was supposed to come up with the solution. "I messed up, sis. I did it good this time."

"Who were you going to sell them to?" she asked, still trying to make some sense of her brother surrounded by guns.

"It doesn't matter."

"It does matter! The owner of those guns is dead! You don't mess with people like that."

"I was going to get us out of this hellhole. I could have made enough money to move us anywhere."

Pegasus leaned across him and took both grenades out of his hands. "I love you, Kenny. I love you for trying. But you have to stop now. It's over."

Otto finally reached Josie on her cell phone on his way out to the campsite. Josie had Kenny handcuffed and was leading him to her jeep. Otto arrived as she reached the road. She loaded Kenny in the back of his jeep, and he transported Winning to the Arroyo County Jail. It was after three in the morning before he was booked and sitting in an interrogation room. Josie sat across the metal table from Kenny and slid him a pack of cigarettes and a lighter. Otto set a cup of instant coffee in front of him and stood in the back of the room. Kenny still wore just a ripped black T-shirt and jeans. He lit a cigarette and inhaled deeply.

After the preliminary information, Josie asked him to explain in detail how he came up with Red's guns. Kenny had lost the angry martyr persona and looked as if he were coming down off a three-day high. His eyes remained bloodshot and unfocused, his words slightly slurred.

"Not much detail to give. I found Red dead on my couch. I figured somebody was going to get the guns, may as well be me. He probably stole the guns to begin with. Turnabout."

"You found Red's body and didn't bother to report it?"

He shrugged.

"You left a dead body in the trailer while your sister lay in the bedroom sleeping?"

He shrugged again. "The guy was dead. Wasn't like he was going to get up and do something to her. I could tell he was dead, so I left to think. That's when I decided to go back to Red's and load the guns in my camper. It was already parked behind Red's place. Why not take something bad and turn it? I rented the storage unit later that day. Check the records."

Josie already knew the records Cammie gave her verified his story.

"Why use Paul Fallow's name?"

"Because Paul Fallow is an ass. He's an arrogant jerk who deserves whatever he gets."

"Did you change the front page in Red's policy manual? Did you take your name off the list to keep us from viewing you as a suspect?"

He lifted a shoulder and sipped at the coffee.

"What makes the most sense to me," Josie said, "is that you shot Red for the guns and then stole them. You took your name out of the manual and added Fallow's name to the rental information to throw suspicion away from you."

"Why would I shoot Red, and then drag his bloody body into my own trailer?"

"Maybe you stuck him on the couch to get the body hidden while you ransacked his house."

"This is stupid. I want a lawyer."

After finishing the paperwork with the intake officer, Josie found Otto looking out the door into the lobby area at the front of the jail.

"What's up?" she asked.

He turned to face Josie, and she couldn't read his expression. He looked lost. "It's my wife. Delores is sitting on the bench with Pegasus Winning. She has a box of Kleenex in one hand and the girl's hand in her other. I'm quite sure my wife has just invited the girl to stay at our house."

Josie smiled and patted Otto on the back. "You're a lucky man. Actually, she's pretty lucky, too."

"Oh, no. I'm not in the same league as that woman." He shook his head as if trying to puzzle out how he had ever married a woman that good.

They watched for a few minutes until Pegasus stood, hugged Delores, and left the building by herself. Josie followed Otto into the waiting room.

"Wouldn't come home with you?" Otto asked his tearful wife.

"I tried. She said she might come to church with us on Sunday. I said we'd be by her house to pick her up at a quarter to ten."

Josie smiled and hoped Delores's optimism paid off.

Otto tried to shoo his wife out the door. "Let's go home. You did what you could."

Delores ignored Otto and turned to Josie. "What is it with you young women? Is it such a crime to let someone help you every once in a while?"

Josie stopped by the gas station on the way home and picked up two cups of diced fruit for a combined supper and breakfast. Standing in her kitchen, she doused the fruit with hot sauce, took two quick shots of bourbon, and ate standing at the sink. By 2 A.M., she decided she was sufficiently tired to try going to bed. She let Chester out to walk the perimeter of the house and then lured him back inside with a dog cookie. She double-locked the front and back doors and stood in her bedroom doorway, debating whether she could do it.

She changed into her nightshirt, washed her face and brushed her teeth, and slid between the clean white sheets with her bedside lamp on. She considered the bourbon again but decided she was stronger than that. She thought of calling Dillon but knew the problem was hers to solve alone. *One night*, she thought. *I'll take it one night at a time.*

EIGHTEEN

The phone rang in the kitchen at nine forty-five in the morning and woke Josie from a sleep so deep, she had to remember where the phone was. She stumbled out of bed and found Sergio Pando on the line calling to check on her.

"Word on the street is that Artemis stopped the Medrano cartel at the border. I wonder if you know what a blow this is to their organization. With the Pope gone, and the Bishop trying to hold together people who no longer believe in his leadership, they are limping along. I hear members are even defecting. Leaving the organization altogether."

Josie sat down at her kitchen table, her brain still fuzzy with sleep. "That's good to hear, Sergio."

"The bad news is, La Bestia has freedom to push forward. They will take advantage of Medrano's weakness and they will put pressure on the people and businesses in Piedra Labrada."

"I'm sure the bribes and protection payments will increase," she said.

"We've put together a Piedra contingent to gather those who are left and willing to fight. We're talking about moving our homes and businesses into a smaller area, arming ourselves to fight back. Maybe we catch a break that way."

"If we can help in Artemis, band together on both sides of the river, we'll do it. I'm behind you one hundred percent," Josie said. It was good to hear optimism from someone living in Piedra. Things had been so grim for such a long time that most had given up hope.

She hung up with Sergio, fixed herself and Chester a half dozen fried eggs, and sat on the back patio and enjoyed the sunny morning. Her body was sore and tired, but she felt the fog clearing from her head and felt her senses sharpening. The pieces and ends of the investigation were weaving together in her mind, and she was ready to log back in to work.

In a moment of self-awareness, maybe pity, she couldn't be sure of the reason, Josie called her mother to check on her, to make sure she made the trip back to Indiana safely.

Her mother sounded surprised at the call and happy to hear from her at first. "The drive wore me out. Too many flat miles with nothing to look at."

"A lot of people don't like all the wide open space. Some people say it makes them nervous," Josie said.

"Didn't make me nervous. Just made me tired. All that interstate driving. I should have planned some highway miles."

"I was surprised you left so soon. I could have helped you plan a route back."

"So, how did it feel, me leaving you without a word?"

Josie's face flushed and she closed her eyes to the fight she could already feel coming. "Let's not do this."

"Hope it made you think about the way you left me with no word."

"We left for different reasons."

"Oh, really? Fill me in, then. 'Cause I don't know one iota why you left the way you did."

The energy Josie had felt was turning to weariness like a switch had been flipped off. "I just called to make sure you made it home. I didn't call for a fight."

"Don't think I can't see the way you judge me. Seems to me you turned out all right. You think I didn't have something to do with that?"

"I was a child. You left me to fend for myself through grade school. There wasn't much parenting involved."

"You think it was easy on me? I had a little girl who was half-crazy over her daddy getting shot. You think I was right in the head, just ready to jump in there and be mother of the year?"

Josie consciously lowered her voice, slowed her speech, and tried to de-escalate the tension. "I was eight. You were an adult. When things get tough, sometimes you need to suck it up and put on a show. First you convince other people you can handle it, and then you convince yourself."

"And did your eight-year-old little mind notice that I did it for us? To get us by? I'd never worked a day in my life! I had no skills. I couldn't type, couldn't run a cash register, couldn't do shit!"

Josie took a breath. "Okay, this is pointless. Maybe someday we can work through this. Not now, though. I'm glad you made it back home."

Her mother remained silent.

"I'll talk to you later." Josie hesitated, heard nothing on the other end, and slowly closed her cell phone.

The conversation burned her insides like battery acid. Even after so many years, she recognized the feeling; she always felt this way after talking to her mother, no matter the topic, and no matter the time between conversations. She had no doubt her mom had the same experience. The only consolation was that it was an improvement over the last two years of silence.

She dialed the hospital and discovered Dell had checked himself out at ten o'clock the night before. She needed a dose of Dell to get herself out of her own head.

Dressed in khaki shorts, a pink tank top, and her favorite pair of walking boots, Josie called Chester, and they set out behind the house through Dell's pasture. The sky was a brilliant blue, the sun not quite high enough to burn.

She found him outside in his ratty jean shorts and cowboy boots, bare chested, sitting on a stump by a fire pit twenty feet from the front of his cabin. He grinned up at her and tossed a few more twigs onto the small fire.

"You think just because you live by a cop that you don't have to abide the burn ban?"

His grin widened. "I got a doctor's excuse. You know the medical marijuana they use over in California? Well, I got medical fire prescribed for me."

Chester shoved his nose up under Dell's hand until he rubbed the dog's ears.

"I hear you made a run for it last night," she said.

"I couldn't take that place. The smell was horrible. It's supposed to smell clean. Does the smell of chemicals smell clean to you?" He sat up straight, breathed deep, and exhaled with a smile. "This is clean. Smell that mesquite smoke? That's what'll cure me. Right here in my own front yard."

Josie sat across from him on a stump that had long ago been designated her own. "I'm sorry I got you involved in that mess."

He glared at her. "Now, don't go and piss me off. Treat me like some old man who can't make a decision for himself. I went because I wanted to. End of discussion."

She nodded. "Fair enough."

"Let me tell you something. I don't like this kind of talk, so I'll make it quick. I was proud to know you the other night. You showed a lot of grit out there. You have honor and integrity, and there aren't too many people I'd say that about."

She let the words settle around her. A lump formed in her throat, and she swallowed hard to keep the emotion out of her voice. "I can see it in other people. I try, but I can't see it in myself. I never feel like I quite get there."

"That's the way it's supposed to be. It keeps you working on being better." Dell leaned forward and tossed a few more gnarled chunks of mesquite onto the fire. "Here's the thing. If we could see ourselves like other people do, it'd do one of two things. We'd either have an ego inflated so big, we'd explode, or we'd be shocked to find out how much people hated us. Either way, it'd kill us. That's why the movie stars are so screwed up. People aren't hardwired to hear all that nonsense. One day they're brilliant; the next, they're a has-been. Nobody ought to hear that. You keep plugging away in life and keep trying to do better by your own standards. You don't worry about what your mom or the mayor or anybody else has to say. You'll be just fine."

Dell paused and stood suddenly, claiming he needed to strain his sun tea. She knew he'd change the subject when he got back. While he was inside his cabin, Josie's pocket vibrated and she took a call from the Arroyo County Jail requesting she come as soon as possible. The ballistics information had come in on the guns Otto had found in Pegasus Winning's trailer.

Josie arrived at the jail at the same time attorney Charlie Givens was getting out of his Oldsmobile sedan. Five years ago, when Charlie turned sixty, he retired from his small private law business in Presidio. He had to resume work for the county just a year later, when his wife was diagnosed with inoperable cancer. She was trying an experimental treatment not covered by their insurance. Givens was a good man and a competent attorney and Josie had always liked him. He reminded her of Andy Griffith, with the same old-fashioned good manners and drawn-out way of talking.

Givens sat his briefcase on the pavement and shook Josie's hand in both of his.

"Good to see you, Chief Gray."

"How's your wife doing, Charlie?"

He nodded slowly. "She's back home again. Next treatment in three weeks. So far, so good."

"I'll be thinking about you both."

Charlie picked his briefcase up again and they walked toward the entrance of the jail. "I'm here to see your boy, Kenny Winning."

Kenny didn't know it, but he had just caught his first break.

Josie found Otto in the central hub talking with Sheriff Martínez. Otto gave Josie the results from ballistics and said Kenny was meeting with Givens for the first time. Josie shared the notes and questions she had prepared to use during the interrogation with Otto and Martínez. They agreed that Martínez need not be present, but that Otto would stand in the back of the room and enter the conversation only if he felt Josie needed support.

Josie noticed the smell in the interrogation room as soon as the jailer unlocked the door. Sweat and fear, the unmistakable odor of a man realizing his life had been forever altered in a horrible and permanent way. A week ago, Kenny Winning had been convinced he had scammed the winning ticket and would cash in. Now the look on his face, not desperation yet, the look of someone trying to fake innocence, made her heart ache. She knew before he spoke his first word that he had done far more than he let on. He couldn't fake innocent any more than she could fake a laugh.

Charlie was sitting at the table on the same side as Kenny with a yellow legal pad and a pen sitting in front of him. A half page of notes were jotted down on the pad.

Josie mirandized Kenny again and set up a tape recorder in the middle of the table. He had not been handcuffed, and he had a pack of cigarettes, a lighter, ashtray, and Styrofoam cup of coffee in front of him. Josie opened her steno pad to the page of questions, though she had committed them to memory.

Givens said Kenny was ready to offer a statement. Josie handed him paper in triplicate and asked him to describe what happened to Red's guns in as much detail as he could remember. The written version was not much different from the abbreviated version he had shared with Josie the day prior. He had found the body and seized the moment. He had seen stealing the guns as a way out. Once Josie moved the questioning back to Red's murder, Kenny's tone of voice altered, moving from weary to cocky and strident, a sure sign Josie was on the right path.

"Let's make sure this is clear. I'm sure Mr. Givens will agree with me. If you cooperate now and tell the truth without days of wasted investigation, your sentencing will reflect your cooperation."

Kenny glanced at Givens, who nodded once gravely. "That is a fact. The truth will often reduce time served if you make it to penalty phase. However, if you have any question about what information to share, I counsel you to confer with me in private. Off the record." Givens looked over his reading glasses at Kenny. "Understood?"

Josie had planned a half dozen approaches for the interview. She followed a hunch and opted for a quick start. "Here's information that may help you decide how we proceed. All of the guns that were confiscated from the rental trailer you rented, and your camper? They've all been sent to ballistics. We've got the gun that shot Red Goff."

Kenny's stare had grown intense and the muscles along his jawline rigid. His thought process was either operating at warp speed or had slowed to a standstill. He stared at Josie as if trying to process the information while his attorney stared at Kenny, trying to process his response. Josie loved this part of an investigation: the end of the chess game, where the opponents locked down for the final move.

Kenny's gaze was unflinching.

Josie went on. "I'll share something with you that we haven't made public yet. We found the bullet. Lodged into the pine tree outside your trailer. Near the picnic table." She paused for a moment, sipped her cold coffee, and maintained her gaze. "You've surely watched enough TV to realize we can match that bullet to the gun. Just like a fingerprint."

No response.

"Or maybe that bullet will match the gun you gave Pegasus. Maybe her fingerprints are all over the gun that killed Red Goff."

Anger flashed on his face.

"Did I mention we found the guns in your sister's trailer? They've been checked. One of those guns matches the bullet that killed Red Goff."

Sweat dripped down the side of his temples as he leaned into the table. "She has nothing to do with this."

"Careful now," Givens said.

"Come on, Kenny. If the bullet comes from a gun in her trailer with her fingerprints all over the gun? Even if it's registered to you, the jury wants a connection between the shooter and the weapon."

"It's my gun!" His hands gripped the handles, and Josie thought he might come up out of the chair. His eyes were wide and unfocused. "I shot the son of a bitch!"

"To get at his guns?"

Givens interrupted, "Mr. Winning, I would recommend you stop right now. We need to talk before you proceed."

Kenny ignored the attorney. Josie had seen it happen before, as if the tension of maintaining a lie had been broken and the truth came rushing out like water.

"The son of a bitch was looking at her! I caught him looking at her through the window. She was walking around clueless, completely naked." Kenny shut his eyes and slammed his back against his seat. "I walked up to him and put a gun to his forehead. He didn't even flinch."

"Did you shoot him then?"

"It was his own fault he got shot!"

Kenny leaned forward suddenly and grabbed a cigarette out of the pack, lit it, and inhaled deeply. He pitched the lighter on the table and ran his hand through his hair.

"I knew Pegasus got off work at seven that morning. I was going to surprise her with breakfast when she got home. She didn't even know I was in town yet."

"Was your trailer set up behind Red's place at that point?" Josie asked.

He nodded, worry lines deeply etched into his forehead. "I set up the camper about a mile behind Red's, where it couldn't be seen. Nobody went out there. I knew Red was too lazy to walk back there. He was supposed to be so prepared, but I was living behind his house. The bastard didn't even know it. I walked around the back of Red's house and saw him sitting at my picnic table. It took me a minute to figure it out. It was a dark morning, overcast. It actually looked like it might rain. I thought he was sitting at the picnic table having breakfast. Maybe taking advantage of the break in the weather. Then I saw him with his camera. She was getting ready for a shower. She had the lights on inside."

Kenny stopped talking and placed the heels of his hands into his eyes as if to stop the images. Givens frowned and looked at Josie as if the depravity in the world would never cease to amaze him.

"He stood up from the picnic table, held his camera up to his face, twisted that lens, slinking around the trees like some private dick. Not even eight o'clock in the morning! The guy was a sick bastard."

"He didn't notice you standing behind him?" Josie asked.

"He was oblivious. I put the gun to the back of his head. He never said a word, just lowered the camera. We stood there in silence and watched her walk into the bathroom and shut the door. She had the windows open, the curtains pulled back. I had to watch my own sister walk in front of the damn window with no clothes on. We watched the door shut and I dropped the gun. I told him what a sick pervert he was."

Kenny stopped talking and stared at his hands on the table, his eyes suddenly distant with memory.

"I was finally getting it together for us. I had a job lined up in New Orleans. A good one, before this happened."

He paused again, and then looked at Givens, who told him to finish his statement. No reason for censure at that point.

"I only put the gun to his head to scare him. I wanted to scare him bad, but I didn't intend to shoot him. That's the crazy part. But he turned around and faced me! He started telling me she liked it! He said she knew he was standing outside her window. That's why she kept the curtains open. She walked around naked for him because she liked it!"

He looked at Josie, his expression full of rage and confusion, something other than regret.

"I threw the first punch. He didn't even bother to punch back—he grabbed for the gun in his front pocket. I saw the handle grip as he reached, and I knew it was him or me, so I brought the gun up and shot. There wasn't even time to think. It was an instinct, my life or that sick bastard's."

"There wasn't a gun on Red when we found him."

"I took it with me. It was in the trailer with the rest of the guns."

"Why did you move the body?" Josie asked.

"I was angry with Pegasus for being so stupid. I wanted to teach her a lesson. Here she was, flaunting around naked in front of windows with no curtains so a pervert like Red could—"

Josie waited a moment for him to finish. When he didn't, she asked, "So you waited until she fell asleep, and then moved him on her couch to teach her a lesson?"

"She thinks she's street smart. She talks like she's been around the block, but here she was, letting this pervert get his porn for free outside her window. She stood there bare assed in front of Red. So, I wanted to teach her a lesson. Look what happens when you leave your door wide open."

"Does she know you shot Red?"

"I went to tell her what had happened, and found the door unlocked. I've told her, padlock it from the inside. I wanted to get her attention, so I got Red's body over my shoulder and carried him into the trailer. Left him for her to find."

"Again, does she know you shot Red?"

"She has no idea."

"Where was she when you brought the body in?"

"The shower."

Josie wasn't sure she bought into the time frame. It had to have been a long shower for Kenny to have fought with Red, killed him, and positioned his body, all pretty noisy activities, while Pegasus was conveniently singing in the shower.

"How did the guns fit into this?"

"I didn't even think about the guns until after it was over. After I left the body, I went back to Red's house to find the pictures he said he had taken. I wanted them destroyed before the cops got there." Kenny's face looked gray as he shook another cigarette out of the pack on the table. "He had hundreds. Some blown up to eight-by-ten size and taped to his dresser mirror."

"Did you search his house?"

He nodded. "His desk drawers, his bedroom, down in his gun cellar. He had them taped all over the walls down there. It was beyond belief. I found two shoe boxes with pictures. They looked like family pictures, but I didn't have time to look, so I pulled the pictures off the walls and turned the faucet on to flood the place. I wanted it destroyed."

"You knew the house from your association with Red as a Gunner?" Josie asked.

A flicker of surprise crossed his face, and he shrugged. "Yeah, I'd been in his house."

"The guns?"

He tapped his cigarette repeatedly, starring at the coal on the end before finally stubbing it out. He finally said, "There were a couple hundred hanging from his living room wall. After what had just happened, it made sense. Steal the guns, sell them, and get us both the hell out of Dodge."

"Were you going to sell them to the Mexicans?"

"A guy from the Medrano cartel somehow figured out I'd talked to Red's connection with La Bestia. I met with La Bestia's gun merchant once, but his offer was too low. An agent from the Medrano organization was supposed to meet me yesterday, but he never showed."

Josie nodded, satisfied she had been the obstacle that had stopped the deal. Medrano's last local connection was on his way to jail for murder.

After work that night, Josie stopped by Colt Goff's apartment downtown. It was eight o'clock, and Colt invited her into the apartment. It had been cleaned, though it still smelled like stale cigarettes. Her hair had been cut, still spiked, but not so long. Josie thought she looked more put together, less defiant and angry.

A book, *Mastering the SAT,* was lying open on the couch. Josie pointed to it. "Going back to school?"

Colt grinned, her expression sheepish. "Maybe. I can't stack books the rest of my life. I'm thinking about training to be a phlebotomist. I've been thinking about it for a long time. Seemed like a good time to make a change in my life."

Chief Gray sat on the chair across from the couch and wished her well. "I just wanted to let you know we found out who killed your dad. I didn't want you to hear about it from gossip on the street." She took a deep breath and dreaded the moment. Colt nodded for her to continue. "It was Kenny Winning."

Colt's face drained of color, her expression changing from shock to denial and confusion. "That can't be. I used to date Kenny! He would never do something like that." She shook her head no repeatedly.

"It had nothing to do with you, Colt. Nothing to do with your relationship with Kenny. He claims he found your dad looking into his sister's windows. Taking pictures of her. They got into a fight over it. Your dad reached for a gun, and Kenny fired first."

"What will happen to him? To Kenny?"

"I don't know. That's not up to me. He was stupid, but I don't think he planned any of it. That will help him some."

"You know the Gunners is why we broke up? I couldn't handle the whole gun thing. I told Kenny no good can come from them. He thought I was just making some statement because I hated my dad." She paused and stared at Josie for a moment. "And look what happens."

Colt slumped back onto the couch, her face slack and lifeless. "Is it true? Did my dad—?"

Josie nodded, wishing she could protect her from the truth, but knowing the story would be front page in the newspaper by the next day. "I've seen the pictures. They came from your dad's camera."

Tears began rolling down Colt's face, but her hands remained limp in her lap. She looked as if all the strength in her body had been drained.

Josie stood from the chair and sat beside Colt on the couch. She pulled the girl into her chest and wrapped her arms around her.

Colt's weak body began to shake, and the tears came for a long time. Josie knew the girl had no one. No family, no boyfriend to call on. Josie's job made it painfully aware to her how alone and lonely so many people were.

After some time, Colt pulled away. She stood up and went into the bathroom and washed her face. When she returned, she'd pulled herself together somewhat.

"You can't let this derail you." Josie pointed to the study guide. "You're on the right track. You deserve better than what you've gotten so far in life."

"I get what you're saying, but what good does that do me? Lots of people deserve better."

"I believe, in the end, people get what they give. If you give hate and grief to people, it's what you get back in return. I see it every day. That's not who you are, though. I'm a pretty good read of people. You stay true to who you are, and someday you'll find your peace."

Colt considered her for a long moment. "Have you found yours?"

Josie looked at her. "I'm still trying. I'll get there one of these days."

On her way home that night, Josie received a phone call from Lou asking her to drop by the department. The sheriff had left a present for her. As Josie got out of her jeep, she saw two metal cages on the sidewalk by the front door of the police department. Lou was bent over one of them, poking her finger through the cage. She stood up, smiling wide, when Josie stepped onto the sidewalk.

"What's up?"

Lou said, "Sheriff thought you needed these."

Josie frowned, shook her head no. "Why would he think I need roosters?"

"They came from Hack Bloster's place. He's in jail now. Somebody's got to take them. Sheriff thought you'd be perfect."

"I don't know anything about raising chickens!"

"They're roosters."

"Lou! I don't know anything about chickens or roosters. Where would I put them?"

"I already called Dell. He said he'd make you a chicken coop." Lou bent down again and put her finger through the cage to ruffle a feather. "Pretty, aren't they?"

Josie sighed and bent down. They were beautiful animals. The fluffed-up feathers were a deep rusty color that reminded her of the streaks of red that ran through the mountains behind her house. Both of them strutted around their cages, sticking their necks out, needing a spot to roam. Lou and Josie stood and loaded the cages into her jeep.

Lou pointed to its back end, now riddled with bullet holes from the trip down the arroyo. "When you going to get your car fixed?" Lou asked.

"Let's just get through one day at a time."

NINETEEN

Over the next two weeks, Artemis returned to a nervous calm. The Medrano and La Bestia cartels were silent—on her side of the border, at least. Josie tried to keep visions of the Bishop out of her head, but like Moss, she was still looking for a way to plug the holes. She figured they would just find another route eventually, but she hoped that route wouldn't include Artemis.

Josie, Martínez, and the mayor agreed to meet each week for a planning session in the mayor's office. It was a concession of sorts for all involved. Josie knew communication had to improve, and they all needed to be working from the same set of plans. As with so many things, only time would tell.

Hack Bloster still hadn't entered a plea. Sheriff Martínez thought Bloster would most likely take it to trial and attempt to lay most of the blame on Red. It was too early to tell what the commissioners planned to do with the sheriff, although community sentiment seemed to be siding with Martínez.

On Friday afternoon, Dillon called Josie at work and offered to grill steaks if she would start the charcoal. She agreed, and managed to leave work on time so that they were able to watch the sun set from her back patio. After a relaxing dinner, they settled into comfortable Adirondack chairs and eventually, inevitably, the conversation turned toward the violence on the border.

Josie said, "I keep thinking, why us? Why Artemis?"

Dillon stretched his long legs out in front of him and turned to Josie. "Quit looking at this as a personal issue. This isn't about Artemis, or you or the community. It's about evil people abusing the system."

Josie felt a twinge of guilt. Dillon had discussed several versions of the question with her several times over the past two weeks, but until she could satisfactorily answer the question, she would find no peace.

"How do you not take it personally when two major drug cartels choose your town as their route into the U.S.?" she asked. "Why here?"

"They want an inroad. Why anywhere? Geographically, we make sense. Medrano tried and made some headway with Bloster and Red. They find the weakest link, and they break through the fence."

Josie bit her lip, her face flushing. "And Medrano approached me."

Dillon reached over and ran a finger down her cheek. "And what happened when he approached you? How did that work out for him?" He watched her concede with a half smile.

After supper, Josie and Dillon followed the hound dog into the back pasture and up into the foothills. Chester took off on a scent and was soon a half mile ahead of them. The setting sun cast a red glow across the face of the mountain and softened its rough façade. Following the fence line toward the base of the mountain, Josie pointed up into the sky as a shadow passed over them. Two birds swirled over-head, checking for prey or predator below, before floating gracefully down to land on the wooden fence just ten feet to their right. Josie and Dillon both froze, afraid to move and disturb the birds. They were a pair of endangered aplomado falcons, who Dell had told her were nesting somewhere on the ranch.

The male, with a slate-colored back and creamy orange chest, turned its face toward them. Black stripes swept back from his eyes, the fierce warrior paint of one who had survived against great odds. Josie felt her heart beating hard in her chest, and reached for Dillon's hand at her side.